GREAT CANADIAN SCIENTISTS

BARRY SHELL

POLESTAR

BOOK PUBLISHERS

For Sam and Davina

Polestar Book Publishers acknowledges the ongoing support of The Canada Council, the British
Columbia Ministry of Small Business, Tourism and Culture, and the Department of Canadian Heritage.

Edited by Suzanne Bastedo
Cover and interior design by Jim Brennan
Printed and bound in Canada

Canadian Cataloguing in Publication Data
Shell, Barry, 1951-
        Great Canadian scientists
ISBN 1-896095-36-4
        1. Scientists--Canada--Biography--Juvenile literature.
        2.Science--Canada--Juvenile literature. Title.
Q141.S53 1997   j509'.2'271   C97-910819-5

Library of Congress Card Catalog Number: 97-80428

Polestar Book Publishers
P.O. Box 5238, Station B
Victoria, British Columbia
Canada
V8R 6N4
http://mypage.direct.ca/p/polestar/

In the United States:
Polestar Book Publishers
P.O. Box 468
Custer, WA
USA
98240-0468

5   4   3   2   1

Contents

Acknowledgements

THERE ARE DOZENS OF PEOPLE I'd like to thank who helped to make *Great Canadian Scientists* (GCS) a reality. First there are the financial sponsors. Without their generous support the research could never have been done. Here they are, in the order in which they helped:

Royal Society of Canada 1993
British Columbia Ministry of Education Learning Resources Branch ... 1993
Science Culture Canada 1993
British Columbia Partners in Science Awareness Program 1994
Federation of Canadian Biological Societies 1994
Blair Family Foundation 1995
SchoolNet 1996

Then there are the many institutions that helped with advice, consultation, editing, hardware and software, or general support:

Simon Fraser University .... Web Server
Sir Winston Churchill High School, Vancouver .... Summer Students
Science World BC .... Consultation
SFU Excite Centre .... Design consultation
BC Science Teachers Association .... Pedagogical consultation
Polestar Book Publishers, Vancouver .... Book Publication
VR Didatech, Burnaby, B C .... CD-ROM Publication

Many people either supported me or worked hard to make the project a reality. A lot of these people were inspired just by the idea of an accessible source on Canadian Scientists for Canadians. In turn, their enthusiasm for the project inspired me to keep plugging away even when things looked bleak.

Thanks especially to my wife, Dorinda Neave, and my children, Sam and Davina, for their love and support over the years this project has consumed. Sam helped with the design of the CD and did all the voices of the animated help character.

A lot of people at Simon Fraser University (SFU) helped make this book a reality. Jamal Deen gave me the idea. Nick Cercone hired me to interview SFU scientists and write about them in the *Centre for Systems Science* newsletter. I must thank him for getting me started interviewing scientists. Tom Calvert, my SFU boss during the project, encouraged me to continue working on the book in my spare time and generously approved the use of SFU Internet computers for the www.science.ca website.

At Science World BC, Sid Katz and David Vogt championed the GCS idea and helped me raise the money to do it.

Thanks to Michelle Benjamin from Polestar Press who found the superb editor, Suzanne Bastedo, and graphic designer, Jim Brennan. Both of them did a great job on the book.

I especially want to thank everyone on the GCS creative team: Jeff Steinbok, star programmer; Gordon Ross, who coded up the online version together with Ian Wojtowicz who also created a lot of the graphics; Marvin Entz, my right-hand man and research associate who did virtually the whole Short Biography section; David Clifford, graphic designer; David Ritter, sound engineer and music composer on the CD; Kyle Kirkwood, pedagogical consultant and research associate on the teacher's guide; Mark Bentley Cohen for editorial help; and Liana Walden for video editing on the CD. What a great bunch of people. I could never have done it without you all.

Above all, I must thank all the great scientists who agreed to be interviewed and who came up with fascinating explanations and ideas for games and activities. Thanks for supporting the project.

Finally, thanks to my mom and dad, who gave me all those "How and Why Wonder Books" to read when I was a kid.

Barry Shell
Vancouver, May 1997

Introduction

CANADIANS HAVE WON THE NOBEL PRIZE in science ten times, most recently in 1989, 1990, 1992, 1993, and 1994. All but one of these Nobel prize-winners are alive today (in 1997), yet hardly anyone can name them. Canadian scientists made many of the discoveries that shape our modern world. Read on to find out who they are, what they did and why it matters.

The Nobel Prizes were begun in 1900 by Alfred Nobel, the Swedish chemist who made a fortune by inventing dynamite. In his later years Nobel was horrified to see his invention and variations of it used mainly in guns and bombs to kill millions of people. To remedy this, he willed his vast fortune to be used to fund six annual cash prizes to men and women who made outstanding contributions that enriched human life in the fields of chemistry, physics, medicine, literature, economics and peace. Winners of the Nobel Prize receive about one million dollars each. Ten Canadians have won the Nobel Prize in science. You will find information about many of them in the long profiles in the first part of this book; the rest are in the short biographies in the second part.

Bert Brockhouse (1994 Physics)

Michael Smith (1993 Chemistry)

Rudolph Marcus (1992 Chemistry)

Richard Taylor (1990 Physics)

Sid Altman (1989 Chemistry)

John Polanyi (1986 Chemistry)

Henry Taube (1983 Chemistry)

David Hubel (1981 Medicine)

Gerhard Herzberg (1971 Chemistry)

Fredrick Banting (1923 Medicine)

The Idea

I'M A SCIENCE WRITER at Simon Fraser University (SFU) in Burnaby, British Columbia, where I publish a newsletter that profiles the work of SFU scientists. One day in the hallway I was talking to an engineering professor. He said that I should apply the same techniques I had been using in the newsletter to a book on the greatest Canadian scientists.

Figuring there must already be a lot of books like this, I went to the public library expecting to bring home an armload. Imagine my surprise when the science librarian at the main branch of the Vancouver Public Library told me that no such book existed. He also said that students were constantly coming into the library with assignments to write about Canadian scientists, and often had trouble finding much information. So I decided to start the Great Canadian Scientists Project. At first it was just going to be this book aimed primarily at students aged ten and up, but the project has now expanded into a site on the World Wide Web (www.science.ca) and a CD-ROM. It's not just for students, either. I hope this book will appeal to everyone interested in science and scientists in Canada

Born, Bred, Matured and First Published on the Internet

I BEGAN COLLECTING INFORMATION for this project in June 1991 by posting in several Internet discussion groups (Newsgroups on Usenet) and calling for nominations for great Canadian scientists. The call quickly generated a list of about 70 scientists. As the months and years went by, the lists grew and I rebroadcast them to the newsgroups, asking for corrections and more nominations. Several responders helped me check the citizenship or career achievements of some scientists.

Sometimes I used email to follow up on information. Once, upon receiving my email query about a certain scientist, a researcher at AT&T Bell labs in New Jersey simply walked down the hall to ask the scientist whether he was a Canadian citizen. The answer came back in just a few minutes. (The scientist was Brian Kernighan, one of the creators of the C computer programming language, and he is Canadian, by the way.)

How This Book Is Organized

THE FIRST PART OF THIS BOOK contains in-depth profiles based on interviews with nineteen great Canadian scientists. The second part contains short biographies of over 120 other great Canadian scientists I could not interview. At the end of the book, you will find information designed to help you: a glossary, which is a list of some of the scientific words used in the profiles; a sources list of the books I used; and an index.

The Profiles

MANY BOOKS HAVE BEEN WRITTEN on pioneer Canadian scientists who were the first to do something, like Banting and Best who discovered insulin, a cure for diabetes; Fessenden, who made the first voice radio broadcast; and Saunders, who developed the Marquis strain of wheat that made Canada famous. I did not want to focus on them, nor did I want to write about inventors. I wanted to include Canadian scientists who were still alive, so I decided to interview some great *living* Canadian scientists.

As a science writer, I always enjoy learning new things and new ideas about how nature works, but to me the people who do science are always at least as interesting as the discoveries they make. It was fun interviewing these nineteen scientists. For the one or two hours of the interview, I had their full attention while they talked about what they loved: science. Most of them were great teachers and I always came away amazed by something. The other day as part of my SFU job I was interviewing a kinesiologist, someone who studies how the body moves. She showed me an incredible electric wand that could send a magnetic pulse into your brain and make your arm jerk. I didn't want to try it, but she was using it to figure out how nerves control muscles.

It was difficult to decide which scientists to approach for the in-depth profiles. I wanted to interview women as well as men, I wanted as many different scientific disciplines as possible represented, and, ideally, the scientists would be from all parts of Canada. A few of the interviews were done when scientists on my list chanced to visit Vancouver, where I live. Partly by planning and partly by chance, the profiles evolved.

Early on, I noticed that many popular science books focus only on *the science.* I wanted to find out not only how the science was done, but also about *the people* behind the science, and I designed my interview questions to bring that out as much as possible. I tried to videotape the interviews so that I could concentrate more on the person. I also took notes, and kept a tape recorder running to have more than one record of the interview.

During each interview I asked the scientist if she or he had a message to give people reading this book. Their answers are right alongside their photographs at the beginning of each profile. Then I asked for basic personal information, demographics about when and where they were born. You can find this information under The Person in each profile. I asked scientists about their families their parents, spouses, children and grandchildren. Most of the scientists interviewed for this book had very supportive parents and spouses. Most had children, and sometimes, though not always, their children became scientists too. The only outstanding pattern in the family life of the scientists in this book is that most of their parents put a high value on education.

I asked every profiled scientist to name a favourite piece of music. My idea was to use this as background music for their screens on the CD-ROM version of *Great Canadian Scientists*, but their music choices are also printed here in the book because the music communicates something about their individual characters. I strongly recommend that you make an effort to find and listen to the musical selections on your own, especially if you are interested in a particular scientist. To complete the demographic questions, I asked each to describe his or her own character. Some answered easily, while others could not. I also asked secretaries, students, and spouses about the scientist's character, and wrote down my own observations.

The next part of the interview was divided into four sections. In the first, The Story, I asked each scientist to tell a story representing a moment in their lives. It did not have to be a moment of discovery, but a tale that would help the reader understand what it feels like to be a scientist. Secondly, for The Young Scientist section, I asked each scientist to say a bit about what they were doing when they were 12 years old. I thought that they would already have been interested in science at this age, but many were not. For the scientists who emigrated to Canada from another country I also tried to find out what made them choose Canada. World War II was usually a factor.

For the third section, The Science, I asked each to explain an aspect of their scientific work and why it mattered to the world. To make the information understandable to as many readers as possible, I encouraged the scientists to produce a simple drawing or picture to explain what was going on. I also asked for a game or activity that would help readers understand the science. Not every scientist could provide one, but most did. Finally, for The Mystery, I asked what big mystery in the scientist's field still remained to be solved. Their answers are thought-provoking and may be interesting especially to younger readers who might want to become Canadian scientists themselves.

Each profile ends with a Further Reading section of books, magazine articles or research papers written by or about the scientist profiled.

The Short Biographies

EARLY DRAFTS OF THIS BOOK were published on the World Wide Web beginning in May 1995. Since then, many thousands of visitors have contributed to Great Canadian Scientists, especially the few hundred who nominated scientists for short biographies. Marvin Entz, one of this book's editors, worked hard on the short biographies. The section lists the contributions that make each scientist great, followed by date and place of birth (and death) if available, and where they do (or did) their scientific work. In some cases, especially if the scientists lived a long time ago, we could not obtain an exact date for birth or death. I encourage readers who find such information to pass it on so we can update the website and the next edition of this book.

In the paragraph about the scientists you will find details of their education, work and awards, as well as something about how their scientific achievements made a difference to the world. At the end of each short biography, we list some sources for more information.

Why Science?

THE THING I LIKE ABOUT SCIENCE is the way you can just add A + B and get C in a predictable way at least most of the time. In a world so confusing, so unfair at times and incomprehensible in so many ways, science can be a comfort for me. I've always liked science. As a kid it made sense to me. I wasn't a superstar in sports, but I won first place in the local science fair. In university I majored in organic chemistry because of all the wonderful glassware you could play with. It was fun mixing up smelly chemicals to see what happened. I enjoyed watching beautiful pure crystals appear as if by magic from a saturated solution.

Science and technology dominate today's society in many ways. Wherever you live, almost everything you do, eat, wear, hear or see is brought to you through scientific discoveries. But how much do you know about these modern-day wonders that rule your life?

Science is not perfect. While it can help answer plenty of questions, there are many areas where science cannot help at all. For example, when it comes to feelings and aspects of life like personal relationships, politics, morals, ethics, beliefs, and metaphysics, science cannot be counted on to solve our problems. In fact, science may create as many problems as it solves. While science has contributed much that helps the world, it also produces things that can cause harm. Nuclear bombs, pollution and eugenics are just a few examples. Even so, I cannot help being fascinated by science and the people who do it. The greatest enjoyment in my work has come from those brief moments while researching or interviewing a scientist when I find myself saying, "That's amazing!" or "So that's how it works!"

People sometimes ask me, "Why does it matter? Why should I care about these scientists and what they've done? What practical value is there to the science?" Real-world applications are important, but almost all the scientists I interviewed do not plan their experiments with a view to making something useful. They experiment mainly to satisfy their innate curiosity about the mysterious workings of nature. Asking one of these scientists, "What's it good for?" would be like asking a great artist the classic question about their masterpiece, "Will it match the sofa?" In a purely practical sense, great science, like great art, isn't good for anything, unless you consider exploring the limits of human genius and creative expression a good thing or unless you value pushing forth the boundaries of human understanding of the natural world.

In fact, the practical applications of science often come long after the scientific discovery itself.

Some discoveries have no practical value. Yet it's still good to know that there are such things as, say, Black Holes out there in the universe, even though at this moment you might not see how such knowledge is of any use at all. Just to know about Black Holes is enough to inspire thoughts and daydreams on any number of other subjects. Science charges our imaginations with ideas. That's what I find so appealing about it.

At its best, science also teaches you to be critical. It encourages you to question the world around you and to examine everything you know over and over again. The great scientists in this book frequently told me how important it was to question science itself. Perhaps this built-in quality of science – the ongoing questioning and criticizing – is what attracted me as a child and remains with me as an adult. By asking questions, never taking anything for granted, and always reviewing your assumptions, you can improve your knowledge and understanding of yourself, others and everything around you. To me that is the essence of the scientific method.

Three Definitions

EVERYONE ASKS, "What do you mean by *Great*? How do you define *Canadian*? And what about the word *Scientist*?" Any book like this is bound to generate debate and is certain to be incomplete. When Isaac Asimov wrote the *Biographical Encyclopedia of Science and Technology* in the 1960s, he did not even let an assistant type it, because he felt that the responsibility for the scientists chosen rested with him alone. In a similar way, I take full responsibility for the choices in this book. There is no committee, just me. I know I have been inconsistent in many ways. From time to time I receive mail from people who suggest, for example, that Roberta Bondar, the first Canadian woman in space, or David Suzuki, the popular environmentalist, should not really be in this book. Strictly speaking, maybe they shouldn't be, but I figure if you can make it into orbit to do some experiments, or if you get your science messages on national TV every week, that's definitely great, and that's why I included them. I welcome your ideas for how to improve the book in subsequent editions. And let me apologize right now for all the great Canadian scientists that I missed this time.

How have I defined *great*? I started with Canadian winners of the Nobel Prize, but also looked for Canadian winners of the King Faisal Prize, the Albert Einstein Award of the World Cultural Council, the Wolfe Prize from Israel, the Welch Foundation in Texas and of course winners of Canada's own Killam, Tory, Gairdner, Manning, Herzberg and Steacie prizes. As much as possible, I also checked with co-workers to see whether a particular scientist's work was considered to be outstanding in the field.

I defined Canadian scientists as researchers who held Canadian citizenship when they made their most outstanding scientific discoveries. That's it. That means that many of the people in this book were not born in Canada, and some were born here, but do not live in Canada any more. If they were

Canadian when they made their great discoveries, then they are Canadian scientists. Arthur Schawlow is not included (though he grew up in Canada and won the 1981 Nobel Prize for Physics) because he was born in the United States and made all his major discoveries there, too. It is doubtful if he was ever a Canadian citizen.

The scientists profiled in the interviews for this book were all alive in the mid-1990s. In fact, most Canadian scientists who ever lived are alive today. Before 1950, most scientists in Canada were really from someplace else, especially England, Scotland, or France. In those days they did not have to take out Canadian citizenship because Canada was a British or French colony.

Of course there are some gray areas here. Gerhard Herzberg may have written his first papers on spectroscopy in Germany before he came to Canada, but the experiment that won him the Nobel Prize was done in Canada in Ottawa, Ontario. Sid Altman, who won the 1989 Nobel Prize for Chemistry, did all his work in the United States or England and has lived in the USA all his adult life, but he has always remained a Canadian citizen. And Alexander Graham Bell, the inventor of the telephone, was a Scotsman who lived in the United States. Although he had a summer home in Nova Scotia and made the first long-distance telephone call from his home in Brantford, Ontario, where he spent many years, he never became a Canadian citizen. I made an exception and included Bell in the short biography section because so many people consider him Canadian. It was difficult to make distinctions, but according to my interpretation, everybody included in this book is a great Canadian scientist.

When most people hear the word scientist, they think of physicists or chemists or biologists. In this book, however, I am defining *scientists* as those who study the nature and behaviour of the physical universe by observing, experimenting and measuring. As a result, while many of the scientists included in this book do work in the physical sciences of physics, chemistry and biology, many others are medical doctors, engineers, computer scientists, psychologists, or anthropologists.

Women Scientists

IF I HAD WRITTEN only about prize-winning scientists, this book would have contained very few women. No Canadian woman has won a Nobel Prize in science, for example. Women have traditionally had a tough time in science, not only in Canada but almost everywhere else. I could not write this book without acknowledging that fact. It's important to remember that some human factors affect how science is done and who does it. In the past, women faced barriers to entering and staying in scientific careers, and it's still true now. For instance, even though the number of women scientists in this book is about 25 percent, the reality is that the number of practising women scientists in Canada is only somewhere around five percent. There are many women scientists whose achievements deserve more acknowledgment, and I hope that the women in this book will serve as inspiration to girls and young women wanting to become scientists.

The Great Canadian Scientists Project Website and CD-ROM

THE GREAT CANADIAN SCIENTIST PROJECT is the first to integrate new and traditional media for learning about Canadian men and women of science. A website and a CD-ROM complement this book. The project fits the mandate of the federal Information Highway Advisory Council to protect Canadians from the loss of Canadian identity because of the American slant of the Internet. It also fits with a new Pan-Canadian Instructional Resource Profile that emphasizes curriculum content about the process of science and Canadian scientists in Canada's school systems.

The CD and the website deliver the material in a different way from the book and each has strengths that the others do not. They work together, not against each other. The book lets you go home and read more about the scientists while you're on your living room couch or at the kitchen table. With the CD-ROM, you can hear and see the scientists talk about themselves and their work. You can explore scientific principles through fun-to-play interactive computer games. With the website, you can send email directly to living scientists and ask questions. You can also play the quiz and compete against others across the country and even the rest of the world. For more information on the project see page 198.

Profiles

Summary

Name	Science	Major Achievement
Sid Altman	Molecular Biologist	Nobel Prize for Chemistry 1989 for Catalytic RNA
Bert Brockhouse	Nuclear Physicist	Nobel Prize for Physics 1994 for Condensed Matter
H.S.M. Coxeter	Mathematician	World's Greatest Classical Geometer
Roger Daley	Meteorologist	Principal Constructor of the Canadian Numerical Weather Forecasting System
Biruté Galdikas	Physical Anthropologist	World's Foremost Authority on Orangutans
Gerhard Herzberg	Physicist	Nobel Prize for Chemistry 1971 for Molecular Spectroscopy
Werner Israel	Cosmologist	Co-Discoverer of Black Hole Theory
Doreen Kimura	Behavioural Psychologist	World Expert on Sex Differences in the Brain
Charles Krebs	Ecologist	Famous for the Krebs Effect
Julia Levy	Microbiologist	Co-discovered Photodynamic Anti-Cancer Drugs
Walter Lewis and Memory Elvin-Lewis	Ethnobotanists	Famous for Researching Drugs from the Rain Forest
Tak Wah Mak	Immunologist	Discovered the T-Cell Receptor
John Polanyi	Chemist	Nobel Prize for Chemistry 1986 for Chemiluminescence
William Ricker	Fisheries Biologist	Invented the Ricker Curve to Describe Fish Population Dynamics
Michael Smith	Chemist	Nobel Prize for Chemistry 1993 for Site-Based Mutagenesis
Lap-Chee Tsui	Geneticist	Discovered the Cystic Fibrosis Gene
Endel Tulving	Cognitive Psychologist	Expert on Human Memory
Irene Uchida	Cytogeneticist	World Famous Researcher on Down syndrome

Sid Altman
Molecular Biologist

Discovered catalytic RNA, for which he won
the 1989 Nobel Prize for Chemistry

"Don't worry if things change. Just do what you do best."

The Person

Birthdate: 8 May 1939
Birthplace: Montreal, Quebec
Residence: New Haven, Connecticut
Office: Biology Department, Yale University, Connectcut
Title: Sterling Professor of Biology
Status: Working
Degrees:
  BSc (Physics), Massachusetts Institute of Technology,
    Cambridge, 1960
  PhD (Biophysics), University of Colorado, Boulder,
    1967
Awards:
  Nobel Prize for Chemistry, 1989

Rosenstiel Award for Basic Biomedical Research, 1989
National Institutes of Health Merit Award, 1989
Yale Science and Engineering Association Award, 1990
Family members:
Father: Victor Altman
Mother: Ray Arlin
Children: one boy and one girl
Mentor: Leonard Lerman, a professor of molecular
biology at the University of Colorado, who got him
interested in **molecular biology** and introduced him to
Francis Crick and Sydney Brenner.
Favourite music: Mozart's *Clarinet Concerto*
Character: Modest, quiet, loyal

The Story

THE YEAR IS 1970 and it's an unusually warm June day. Sid Altman is worried. He has no job prospects and little to show for a year of work in Francis Crick and Sydney Brenner's laboratory in Cambridge, England. Crick was the co-discoverer of **DNA** (DeoxyriboNucleic Acid), the molecule that encodes the genetic information that tells **cells** how to function and grow. It's an incredible honour for Altman to have been invited to this famous laboratory. At the moment, it's probably the best place in the world for genetic research, but Altman has only two weeks left before he must leave. And he has no idea where he will go or what he will do next.

Altman is working on mutant cells with malfunctioning **t-RNA** (transfer RiboNucleic Acid) a substance that is part of the machinery in a cell that decodes instructions in DNA. DNA and RNA are long twisty chain-like molecules. (For more information about these, see the profile on Michael Smith.) For about the thousandth time, Altman picks up a glass plate on which there is a thin layer of gel. But this plate is special. Altman is trying a new experiment, something no one has ever tried before. If he can just isolate a special type of RNA called **precursor-RNA** it would explain a lot about the process of reading the genetic code from a strand of DNA.

After putting a few drops of material prepared from the mutant cells onto the gel, Altman places the plate into a strong electric field. This technique, called **electrophoresis**, is a standard method for separating chemical compounds. The electric field causes different compounds to move across the gel at different speeds. Altman waits several hours, and then lays photographic film on top of the gel. Tiny amounts of radioactive **tracer atoms** in the RNA emit **X-rays** that will leave characteristic bands on the film.

With a friend, Altman takes this latest piece of film into the darkroom to develop it. Within minutes the two young scientists both see the same thing. It's just a white splotch on the negative but it gives Altman one overwhelming thought: *Now I know I can get a job*. He has taken the first step in a long series of experiments that will lead to the discovery of **catalytic RNA.**

Altman was hired for one more year in Crick's lab, then became a biology professor at Yale University. His work over the next two decades resulted in his winning the Nobel Prize in 1989 for discovering catalytic RNA. He is still working on aspects of the same molecular biology system today.

The Young Scientist

SIDNEY ALTMAN GREW UP in the Notre Dame de Grace suburb of Montreal. As a boy he loved books. He liked sports and writing, too, but the library was one of his favourite places. He read novels, sports books, and science. "I read everything I could get my hands on," Altman remembers.

When he was 12 years old someone gave him a book called *Explaining The Atom* by Selig Hecht. The book showed Altman the power of science to predict things. From then on he was a confirmed scientist. "I wasn't interested in biology at the time. I liked nuclear physics," says Altman today.

One Saturday afternoon while Altman was still in high school a friend of his suggested, "Why don't you come with me to McGill? I'm going to take the American **SAT** exams." These Scholastic Aptitude Tests are a required part of any application to an American university. Altman had always thought he would go to McGill for university, but on a whim he wrote the SAT and he and his friend both applied to the Massachusetts Institute of Technology (MIT) near Boston. As it turned out, Altman got in but his friend did not.

Altman's family had to scramble to get the money together to send him to this great school, and he wasn't even sure he wanted to go. There was a big debate in the Altman household. But within three weeks at MIT Altman knew he wanted to stay. He was impressed by the high calibre of the students and he really enjoyed living away from home.

At MIT he received a BSc. Then he went to the University of Colorado medical school where he obtained a PhD in Molecular Biology and met Leonard Lerman, a professor of molecular biology. Lerman was instrumental in helping Altman win a fellowship to work in Crick and Brenner's lab in England where he began his Nobel Prize-winning research. After these early discoveries, Altman went back to the United States and became a professor at Yale University.

Altman never renounced his Canadian citizenship, but now holds dual citizenship in Canada and the United States.

The Science

MOLECULAR BIOLOGISTS STUDY the thousands of chemical reactions that go on inside cells to create and sustain life. Altman specializes in the chemical processes involved in copying information from DNA and using it to make **proteins**, the building blocks of cells. Information is copied from DNA by a **molecule** called RNA. About six different types of RNA are involved in

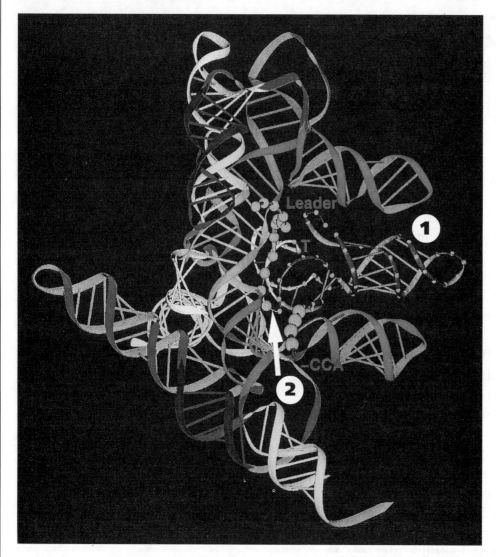

A 3D model of M1 RNA, the catalytic RNA molecule that Altman discovered.

1. The t-RNA precursor molecule whose tail is chopped off by the catalytic RNA.

2. The arrow points to the site of cleavage where the t-RNA molecule is severed.

(Model produced with DRAWNA software by Eric Westhof, Institut de Biologie Moléculaire et Cellulaire, Centre National de la Récherche Scientifique, Strasbourg, France.)

this transcription process.

In Crick and Brenner's lab, Altman was investigating part of this complex process. He discovered an enzyme called RNase P that chops a little tail off the end of an intermediate molecule of RNA called precursor-tRNA. **Enzymes** are special protein molecules that make chemical reactions go faster, a process called **catalysis**. Enzymes usually do

this by holding or bending a molecule in a certain way so that one of its chemical bonds breaks easily. It took about a decade, but Altman eventually discovered that the enzyme he was after was not your average enzyme. Instead of being a protein like all other enzymes, it was made of two parts – one strand of RNA and one protein. Furthermore it was the RNA portion that provided the catalysis.

This was a significant discovery because RNA molecules are much more primitive than protein molecules. Besides offering an explanation for how life might have begun billions of years ago before proteins existed, it also hints at a way to beat a very troublesome primitive life form: the **virus** that causes the common cold. Cold viruses are made of RNA. It may be possible to design catalytic RNA-based vaccines that kill cold viruses by chopping up their RNA.

Mystery

ALTMAN FEELS THAT PERHAPS the biggest mystery to be solved by the next generation will be the understanding of the human brain.

Further Reading

Altman, S. Enzymatic cleavage of RNA by RNA (Nobel Lecture). *Angew.* Chem.Int. Ed. Engl. 29 749-758, 1990.

Altman, S. and Y. Yuan. Differential evolution of substrates for an RNA enzyme in the presence and absence of its protein cofactor. *Cell*, 77: 1093, 1994.

Altman, S. and E. Westhof. Three dimensional working model of M1 RNA, the catalytic RNA subunit of ribonuclease P from Escherichia Coli. Proc. *Nat. Acad. Sci. USA*, 91: 5133-5137, 1994.

Altman, S. and Y. Yuan. Selection of guide sequences that direct efficient cleavage of mRNA by human ribonuclease P. *Science*, 263: 1269-1273, 1994.

Bert Brockhouse
Nuclear Physicist

Won the Nobel Prize for Physics in 1994 for designing the Triple-Axis Neutron Spectroscope and using it to investigate Condensed Matter

"Your mind is your most valuable survival organ. Learn to tune your mind like a radio, filtering out all the noise and other channels, focusing on one thing."

The Person

Birthdate: 15 July 1918
Birthplace: Lethbridge, Alberta
Residence: Ancaster, Ontario
Office: Works at home
Title: Professor **Emeritus**, McMaster University, Hamilton, Ontario
Status: Retired
Degrees:
  BA (Physics and Mathematics), University of British Columbia, Vancouver, 1947
  PhD (Physics), University of Toronto, Ontario, 1950
Awards:
  Henry Marshall Tory Medal, Royal Society of Canada
  Buckley Prize, American Physical Society
  Duddell Medal and Prize of the British Institute of Physics and Physical Society
  Centennial Medal of Canada
  Fellow of the Royal Society of Canada
  Companion of the Order of Canada
  Foreign member of the Royal Swedish Academy
  Fellow, The Royal Society of London
  Silver Jubilee Medal
  Nobel Prize for Physics, 1994
Family members:
  Father: Israel Brockhouse
  Mother: Mabel Emily Neville
  Spouse: Doris Miller
  Children: Anne, Gordon, Ian, James, Beth, and Charles
  Grandchildren: eight
Mentor: Donald Hurst, his boss at the Chalk River Atomic Energy Project who supported him in his study of neutron beams.
Favourite music: Gilbert and Sullivan's *Mikado*, "A Wandering Minstrel I" or *Yeoman of the Guard*, "I Have A Song to Sing Oh"
Other interests: Family, reading, bridge, computers
Character: Modest, honest, absent-minded, frugal, kind, opinionated

The Story

ON AN ORDINARY WEDNESDAY morning in October 1994, Bert Brockhouse gets out of bed at his usual time, about 6:45. As he stretches a bit to loosen the overnight aches of his 76-year-old body, he sees the little red light blinking on the answering machine.

Who could have called in the middle of the night? he wonders, as he presses the play button. He listens to a voice announcing that it is from Stockholm: "B. N. Brockhouse and C. G. Shull have been selected as recipients of the 1994 Nobel Prize for **Physics**." Brockhouse is stunned. For a moment he thinks, *Oh that's interesting*, but then he realizes, *I am B. N. Brockhouse*, and he calls his wife, Dorie, to listen to the tape again with him.

The rest of the day is filled with phone calls, telegrams, and interviews, and the next year is one of travel, awards, banquets, and lectures. Brockhouse is simply beamed out of quiet retirement. In his annual Christmas letter to friends that year, after describing all the festivities in Stockholm, Brockhouse says, "If anyone cares, we got a new car in the summer, a Chrysler Neon."

The origins of Brockhouse's Nobel Prize could be traced back to 1951. Fresh out of the University of Toronto with a PhD in Physics, Brockhouse sat at his desk in a faded blue-shingled wartime hut at Chalk River, Ontario, home of Canada's Atomic Energy Project, which was funded by the National Research Council.

He gazed out the window at the snow. It was winter, but he felt warm inside the hut. He just sat there thinking, mulling things over in his mind. The other night he had been at the home of Donald Hurst, his boss and head of the Neutron **Spectrometer** section. They had been reading a 1944 paper about **neutrons** – subatomic particles with no electric charge that, together with **protons**, make up the nucleus of an **atom**. The existence of neutrons had only been verified about 12 years before. Not much was known about them. Brockhouse didn't quite understand the theories in the paper, but he felt it had a lot of interesting ideas. He was supposed to be working on something else, but he couldn't stop thinking about the concepts in the paper and how he could do experiments at Chalk River to try out some of the new theories.

He fiddled with some math on his notepad for a while and then went to the coffee room. As he passed the lab that housed the **radioactive nuclear pile**, a controlled nuclear reaction that emitted one of the most powerful sources of neutrons in the world at the time, he wondered whether he could put it to use. In the coffee room he met Hurst. Brockhouse went up to the blackboard and said, "Don, there's something I'd like to show you." He sketched out some equations on the blackboard. The math described a device they could build that would use a neutron beam as a better type of spectrometer, a kind of flashlight that could probe into the mysteries of crystal structures and other solids such as metals, minerals, gems, and rocks.

The Young Scientist

IN THE 1920s Bert Brockhouse's family moved to Vancouver, British Columbia. They operated a rooming house in Vancouver's West End and Bert had a paper route to help supplement the family income. He liked fishing and went with his buddies to catch shiners, cod, and salmon off the pier at English Bay. He fooled around with radios a lot as a teenager, hanging out at radio repair shops and making home-made radios from designs in popular electronics magazines. After highschool, instead of going to university, Brockhouse worked as a radio repairman. Then World War II came along and he used his radio skills as an electronics technician in the Canadian Naval Reserve.

When the war ended, Brockhouse went to the University of British Columbia, majoring in mathematics and physics. After marrying Doris Miller, a film cutter at the National Film Board, Brockhouse finished his PhD and the newlyweds moved to Chalk River. Brockhouse spent his working life as a researcher at Chalk River, perfecting neutron spectroscopes and their applications. He solved problems in controlling the source of the neutron beam; limited the beam to neutrons of only one **energy**; got rid of background **radiation** from other experiments in the lab; and solved problems with the sensitivity of the detectors. The resulting **Triple-Axis Neutron Spectroscope** is now used worldwide to investigate **crystal structures**.

The Science

BROCKHOUSE CONDUCTED EXPERIMENTS in the physics of solids like metals and crystals. This kind of physics is called **Solid State Physics**. As his tool he used the Neutron Spectrometer that he developed at Chalk River, which allowed him to look right inside the crystalline structure of solids to find out how solid things like rocks and gems are held together.

Imagine shining a beam of light on an object. Your concept of that object is based on the light reflected from it. But at the atomic level, the wavelength of the light beam is "too big." The wavelength (or the size) of the light from a flashlight is about 7000 Angstroms (one **Angstrom** is roughly the width of a hydrogen atom or 10^{-10} metre), while the wavelength of a neutron beam is only around 1 to 4 Angstroms. In other words, if you could use a beam of neutron light, you could see details thousands of times finer than you can see with ordinary light. Incidentally, in the same way, the shorter wavelength of **X-rays** is what gives them the power to penetrate through

1. **The original triple-axis spectrometer** (1959). A spectrometer is a device that measures the angle, wavelength and energy of light or other type of radiation, in this case neutron radiation. The panel of 52 rotary switches in the upper centre of the picture could be preset to go through an energy scan of up to 26 points. A feature of Brockhouse's spectrometer was the way he could vary three angles: the direction of the neutron beam, the position of the specimen, and the angle of the detector. Add to this the ability to vary the energy of the incoming neutrons and the sensitivity of the detector and he had a Nobel Prize-winning creation.

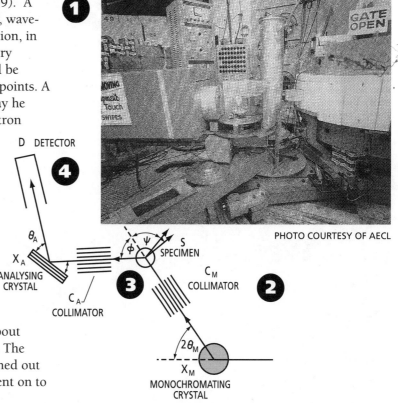

PHOTO COURTESY OF AECL

2. **Monochromating Crystal**. Monochromating literally means "making one colour." A special crystal of aluminum was used to separate out neutrons of one particular energy or colour. Knowing the exact colour of the beam going in can tell you more about what is inside the material you are investigating. The beam was then aimed and **collimated** (straightened out by going through a series of slits) before being sent on to the target.

3. **Specimen**. The position of the target metal or crystal can be varied on two axes (twirled around sidewise or vertically, for instance). The beam of neutrons bounces off the target in different directions that tell something about the atomic structure of the material if they can be detected.

4. **Detector**. The analyzing crystal, similar to the monochromating crystal, can be tuned to pass only neutrons of particular energies. These neutrons then pass through the analyzing crystal on to the detector which counts them. By knowing the energy, quantity, and angle of the neutrons that go into the specimen and then measuring the energy, quantity, and angle of the neutrons that come out, physicists can calculate things about the internal structure of the specimen.

things and reveal inner details that you cannot see with normal light.

According to Brockhouse, "The virtue of neutrons is you can say a great deal about a material by using a neutron beam. You can work out the distance between atoms, the angle of bonds between atoms, the strength and energy of atomic bonds holding the atoms of a solid together, and much more. All these things are very handy and can be applied to working with metal, rocks, gems, and other solid materials." But fundamentally, Brockhouse was just trying to satisfy his natural human curiosity. He wanted to know what things were made of, and to look inside things—like rocks.

Activities

Two activities are suggested here. The first is very simple and can be done by anyone. The second activity is for older students, teachers, and adults with access to equipment that might not be available in every home or classroom.

Activity 1

Object:

To pretend you are a physicist trying to figure out the inner workings of an object or specimen.

You need:

- *An old watch or alarm clock. (Even new ones can be found for $10 in most drug stores.)*
- *A large pile of stones and rocks of various sizes.*
- *A tape measure or ruler.*

What to do:

Put the clock or watch on a dry concrete surface inside or outside, someplace where it's safe to throw stones. Now try throwing small stones from a certain distance towards the watch. You can use the tape measure to be sure you are throwing from a constant distance and direction. Write down your distance and also the size of your rocks. When you hit the watch, what happens? Write down what you observe. If you are lucky, you will smash the watch to pieces and parts will fly in all directions. From this you can determine what was inside the watch and if you are careful and clever, you might be able to figure out how the watch was made and how it worked.

If the watch does not get smashed with small stones, you can increase the energy of your "neutron beam" by using bigger rocks, or you can try a different direction of throw or distance. You can also turn the specimen in another direction. This is a very crude analogy of what physicists like Bert Brockhouse do, but they use neutrons instead of rocks and they use very complicated equipment to carefully measure the energy of their rocks as they are thrown and to measure the pieces that come out of the target specimen.

Activity 2

This activity is a better example of the way experimental physicists really work. They use measurements to infer properties of the material they are examining.

Object:

To use a laser to count the number of lines on a CD.

You need:

- *A laser light source like a red laser pointer or a high school lab laser. Ideally you need to know the wavelength of the laser exactly. (It will probably be around 665 nanometres and will be written on the laser.)*

- *Any diffraction grating – for example, mylar, rainbow wrapping paper, an ordinary audio CD, or a high school diffraction grating of known line number.*

- *A tape measure or ruler.*

- *A table with a simple chemistry equipment stand to mount the laser.*

What to do:

Set up the laser light source and the target grating (for example, the "rainbow" side of an audio CD) as shown in the diagram on page 28.

The screen or wall must be perpendicular to the grating on the table. Use a very low angle of incidence for the light source – somewhere between 5 degrees and 20 degrees. (Keeping a shallow angle lets you ignore angle measurements for the calculations that come later.) Turn down the lights in the room, switch on the laser and rotate the grating until you get a series of red laser dots on the wall, blackboard, a sheet, or anything perpendicular to the table. You might want to put marks on this screen later when you do the measurements. You may have to rotate the laser in the stand and generally fiddle with things to get it right.

The first dot on the wall is called the specular dot and is just the direct reflection of the laser beam from the CD. The rest of the dots above it

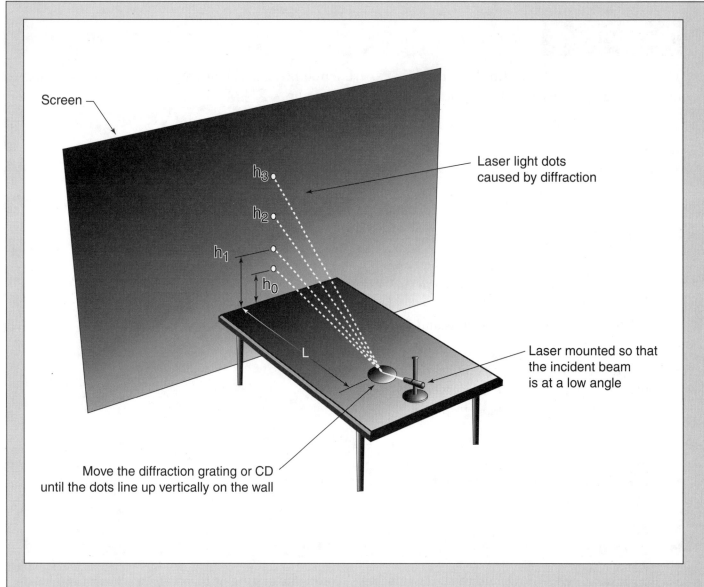

Screen

h_3

h_2

h_1

h_0

L

Laser light dots
caused by diffraction

Laser mounted so that
the incident beam
is at a low angle

Move the diffraction grating or CD
until the dots line up vertically on the wall

are caused by diffraction so you start the numbering from the first one of those. The specular spot is the zero spot. You might have to adjust the angle of the incoming laser light to get the series of dots to appear. By the way, you need a laser light source for this experiment because laser light is collimated, which means the light is all nicely straightened out into a solid beam. Note that Brockhouse had to use collimators in his neutron spectrometer. Neither your experiment nor Brockhouse's will work without collimated beams.

After you can see the dots you need to make a few measurements. First of all, you must establish the baseline, which is the place on the screen that is the same height as the top surface of the CD on the table. Draw the baseline on the wall. Measure the following:

L (The length from the laser spot on the CD to the wall or projection screen.) ...... _____

h_0 (The height from the baseline to the lowest red spot on the wall.) .... _____

h_1 (The height from the baseline to the second red spot on the wall.) .... _____

h_2 (The height from the baseline to the third red spot on the wall.) .... _____

h_3 (The height from the baseline to the fourth red spot on the wall.) .... _____

...and any other dots you want. (Note: if you only get h_0 and h_1 that's enough)

You also need to know either:

λ (lambda, the wavelength of the laser) .... _____

d (the spacing of the grating) .... _____

And finally:

n (the number of the dot on the wall, e.g.: 0, 1, 2, 3, 4, etc.) .... _____

If you know the number of lines in the diffraction grating (or CD), you can infer the wavelength of the laser light. If you know the wavelength, you can figure out how many lines in the grating. Use the formulas:

$$\lambda = \frac{d\,(h_n^2 - h_o^2)}{2nL^2} \qquad d = \frac{2nL^2\,\lambda}{(h_n^2 - h_o^2)}$$

In Brockhouse's triple axis spectrometer, he could make these measurements in three dimensions, plus he also measured the shift in energy of the neutron beam which told him more about the vibration of atoms within solids. Using similar techniques, solid state physicists employ beams of radiation to measure physical properties like the spacing of atoms within crystals.

In your experiment, try turning the grating 90 degrees. What happens to the dots on the screen? If it makes you curious to know why they form an arc, you might want to find out more about solid state physics.

Mystery

LIKE MANY RETIRED PHYSICISTS, Brockhouse likes to explore **metaphysical** ideas – things like spirit, morality, ethics, and beliefs. Regarding his current work, he speaks cryptically of "The Grand Atlas," a sort of rulebook for nature incorporating theories both physical and metaphysical. Brockhouse is a religious man. His belief in physics theory coexists with his spiritual beliefs. "Science is an act of faith," he says. Without faith, how can understanding the existence of a neutron help with the larger moral issues in life?

Brockhouse's example of a moral problem is **Kantian Doom** – the idea that we are doomed because even though we know that something is bad for us, we do it anyway because everyone else is doing it. Examples might be driving cars, using computers, or watching television. Brockhouse believes such problems may require metaphysical solutions, not scientific ones.

Further Reading

Brockhouse, B. Slow neutron spectroscopy and the grand atlas of the physical world. *Reviews of Modern Physics*, vol. 67, no. 4, October 1995.

Harold Scott Macdonald (H. S. M.) Coxeter

Mathematician and Geometer

World's Greatest Living Classical **Geometer** (as of 1997)

*"If you are keen on mathematics...
You have to love it, dream about it all the time."*

The Person

Birthdate: 2 February 1907
Birthplace: London, England
Residence: Toronto, Ontario
Office: Mathematics Department, University of Toronto, Ontario
Title: Professor Emeritus
Status: Working
Degrees:
  BA, Cambridge University, England, 1929
  PhD, Cambridge University, England, 1931
Honorary Degrees:
  University of Alberta, 1957
  University of Waterloo, 1969
  Acadia University, 1971
  Trent University, 1973
  University of Toronto, 1979
  Carleton University, 1984
  University of Giessen, 1984

McMaster University, 1988
Awards:
  Henry Marshall Tory Medal, Royal Society of Canada, 1950
  Fields Institute/CRM Prize 1995
Family members:
  Mother: Lucy Gee
  Father: Harold S.
  Spouse: Hendrina Johanna (Brouwer)
  Children: Edgar H., Susan
  Grandchildren: four
Mentor: Professor H. F. Baker at Cambridge University, England
Favourite music: Bruckner's Ninth Symphony, Third Movement, *Te Deum*
Other interests: Art of Escher, music of Bruckner, novels of Ethel Voynich, plays of Bernard Shaw
Character: Obstinate, optimistic

The Story

THE AROMA OF ANTISEPTIC and crisp sheets mingles with the sooty smell of a small coal-burning fireplace at the end of the infirmary room. Two fourteen-year-old boys are in side-by-side beds recovering from the flu in their private school's sick-room.

"Coxeter, how do you imagine time-travel would work?" asks John Petrie, one of the boys.

"You mean as in H.G. Wells?" says Donald Coxeter, the other boy. **H.G. Wells's** classic science fiction book, *The Time Machine*, is a popular topic of conversation. Both boys believe **time travel** will eventually be possible. After a few sec-onds Coxeter says, "I suppose one might find it necessary to pass into the **fourth dimension**." This is the moment when he begins forming ideas about **hyperdimensional geometries**.

Both boys are very bright. They start using the books and games by their beds to play around with ideas of higher dimensional space – spaces and dimensions that go beyond the ordinary three dimensions of natural space as we see it. These early musings lead Coxeter to later discoveries about regular **polytopes** – geometric shapes that extend into the fourth **dimension** and beyond.

The Young Scientist

SOON AFTER HE RECOVERED from the flu, Coxeter wrote a school essay on the idea of projecting geometric shapes into higher dimensions. Impressed by his son's geometrical talents and wishing to help Coxeter's mind develop, his father took him to visit Bertrand Russell, the brilliant English philosopher and educator. Russell helped the Coxeters find an excellent math tutor, who worked with Coxeter, enabling him to enter the famous Cambridge University.

At 19, in 1926, before Coxeter had a university degree, he discovered a new regular **polyhedron**, a shape having six **hexagonal** faces at each **vertex**. He went on to study the mathematics of **kaleidoscopes** which are instruments that use mirrors and bits of glass to create an endlessly changing pattern of repeating reflections. By 1933 he had counted and specified the **n-dimensional** kaleidoscopes (n-dimensions means 1-dimension, 2-dimension, 3-dimension, etc. up to any number (n) dimensions).

Around 1937 Coxeter received a completely unexpected invitation from Sam Beatty at the University of Toronto offering him an assistant professorship there. His father, foreseeing World War II, advised Coxeter to accept the offer. As Coxeter says, "Rien and I were married and we sailed off to begin our life together in the safe country of Canada."

Throughout his career, Coxeter has not used any of his first names, but has been known as H. S. M. Coxeter.

The Science

GEOMETRY IS A BRANCH OF MATHEMATICS that deals with points, lines, angles, surfaces, and solids. Coxeter's major contribution to geometry was in the area of **dimensional analogy**, the process of stretching geometrical shapes into higher dimensions. He is also famous for Coxeter groups, the inversive distance between two disjoint circles (or spheres), and for the six books he has written on geometry.

①

②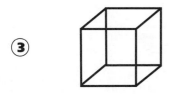

③

④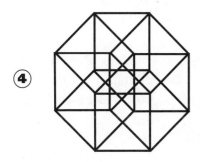

⑤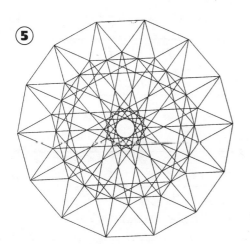

1 **Line:** A line is a one-dimensional shape. You can only move along a line in one direction: forward or back. If you sweep a line sidewise in the second dimension, you create a square. Four lines at right angles make a square. A square (**2**) has a two-dimensional surface. You can move in two directions – forward and backward, and right or left.

3 **Cube:** If you pull a square upwards, you are moving into the third dimension. The result is a cube. Six squares make a cube. Inside a cube you can move forward and backwards, right and left, or up and down – three directions or three dimensions.

4 **Hypercube:** If you pull a cube into the fourth dimension you get a **hypercube**. Eight cubes make a hypercube. The figure you see here cannot exist in the real world, which only has three-dimensional space. It is a projection of a four-dimensional object onto two dimensions just like the cube below it is a projection from three-dimensional space to the two-dimensional flat space of the paper.

5 **Regular Polytope:** If you keep pulling the hypercube into higher and higher dimensions you get a **polytope**. Coxeter is famous for his work on regular polytopes. When they involve **coordinates** made of **complex numbers** they are called complex polytopes.

Activity

Object:

Make **rhombus** *tiles and use them to make various designs.*

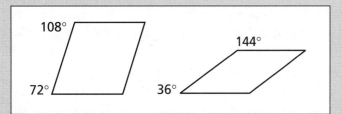

You need:

- *Cardboard or construction paper.*
- *A straight edge or ruler.*
- *A protractor to measure angles.*
- *Scissors or a utility knife.*

What to do:

A rhombus is a squashed square. Try making some rhombus tiles. Make two diamond-shaped rhombuses, each having four sides of equal length. One rhombus has two angles of 36 degrees and two of 144 degrees. The other one has two angles of 72 degrees and two angles of 108 degrees. It's very important that you use the protractor to measure these exact angles when you draw your rhombus shapes or else they won't fit together properly to make patterns. You can use this pattern below as a guide. Just photocopy it onto some coloured paper.

Measure, draw and cut out several dozen of these rhombus shapes. Then move them around on a table to make patterns and shapes or glue them in various designs to another sheet of paper.

A rhombus is a two-dimensional or 2D shape. You can make shapes that look like three-dimensional (**3D**) cubes projected onto the 2D surface of the paper. Try to make 3D cube projections from these 2D rhomboids. How many different ones can you make? What other shapes can you make?

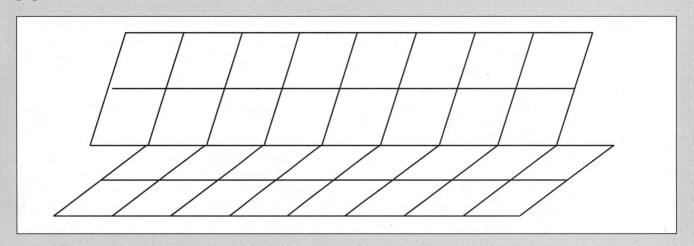

Roger Penrose, the brilliant English mathematician and physicist (born in 1931 and currently a professor of mathematics at Oxford University in England), has shown how these shapes can be used to make an aperiodic tiling of the plane. That means you can tile a flat area with these shapes in a pattern that never repeats. Here's what one looks like. Try it.

If you love this and it gets you thinking and dreaming about shapes and numbers, consider this: multiples of the same 36-degree angle make up all the angles in the two shapes! That is, 36 x 2 = 72; 36 x 3 = 108; 36 x 4 = 144. These are all the angles we started out with! If you think this is cool, you may have a future in math and geometry.

Mystery

COXETER HOPES THAT SOMEBODY might come up with a good proof for the four-colour map problem which simply says that if you have any map in two dimensions and the countries are any shape, you need only four colours for the countries so that two countries of the same colour never touch each other. Though it can be demonstrated easily with some paper and coloured pencils, nobody has ever proved (or disproved) this idea with pure geometry and math. A controversial computer proof has recently been presented that claims to prove the four-colour map problem. The computer tested millions of different maps by brute force, but to Coxeter this proof is not satisfying. Coxeter is a Platonist, a person who believes that beautiful explanations exist for all puzzles; it's just a matter of someone finding them. A more elegant proof of the four-colour map problem would be one that uses simple mathematical or geometrical ideas presented in a clear and logical way.

Further Reading

Coxeter, H.S.M. *Introduction to Geometry (2nd Ed.)*. Wiley, New York, 1969.

Coxeter, H.S.M. *Regular Polytopes (3rd Ed.)*. Dover, New York, 1973.

Coxeter, H.S.M. *Projective Geometry (2nd Ed.)*. University of Toronto Press, Toronto, 1974.

Coxeter, H.S.M. and M.C. Escher. *Art and Science*. 1986.

Coxeter, H.S.M. *Regular Complex Polytopes*. Cambridge University Press, London, 1991.

Also interviewed in *Mathematical People: Profiles and Interviews*. Edited by Donald J. Albers and G.L. Alexanderson. Birkhauser, Boston, 1985.

Roger Daley
Meteorologist

Retired Chief Scientist, Atmospheric Environment Service of Canada

"Don't worry if you have not made a choice of career. It can come anytime from grade school to graduate school. But for a career in the natural sciences you will need a strong curiosity about the world around you, and an ability to analyze and describe what you see. Mathematics provides the basis for all the sciences, even environmental science, so get a good foundation in math."

The Person

Birthdate: 25 January 1943
Birthplace: London, England, but grew up in West Vancouver, British Columbia
Residence: Monterey, CA
Office: Naval Research Laboratory, Monterey, CA
Title: Chief Scientist, Atmospheric Environment Service of Canada
Status: Working. Daley is currently designing and building a new data assimilation system for global forecasting for the US Navy. The system will run on special supercomputers. A similar shipboard forecasting system will work on computer workstations on aircraft carriers.
Degrees:
  BSc (Honours Physics), University of British Columbia, Vancouver, 1964

MSc, McGill University, Montreal, Quebec, 1966
PhD, McGill University, 1971
Awards:
  Fellow of the Royal Society of Canada, 1993
  Outstanding Scientist (National Centre for Atmospheric Research, Boulder, Colorado), 1994
Family members:
  Mother: Mary Daley
  Father: Eric Daley
  Spouse: Lucia Tudor Daley
  Children: Kate, Charlie
Mentor: Professor Robert Stewart
Favourite music: Handel's *Water Music*
Other interests: History, family, travel
Character: Curious, hard-working

The Story

ROGER DALEY IS IN GOOSE BAY, Labrador, on apprenticeship for the Canadian Weather Service. It's 1966 and Goose Bay is a US airforce base as well as a Canadian weather station. Daley is lonely, spending a lot of time alone in his humble room in the barracks. It's cold and there's not much to do. The smell of jet fuel is everywhere and the Delta Dagger Interceptors and KC 135 tankers that refuel B52 bombers in flight roar overhead at all hours of the day and night.

Daley decides to try an experiment. Working alone in his room at night, he makes up little blue cards for all the American pilots to fill out while flying missions in the area. The pilots have to write down things like dates, times, temperatures, altitudes, wind direction, wind **velocity**, and also their own general impression of the bumpiness of the flight. To Daley, the air is like an ocean of flowing currents and bubbles of different gasses constantly jostling about. It's a fluid like water, but much thinner. He spends a lot of time poring over maps spread out on his bed late at night, entering the information from the cards onto the maps to get a picture of this ocean of air around him – the **atmosphere**. Partly out of curiosity and partly just to have something to do, he takes the information on these cards and works out some mathematical formulas that relate the complicated interactions of winds, temperatures, altitudes, and

other factors to create **atmospheric turbulence** – that bumpy feeling you get in airplanes sometimes.

The pilots are very interested and cooperative because knowing the patterns of upper level turbulence along the Labrador coast will help them fly more safely. They start hanging around his room and talking about the air in which they fly. Daley realizes he loves this research and though he never publishes it, he decides to go back to university to get a degree in meteorology, the science of weather.

The government of Canada paid for Daley's training as a weather forecaster. In return, Daley had to go wherever the government sent him. That's how he ended up in Goose Bay. Daley decided to become a **weather forecaster** because, as he says, "I wanted to do something practical with my education, something that would help people in ordinary life." The physics of weather seemed more practical to him than nuclear physics, for instance.

After Goose Bay, Daley went to McGill University for a PhD in **meteorology**. Then he spent some time in Copenhagen, Denmark, doing research on the mathematics of wind patterns. From 1972 to 1978 he worked at the Canadian Meteorological Centre in Montreal. He headed a research group that developed mathematical techniques and computer programs that could predict the weather for about three days. These numerical descriptions of the atmosphere or variations of them form the basis of virtually all forecasting and long-term climate simulations in use everywhere in the world to this day.

In 1978 Daley took on the job of Senior Scientist of the US National Center for Atmospheric Research in Boulder, Colorado – perhaps the world's leading atmospheric research centre. In 1985 he came back to Canada to work as Chief Scientist at the Canadian Climate Centre in Downsview, Ontario. In 1991 he wrote a book on atmospheric data analysis which is considered by many to be *the* book on atmospheric modelling. Daley is now working for the US Navy on an advanced computerized global weather forecasting system.

The Young Scientist

WHILE DALEY WAS GROWING UP in West Vancouver, the Coast Mountains were his backyard. He climbed, skied and boated. His best subject in high school was history but he was always good in math. Although he saw math as a doorway to science, he never wanted to be a research scientist. He always wanted to do something that related to "normal" life. In Grade 12 he had no intention of studying science.

The Science

METOROLOGY IS THE STUDY of the earth's atmosphere and weather. If you ever listen to a weather forecast, chances are you are probably enjoying the results of Roger Daley's research. Among other things, Daley developed a mathematical technique called spherical harmonic expansion which is now used worldwide in computerized global atmospheric **simulation** models. Just like you can make a small plastic model of a car or an airplane, **meteorologists** can make models of how the temperature, wind, rain, and other things in the atmosphere change over time and space. Instead of plastic, meteorologists use numbers and equations inside a computer to model the real atmosphere. Even though your model car can be very detailed, it's not a real car. By playing with it, however, you can get an idea of what it would be like to have a real car. In the same way, the atmospheric models used by meteorologists are not real, but can help meteorologists get an idea of what the real atmosphere might be like under certain conditions. Daley's models are used every day to predict the weather across Canada and most other countries. Good weather forecasts are essential for agriculture and all forms of transportation, among many other human endeavors.

Daley's models are also used in studies of **global warming** – the idea that coal, oil, and gas burning might cause a large enough increase in **carbon dioxide** over the next 100 years to cause a **greenhouse effect**, warming the planet by a few degrees Centigrade. Ice caps would melt and the ocean would rise, drastically changing the world as we know it. Daley is somewhat skeptical about the potential for global warming. He feels there are many questions which have not been considered yet, and that a lot of the science is "for show," for sensational effect, rather than good science. Why scientists might be interested in sensationalism is anyone's guess, but it could be to attract more money and fame. Or it might be a way of drawing public attention to certain questionable human behaviours like burning too much gas and oil.

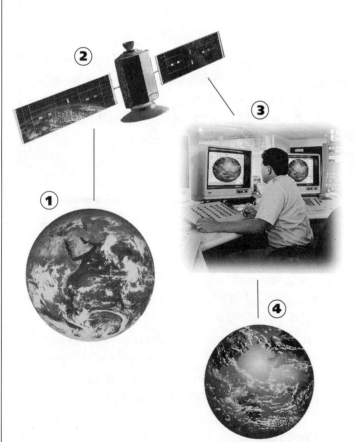

1. Real Earth
The earth's weather is a very complex system affected by ocean currents, temperature, pressure, wind, and many other things.

2. Weather Satellite
Several Canadian weather satellites detect many of the factors that create weather. They send this information back to Earth.

3. Super computer
A supercomputer in Montreal (programmed in part by Roger Daley) records and interprets information from the satellite and other sources.

4. Model Earth
The weather computer constructs a model of the earth based on very complicated mathematical formulas. This model can be used to help predict the weather.

Activity

Object:

To simulate how meteorologists track storm clouds.

You need:

- *A cup of black coffee*
  (preferably a clear glass cup).
- *A little bit of milk or cream.*
- *A ruler.*
- *A watch or stopwatch.*

What to do:

In this experiment you will track a drop of white milk as it moves in a cup of very gently stirred black coffee. Imagine that the coffee represents the motion of air in the atmosphere. The drop of milk in the coffee represents a trace gas. By following the motion of the milk, knowing where you dropped it, and using a stopwatch to measure the passage of time, you can determine the velocity or speed of the moving coffee.

It's important to stir the coffee very, very slowly. Before you drop in the milk from the end of a stir stick, lay a ruler across the top of the cup and measure the exact distance in centimetres from the centre of the cup to the spot where the drop will fall. This is the radius (r). Before you let the drop of milk fall, get ready with the stopwatch so you can time exactly how long it takes to go all the way around the cup and back to where it started. When the experiment is over you should have two numbers: r, the radius of the circle, and t, the time it takes to go around the circle one

time. You can use the formula $2\pi r$ to get the distance the milk travels in one trip around the cup, one **rotation**. (π **or Pi** is a mathematical constant that is roughly 3.14159, so 2π is about 6.28. If the radius you measure is 2 cm, then the distance the drop travels in one rotation would be 6.28 x 2 = 12.56 cm.) The speed of the slowly moving mixture is the distance divided by the time, so divide the distance the milk travels (say 12.56 cm) by the time, (say 5 seconds) to get 2.51 cm/sec. Now you try your own measurements and calculations. How good are your velocity measurements when the milk and coffee become well mixed?

This is how meteorologists work out the speed of moving clouds, winds and storms in the upper atmosphere. They have satellites that can "see" certain naturally occurring gasses in the atmosphere. One such gas is natural gas, or **methane**, that sometimes seeps from bogs. Meteorologists use the satellites to "track" this methane as it moves about in the atmosphere, just like you tracked the milk in the coffee cup. If they can calculate how fast the methane is moving, they can figure out wind speeds in the upper atmosphere exactly the same way you calculated the speed of the moving coffee in the experiment. Knowing these wind speeds is very important for jet pilots because the wind speed and direction can make for a late or early arrival time at the plane's destination.

Mystery

DALEY HOPES FUTURE GENERATIONS will help develop a huge computer system that will be able to model all the **geophysical** systems in the world. Geophysical systems are the forces and motions that affect the earth's air, its lakes and oceans, and even continents through earthquakes and volcanoes. Among other things, such a system would allow us to accurately predict trends in global warming and the formation of **ozone holes** – gaps in the upper atmosphere that appear seasonally over the North and South Pole ice caps.

Further Reading

Daley, Roger. *Atmospheric Data Analysis*. Cambridge University Press, Cambridge, 1991.

Biruté Galdikas

Anthropologist

World's foremost authority on orangutans

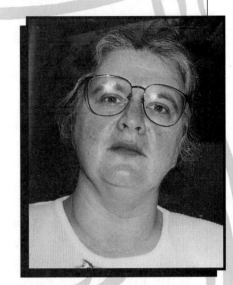

"I've always wanted to study the one primate who never left the Garden of Eden. I want to know what we left behind."

The Person

Birthdate: 10 May 1946

Birthplace: Born in Germany while her parents were enroute from Lithuania to Canada, but grew up in Toronto

Residence: Coquitlam, British Columbia; Los Angeles, California; Borneo

Office: Simon Fraser University, Burnaby, British Columbia

Title: Professor of **Anthropology**

Status: Working

Degrees:
BA (Psychology/Biology), University of British Columbia (UBC) and University of California at Los Angeles (UCLA), 1966
MA (Anthropology), UCLA, 1969
PhD (Anthropology), UCLA, 1978

Awards:
PETA Humanitarian Award, 1990
Eddie Bauer Hero of the Earth, 1991
Sierra Club Chico Mendes Award, 1992
United Nations Global 500 Award, 1993
Tyler Prize (University of Southern California), 1997

Family members:
Father: Antanas Galdikas
Mother: Filomena Galdikas
Spouse: Pak Bohap
Children: three

Mentor: Louis Leakey, the world-famous anthropologist who supported Galdikas's research efforts

Favourite music: Indonesian native folk songs

Other interests: Children, reading, walking, Indonesian culture

Character: Patient, determined, loyal

The Story

SWEAT POURS DOWN HER FACE. She feels thirsty. Swatting at mosquitoes, Biruté Galdikas balances on a slippery log. The logs are always slippery. *I don't know why, but they always are*, she thinks. She tries to avoid a thorn vine and a tree with toxic bark as she trudges through the dark, dank **rain forest**. Then she stands waist-deep in tea-coloured swamp water, her joggers, socks and jeans soaking wet. Two pairs of socks, one tucked under and one pulled over her jeans, keep out leeches and other unspeakable menaces which thrive in the murky water. She's wearing a khaki long-sleeved shirt with lots of pockets and a cotton jungle hat she bought at an army surplus store.

Catching her breath as she stands in the swamp, she spots two huge male **orangutans** standing face to face, glaring at each other's massive cheek pads. They're not that close, but she can tell they are ready to fight for the chance to mate with the female that Galdikas has been tracking for days. Actually, she can only glimpse their shifting shadowy forms in the dense foliage. The sounds are horrific: snarling, grunting – loud and frightening. The orangutans wrestle and tumble, smashing through the brush, trying to bite each other on the head and shoulders. Finally, one flees into the bush. Moving forward to see, Galdikas snaps a twig, distracting the other one. Suddenly, he grabs two thick vines, swings down until he hangs only a metre above her head and stares into her eyes, so close that her nostrils tingle from the stale

The Young Scientist

EVER SINCE SHE WAS FIVE, Biruté Galdikas wondered where human beings came from. She knew they came from ancient apes but she wanted to know more. When she was 12 years old she loved to go into the wilder sections of High Park in Toronto. She would pretend she was a Huron or Iroquois Native slipping through the woods, at one with nature. She spent hours like this, quietly and secretly observing the wild animals in the park.

When she went to university, she combined her love of nature with her curiosity about the great apes and studied psychology and biology. At 22, while she was working on her master's degree in anthropology at UCLA, Galdikas met Dr. Louis Leakey, who is famous for discovering fossils of early humans in Africa. Leakey and the National Geographic Society helped Galdikas set up a research camp in **Borneo** to study orangutans. Her husband, Pak Bohap, a Dayak rice farmer in Borneo, is a tribal president and co-director of the orangutan program there.

odour of his sweat.

In 22 years of jungle observations, Galdikas has had only a handful of such close encounters, so rare are orangutans's meetings with humans or even with each other. But this fellow's message is clear: "Leave me alone."

Galdikas has learned more than any other human being about what it means to be an orangutan, and what she has found out is that orangutans do like to be left alone. An adult male's range is at least 40 square kilometres and he can spend weeks loping slowly from tree to tree, eating fruits, nuts, insects, leaves, and bark without ever meeting any of his kin.

Galdikas has devoted her life to studying orangutans. She wanted to know why these great apes did not evolve the way our ancestors did into human beings. Human beings evolved from a different type of ancestral ape that learned how to live together in communities. Orangutans never learned this. They have not changed in millions of years because the forests where they live have not changed. They have always had enough food and space to continue their solitary existence.

The Science

GALDIKAS IS AN ANTHROPOLOGIST. Anthropology is the study of human beings, but Galdikas is a physical anthropologist, who looks to our evolutionary ancestors and relatives, the great apes, to help understand the mysteries of human nature. Galdikas has been living in the rain forest among the orangutans for the last 24 years. During this time she has founded orangutan support groups all over the world and has become a professor at Simon Fraser University. She has written articles for *National Geographic*, *Science* and other journals and has just finished a book on orangutans.

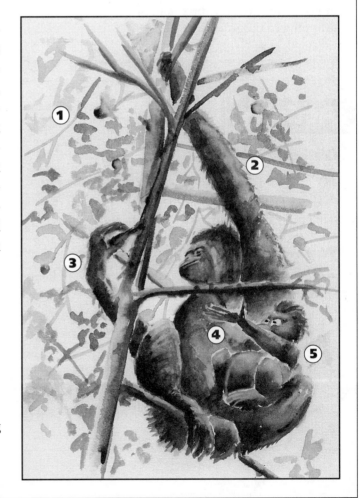

1. The Rain Forest

The tropical rain forest is one of the most stable natural places on the planet. A huge variety of plants and animals thrive there, and nothing has changed for millions of years. This is why the common ancestor for all apes, including humans, may have been somewhat like an orangutan. Orangutans have no serious predators except humans. Their dietary knowledge of the irregular fruiting patterns of tropical plants indicates how intelligent they are. It also explains their solitary lifestyle and the eight-year interval between births. A big animal needs a lot of foraging territory without too many others around who eat the same kinds of food.

2. Structural Brachiators

Orangutans are structural brachiators, which means they are built to swing from branches with their upper limbs, but they have become too heavy to move quickly like this. Adult orangutans are the largest tree-dwelling animals on earth, averaging about 100 kilograms for males.

3. Food Collecting

In this photograph a mother orangutan is collecting sweet habu-habu bark for her baby, one of over 400 types of food orangutans enjoy in the rain forest. Galdikas has tried many of these foods herself. One way she has learned to spot orangutans in the dense foliage is to listen for the sound of fruit peels and pits dropping to the ground.

4. The baby is reaching for the food

Through the repeated transfer of food between mother and baby, young orangutans learn what kinds of food are good to eat and how you eat them. They watch and imitate. They learn by trial and error. For instance, they might try eating the peel of a fruit and discover that it is too bitter. After making this error once or twice, they don't try it again.

5. Babies

Until they are four years old, baby orangutans cling to their mother's fur They are very dependent and remain with the mother for nine years. Females have perhaps four offspring in a lifetime. Orangutan males live solitary lives, looking for other orangutans only to mate. The orangutan's natural life-span is unknown, but in zoos they have lived for up to 60 years.

Activity

Object:

*Try being a physical anthropologist and make an **activity budget** for an animal you can observe. You will call this animal your **focal animal**.*

You need:

- *A focal animal, whether it's a pet, a human being or a squirrel in the park.*
- *A notebook.*
- *A pencil.*
- *A watch.*

What to do:

Observe your focal animal for at least one hour, writing down what time each new activity starts and how long it lasts. Note what the animal does, how it holds things, posture, utterances – everything you can think of. Make two columns: one for the exact time and one for the activity. For instance:

Time	Activity
11:02	Left hand picks up cup
11:02:05	Sips about 5 millilitres

Afterwards, break down the activities into categories like Eating, Moving, or Resting, and add up how much time the animal spent on each. Categories can be divided further. For instance,

"Eating" could show time spent on each type of food. Finally draw a **graph** to display your results. Your graph could look like this **pie chart** where each slice represents an activity:

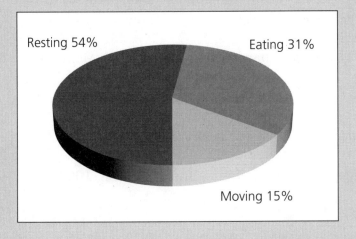

Resting 54% Eating 31% Moving 15%

You could also do a graph to show the breakdown of food types, where each column represents a type of food:

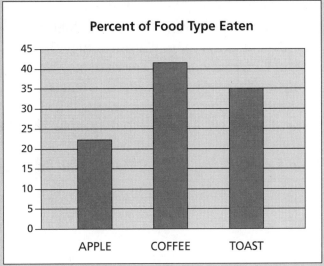

Percent of Food Type Eaten

Mystery

WHAT BOTHERS GALDIKAS is that she sees orangutan behaviour appearing in modern men and women. It's a mystery to her why human beings, who are normally social, gregarious creatures, are becoming more individualistic like orangutans. She says, "What I have learned from orangutans is that we humans must not turn our backs on our own biological heritage. Modern society promotes the ideal of the rugged individual. For men, you have the Clint Eastwood persona – the Marlborough Man. For women, you have single moms raising their kids alone. The ideal Western male rides into town, fights the bad guys, falls in love, and then heads off into the sunset. He is strong and solitary just like an orangutan but he represents an evolutionary dead-end. Many of today's problems are a result of abandoning our human biological roots. We must look to our distinctive gregarious human heritage: living and working in family groups and communities if we want to be successful. Otherwise we are just stressed out 'orangutans' in an urban setting."

Further Reading

Galdikas, B., and A. Russon. Imitation in free-ranging rehabilitant orangutans. *Journal of Comparative Psychology*, June 1993.

Galdikas, B. and P. Vasey. Why Are Orangutans So Smart? Ecological and Social Hypotheses. In *Social Processes and Mental Abilities in Non-Human Primates: Evidences from Longitudinal Field Studies*. Edited by F.D. Burton. The Edwin Mellen Press,1992

Galdikas, B. and P. Vasey. Primatology. In *The Sociobiological Imagination*. Edited by M. Maxwell. State University of New York Press, 1991.

Mongomery, Sy. *Walking with the Great Apes. Jane Goodall, Dian Fossey, Biruté Galdikas.* Houghton Mifflin Co., Boston, Massachusetts, 1991.

Gallardo, Evelyn. *Among the Orangutans. The Biruté Galdikas Story.* Chronicle Books, San Francisco, 1993.

Galdikas, B. *Return to Eden: My Life with the Orangutans of Borneo.* Little, Brown, Boston, 1995.

Gerhard Herzberg
Spectroscopist

Won the 1971 Nobel Prize for Chemistry for using spectroscopy to discover the internal geometry and energy states in simple molecules, and in particular the structure and characteristics of free radicals

"You shouldn't do science just to improve wealth – do science for the sake of human culture and knowledge. There must be some purpose in life that is higher than just surviving."

The Person

Birthdate: 25 December 1904
Birthplace: Hamburg, Germany
Residence: Ottawa, Ontario
Office: Herzberg Institute of Astrophysics, National Research Council of Canada, Ottawa
Title: Distinguished Research Scientist
Status: Working on the study of **molecular ions**
Degrees:
  Diplom Ingenieur, Darmstadt Institute of Technology, Germany, 1927
  PhD, Darmstadt Institute of Technology, 1928
  Privatdozent (post Doctorate), University of Goettingen, Germany, 1929
  Honorary degrees from universities of Oxford University, Cambridge University and the University of Chicago, including many others
Awards:
  Medaille de L'Université de Liege, 1950
  Henry Marshall Tory Medal, Royal Society of Canada, 1953
  Joy Kissen Mookerjee Gold Medal, Indian Association for the Cultivation of Science, 1954

Gold Medal, Canadian Association of Physicists, 1957
Medal of the Society for Applied Spectroscopy, 1959
Medaille de l'Université de Liege (silver), 1960
Medaille de l'Université de Bruxelles, 1960
Pittsburgh Spectroscopy Award, Spectroscopy Society of Pittsburgh, 1962
Frederic Ives Medal, Optical Society of America, 1964
Willard Gibbs Medal, American Chemical Society, 1969
Gold Medal, Professional Institute of the Public Service of Canada, 1969
Faraday Medal, Chemical Society of London, 1970
Royal Medal, Royal Society of London, 1971
Linus Pauling Medal, American Chemical Society, 1971
Nobel Prize for Chemistry, 1971
Chemical Institute of Canada Medal, 1972
Madison Marshall Award, American Chemical Society (North Alabama Section), 1974
Earle K. Plyler prize, American Physical Society, 1985
Jan Marcus Marci Memorial Medal, Czechoslovak Spectroscopy Society, 1987
Minor Planet 3316=1984 CN1 officially named "Herzberg" in 1987

Family members:
  Father: Albin H. Herzberg
  Mother: Ella Biber
  Spouse: Monika Tenthoff
  Children: Paul and Agnes
Mentor: Hans Rau, Herzberg's thesis advisor at Darmstadt, who inspired him to find his own problem to study, then supported his early studies of molecular spectroscopy and sent him to meet Schrödinger, the brilliant Viennese physicist

Favourite music: Mozart's *Quartet for Flute, Violin, Viola, and Cello*
Other interests: Singing, music, mountain hiking
Character: Jovial, modest

The Story

GERHARD HERZBERG BENDS OVER the piles of paper on his big desk. He is overwhelmed. As director of Pure **Physics** at Canada's National Research Council, the fall of 1959 is a very busy time for him. Jack Shoesmith, his research technician, comes into the sun-filled office and walks up to the tall windows overlooking the Ottawa River. He says casually, "I have an interesting **spectrum** to show you."

Herzberg thinks of all the meetings and conferences he has to organize, the paper he is writing, presentations he is preparing and the book he is trying to finish, the third volume of his series, *Molecular Spectra and Molecular Structure. I don't have time for this*, he thinks.

"It's good," says Jack.

Reluctantly, Herzberg gets up from his chair and follows the young technician down a flight of stairs to the lab below. It's a big high-ceilinged room, dimly lit and smelling of ammonia and hot electric wiring. There's a hint of **ozone** in the air, like just before a thunderstorm. They walk past the special **spectrograph** that Shoesmith has built – a long steel tube about 50 cm high and 3 m long. Vacuum hoses and electrical wires snake around the base of the apparatus, but the pumps and electricity have been turned off. The big room is quiet except for the murmurs of a small crowd gathered in the corner.

Herzberg hurries over to see what they are looking at. A long thin strip of glass with a seemingly random pattern of vertical lines blackening its surface – a **spectrogram** – lies on a viewing screen. Recognizing it at once, Herzberg picks it up for a closer look. Instantly he shouts, "That's it!" and breaks out laughing. *Eighteen years*, he thinks, *I've been looking for you for eighteen years.*

What Herzberg held that day was the first spectrogram of a simple **chemical** called **methylene** – a **molecule** consisting of a carbon **atom** with two hydrogen atoms, one on either side, written "CH_2." What was special about this? Methylene is a very unstable molecule, a **free radical** – a transition molecule created briefly in a **chemical reaction** when molecules come together and transform themselves into something new. Free radicals last only for the length of time it takes for their constituent atoms to rearrange themselves with other molecules into new molecules – a few millionths of a second – so it's very difficult to obtain a spectrum of such fleeting entities. Herzberg was delighted because the spectrum of the CH_2 free radical was a key to proving many theories concerning the internal structure and energy states of molecules. That particular spectrum which Herzberg identified in 1959 eventually resulted in his winning a Nobel Prize in 1972.

The Young Scientist

AS A 12-YEAR-OLD in Hamburg, Germany, Herzberg and a friend named Alfred Schulz constructed a home-made **telescope**. They patiently ground the glass lenses, and set them in hand-made mounts in a metal tube. On clear nights they used to take the streetcar to the city park and set up the telescope to look at the moon and planets.

In 1933, Herzberg was working as a lecturer at the university in Darmstadt, Germany, when the Nazis introduced a law banning men with Jewish wives from teaching at universities. Since Herzberg had married a Jewish woman in 1929 – Luise Oettinger, a spectroscopist who collaborated with Herzberg on some of his early experiments – he began making plans to leave Germany. Earlier that year he had worked with a visiting physical chemist from the University of Saskatchewan in Saskatoon. This fellow was named John Spinks and he helped Herzberg get a job at the University of Saskatchewan. It was very difficult for German scientists to find jobs outside of Germany. Thousands of them were leaving Germany to escape the Nazis and they were all looking for jobs in the United States and Canada at the same time. When Herzberg and his wife left Germany in 1935, the Nazis only let them take the equivalent of $2.50 each, as well as their personal belongings. Fortunately, before he left, Herzberg was able to buy some excellent German spectroscopic equipment to take with him to Saskatoon. At the time you couldn't buy such equipment in Canada.

Leaving Germany was very painful for the Herzbergs since they had no idea what they would find in Saskatoon. It turned out to be a good experience for the Herzbergs, although Saskatchewan was very different from Germany. They had to get used to many new things. During the ten years they lived there, Herzberg taught physics and wrote the first edition of his famous book, *Molecular Spectra*. His two children were born in Saskatoon.

After moving to Chicago for a few years, Herzberg accepted a position with Canada's National Research Council in Ottawa and was the Director of Physics there from 1949 to 1969. During this time he made his Nobel Prize-winning discoveries in molecular **spectroscopy**.

The Science

HERZBERG IS A PHYSICIST but his discoveries, which involve the internal geometry and energy states of molecules, are important to chemists, too. You have to remember: when Herzberg was born, the notion of an **electron** was just catching on. When he graduated from university, people had yet to discover how atoms combined to form molecules. It was all new theory. Very little had been proven.

To try to prove all these exciting new ideas, Herzberg became a pioneer in the field of molecular spectroscopy, the study of how atoms and molecules emit or absorb light. By analyzing a spectrogram – a sort of photograph of the way a molecule emits and absorbs light – he was able to tell a lot about molecules. For example, by measuring the distance between the lines on a spec-

trogram and counting how many lines there were, he was able to apply some mathematical formulas which described the energy levels and probable locations of the electrons in the molecule. This was very useful to chemists because the knowledge helped them to imagine ways to combine chemicals to create new substances.

Once the spectrum of a molecule is known, it can also be used by astronomers. They can characterize the composition of distant stars and **nebulae** by training spectrographs on them through telescopes. This is handy if you are interested in knowing what stars are made of. It's a way to learn what is out there, millions of light years away, without having to make the impossibly long trip to visit a place and take samples. (This is one thing that really interested Herzberg because his first love was astronomy.)

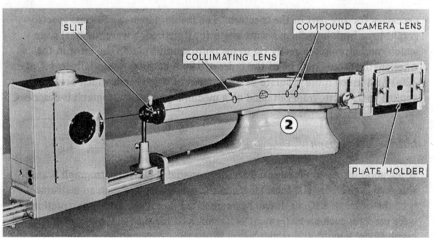

1. A spectrogram is a long piece of plate glass coated with photographic chemicals. After they have been exposed in a spectrograph and developed, the plates have dark vertical lines. By measuring the spacing and thickness of the lines, physicists can apply mathematical formulas and determine some of the energy states of the molecules whose light produced the spectrogram.

2. A spectrogram is created with a machine called a spectrograph.

It takes a beam of light created by burning the chemical you wish to investigate. The light is focused by a lens, then passed through a **prism** and spread out into its component parts like a rainbow. But this rainbow is very precise and appears as dark and light vertical lines that you can measure.

3. The distance between the larger lines in the spectrum is proportional to the molecule's "vibrational" energy. The small groups of lines clustered around the major lines represent the "rotational" energy of the molecule.

These lines and their mathematical relationships are called **Balmer lines** after the Swiss high-school teacher who figured them out in 1885.

4. The molecule CH_2 or methylene. Methylene is a free radical, which means it has an extra pair of electrons that it tries to share with another molecule. These extra electrons make the free radical very reactive, which means it will combine quickly, usually within a few millionths of a second, with some other molecule.

Activity

Object:

To demonstrate the conservation of angular momentum, a basic principle of physics. (Angular momentum can be thought of as the energy of turning. When a car is turning, you feel angular momentum as a pulling force to the outside. It's why you lean into a turn.)

You need:

• *A revolving chair or stool.*

What to do:

Sit in the revolving chair or stool. Now, holding your arms stretched out at your sides, spin yourself around, or have someone else spin you. As you spin, quickly bring your arms in. You should notice a change in your rate of rotation. Is it faster or slower? This change you feel is caused by the conservation of angular momentum, a basic principle of physics. When you tighten the circle of turning, the energy of turning has to go somewhere and it ends up making you turn faster. Figure skaters use this too, when they bring their arms in to spin faster and faster.

Conservation of energy is a law of nature according to modern science. The energy of turning which is present in all spinning molecules and atoms must go somewhere when things change, like they do in a chemical reaction or in burning, heating, or freezing. Among other things, Herzberg showed exactly how the lines in a spectrogram represent the conservation of angular momentum in a molecule as its spinning electrons move between different quantum levels of energy. Certain lines in a spectrogram show the different energy levels that a molecule can have and they also fit into a clever mathematical system called **quantum mechanics**, a theory that underlies most of modern physics. Quantum mechanics says that many things in nature happen in steps called quantum levels.

Mystery

HERZBERG IS FOND OF REMINDING everyone that you should not do science for the purpose of doing something useful. "That's not why I did it," he says. "Scientists wonder how certain things work, so they try more and more to find out how and why. Whether or not their work will lead to something useful, they don't care, because they don't know, and for that matter, they're not that interested. If you develop science only with the idea of doing something useful, then your chances of discovering something useful are less than if you apply your mind to finding something essential." According to Herzberg, a true scientist tries to uncover the mysteries of nature for the sole purpose of advancing human knowledge. The usefulness of this knowledge becomes self-evident after it is discovered.

Further Reading

Herzberg, G. Molecular spectroscopy: A personal history. *Annual Revue of Physical Chemistry* 36: 1-30, 1985.

Herzberg, G. *Molecular Spectra and Molecular Structure, I - IV*. I-III, Krieger Publishing Co., Florida, 1989, 1991; IV, Van Nostrand Reinhold Co., New York, 1979.

Herzberg, G. *Atomic Spectra and Atomic Structure (2nd Ed)*. Dover Publications, New York, 1944.

Herzberg, G. *The Spectra and Structures of Simple Free Radicals: An Introduction to Molecular Spectroscopy (2nd Ed.)*. Dover Publications, New York, 1988.

Werner Israel
Physicist and cosmologist

Developed first logically precise theory for the
simplicity of black holes (1967)

"If you really enjoy your work you never need a holiday."

The Person

Birthdate: 4 October 1931

Birthplace: Berlin, Germany, but grew up in Cape
Town, South Africa

Residence: Victoria, British Columbia, but spent
most of his working life in Edmonton, Alberta

Office: Department of Physics, University of Victoria,
British Columbia

Title: Professor **Emeritus** (Physics)

Status: Retired, but still working

Degrees:
BSc (Physics and Mathematics), University of Cape
Town, South Africa, 1951
MSc (Mathematics), University of Cape Town, 1954
PhD (Mathematics), Trinity College, Dublin, Ireland,
1960

Awards:
Fellow, Royal Society of Canada, 1972
Canadian Association of Physicists Medal of
Achievement in Physics, 1981
University of Alberta Research Prize in Science and
Engineering, 1983
Izaak Walton Killam Memorial Prize, 1984

Fellow of the Royal Society (London, England),1986
Officer of the Order of Canada, 1994
Medal in Mathematical Physics, Canadian Association of
Physicists, 1995

Family members:
Father: Arthur Israel
Mother: Marie Kappauf
Spouse: Inge Margulies
Children: Mark and Pia
Grandchild: Allison

Mentor: John Lighton Synge, the great Irish mathematician in Dublin, who taught him a style of reasoning
and how to draw pictures to understand **relativity**
theory

Favourite music: Arthur Schnabel's recordings of
Beethoven's piano sonatas

Other interests: Has a huge recorded music
collection; collects second-hand books; enjoys
swimming, jogging, and hiking

Character: Self-deprecating, enthusiastic, obsessive,
and absent-minded; has a wry sense of humour

The Story

WERNER ISRAEL RELAXES into the barber chair, daydreaming. He's thinking about his pending retirement and move to Victoria, British Columbia, while the hair stylist throws a protective cape over his chest and fastens it behind his neck. The stylist has been cutting his hair for about two years. The shop is on 87th Avenue in an Edmonton strip mall not far from the University of Alberta where Israel works. He's just gazing out the window when the stylist draws him out of his thoughts by saying, "So what do you actually teach?"

Israel teaches **cosmology** but he doesn't answer right away. A few weeks ago he had been interviewed for a TV show and the interviewer had mistakenly prepared all sorts of questions about make-up and cosmetics. He doesn't want that to happen again, so he decides to tell the stylist about the difference between cosmology and cosmetology. He launches into some basic ideas. Cosmology is a branch of **physics** concerned with the origins of the universe, not anything to do with lipstick or eye shadow. He goes on about how the universe could have come from nothing. This is the **big-bang theory**, the idea that a false vacuum state could be the source of the enormous amount of energy that must have come from nowhere to create everything in an instant. He talks about how cosmologists can accurately predict the relative amounts of **elements** manufactured in that moment of creation.

Meanwhile the stylist cuts his hair, listening attentively.

Israel then describes his own research into **black holes**, how they are incredibly massive objects with so much gravity that anything near them falls in, even light. He gets carried away as he explains some of his theories about what happens if you fall into a black hole, and he doesn't even notice that the haircut is over.

"I'm terribly sorry if I've been boring you with all this physics," he says apologetically to the stylist.

"Oh no, that was absolutely awesome, what you were telling me about cosmosis," the stylist replies.

Israel quietly pays the usual $12.00 and his customary tip and walks out into the springtime sunshine wondering about the meaning of this interesting new word the stylist has invented. At least he wasn't a cosmetologist this time.

The Young Scientist

WHEN WERNER ISRAEL was about nine years old, both his parents became very sick and had to be hospitalized. Werner and his brother ended up living in the Cape Jewish Orphanage for four years. But they were not unhappy years. Israel remembers how one day his father showed up with a set of encyclopedias he had obtained from a peddler in exchange for an old suit. His father had been astute in recognizing his son's talents, for the young Israel spent many hours poring over the books.

Israel became fascinated by stars and cosmology as a boy but he had to teach himself some mathematics to understand what he was reading. He remembers sitting on the beach in Cape Town when he was 12 years old studying *Calculus Made Easy* by Silvanus P. Thompson, and he has never forgotten the epigram on its first page: "What one fool can do, another can."

By the late 1950s, Israel was working at the Dublin Institute as a research scholar. When his term was almost up, he began looking for a job and discovered an assistant professorship available in Edmonton. He had no idea where Edmonton was at the time, but he knew it was where Max Wyman worked. Wyman's papers on the theory of relativity were well known to Israel. In 1958, Israel and his wife moved to Edmonton where they stayed for almost 40 years.

The Science

COSMOLOGY IS THE STUDY OF STARS and other heavenly bodies. Cosmologists ask: How was the universe created? When will it end? How big is the universe? Israel is particularly famous for some of his theories about black holes.

A black hole is not really a hole. It's a region of space that has so much mass concentrated in it that nothing can escape its gravitational pull. Black holes are thought to be formed when very old stars collapse in upon themselves. Scientists believe that black holes have such strong gravity that they act like gigantic vacuum cleaners, sucking in any matter that comes too close. Whether it is a comet, a planet, or a cloud of gas, that matter is crushed to infinite density and disappears forever. The gravity is so intense that it slows down time and stretches out space. Not even light can escape from a black hole, so it's impossible to see one. That's why the American physicist John Wheeler named them black holes.

Despite all this, Werner Israel had the idea that a black hole is actually a very simple thing. Up until he published this theory in 1967, it was believed that the only truly simple things in nature were elementary particles like **electrons** or **neutrons**. An electron simply has three properties: mass, spin and charge. Virtually everything in nature is much more complicated and cannot be described so easily. Rocks have jagged cracks. Planets have rugged mountains. Stars have complex magnetic fields. Israel used mathematical techniques to show that black holes are the simplest *big* objects in the universe. Like an electron, a black hole can be completely described by only its mass, spin and charge. "The surface of a black hole is as smooth as a soap bubble," says Israel. (But you'd never be able to see this, since light is not reflected by a black hole!)

Israel is currently working on several projects involving the internal geometric structure of black holes. He wants to know what goes on inside a black hole. To answer this question he hopes eventually to use **superstring** theory – the idea that instead of using tiny point-like particles to describe matter as we have done up to now, perhaps things can be broken down into tiny line-like superstrings. Israel says, "Einstein's theory of relativity is OK for everything until you get very deep inside a black hole." You need another approach because relativity theory does not handle infinity very well, and a lot of things become infinite inside a black hole.

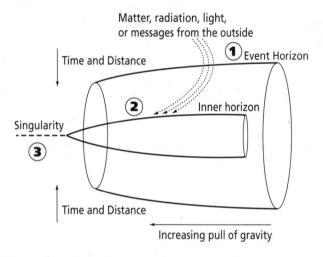

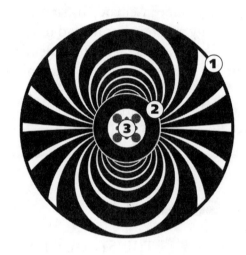

1. If you could watch from the outside as someone else falls into a black hole, it would seem to you that they never get there. The closer the person approaches the hole's **event horizon**, the slower they seem to travel. You can think of the event horizon as the surface of the black hole but it's not solid. To you, the person would appear to stop, seemingly forever suspended at the event horizon. They would begin to turn orange, then red, then fade fairly rapidly from view. Though the person would be gone, you would never have seen where or how they disappeared. If you yourself fell into a black hole you would not even notice the event horizon. From the event horizon onwards everything only goes one way: in. You cannot send out messages for help. However, you can still receive messages from outside, so, to you, everything would seem OK. You would never know when you had crossed the event horizon except that the increasing gravity would draw your body longer and longer, squeezing you in from the sides. You wouldn't last long, which is too bad, because time and space are so weird in a black hole that some scientists think time travel might be possible. Or you might be able to travel to a parallel universe through a **wormhole** – holes in the fabric of space and time. The only problem is: how do you survive the tremendous gravity?

2. As you fall deeper into the black hole you come to the **inner horizon**. This is the point beyond which you cannot even see out. As you reach the inner horizon all events in the universe that have ever happened throughout all of time seem to accelerate and appear to you in a fraction of a second.

3. Nobody knows what happens in the inner regions of a black hole. Theorists like Israel cannot predict what goes on beyond the inner horizon. Ultimately, the black hole becomes a **singularity** – an infinitely massive point in space.

4. The fuzzy blob to the left of the "4" is a ground-based photo of the giant elliptical galaxy NGC 4261 as it appears through a telescope in ordinary light. It is one of the twelve brightest galaxies in the Virgo cluster, located 45 million light-years away from Earth. It contains hundreds of billions of stars. A superimposed radio image shows a pair of opposed jets shooting out of the galaxy, spanning a distance of 88,000 light-years. The image on the right is an enlarged view of the same galaxy taken by the Hubble space telescope. The fuzzy blob turns out to be a giant disk with a 300 light-year ring of cold gas and dust around a bright central core which is probably feeding matter into a black hole, where gravity compresses and heats the material. Hot gas rushes from the vicinity of the black hole are creating the radio jets. These jets provide strong evidence for a black hole in the centre of NGC 4261. The Hubble space telescope has now provided fairly convincing evidence like this for black holes at the centre of many galaxies, including ours.

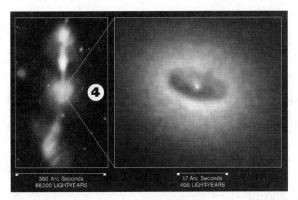

380 Arc Seconds
88,000 LIGHT-YEARS

17 Arc Seconds
400 LIGHT-YEARS

Activity

Object:

To calculate the mass of a typical black hole.

You need:

- *A calculator.*
- *This information: If gas and stars can be observed orbiting a black hole at a velocity of v kilometres per second, and if the orbiting objects are at a distance of r light years from the black hole, then the mass of the black hole in units of **solar masses** (M) can be calculated with the formula:*

$$M = 75 \times v^2 \times r$$

What to do:

In a nearby active spiral galaxy (NGC 4258), 21 million light-years away from Earth, there is an object called a **maser** – sort of a giant natural microwave laser that can be observed orbiting something at the centre of the galaxy that is probably a black hole. The maser is 0.3 light-years from the black hole (**r**) and is orbiting it at a speed of 900 km/sec (**v**). Calculate the size (that is, the number of solar masses) of the black hole at the centre of this galaxy. (Note: You can look up more about this system in *Nature* magazine #373, p. 103, 12 January 1996.)

There is a giant galaxy called M87 in the centre of the Virgo cluster 65 million light years from Earth. Similar observations and calculations show a black hole at the centre of M87 with a mass of two billion suns!

Mystery

A GOOD THEORY EXPLAINING gravity remains one of the biggest mysteries in physics today. Because we don't really understand how gravity works, nobody knows what happens inside black holes, which are the biggest sources of gravity in the universe. Israel feels that a quantum theory of gravity is needed to explain what happens to things that fall into black holes. Though people have been working towards this goal since Einstein's time (for 80 years), a quantum theory of gravity has remained elusive because of problems dealing with infinities of mass, energy, and other physical quantities. Israel believes superstring theory may hold the answer.

Further Reading

Israel, W. and S. Hawking. *300 Years of Gravitation*. Cambridge University Press, England, 1987.

Israel, W. Imploding stars, shifting continents, and the inconstancy of matter. *Foundations of Physics*, vol. 26, no. 5, May 1996.

Droz, S., W. Israel and S. Morsink. Black holes: The inside story. *Physics World*, January 1996.

Susskind, L. Black holes and the information paradox. *Scientific American*, April 1997.

Doreen Kimura
Behavioural Psychologist

World expert on sex differences in the brain

"Don't take too seriously the advice of people who supposedly know better than you do. As long as you are finding out things we didn't know before, you are doing something right."

The Person

Birthdate: Not available
Birthplace: Winnipeg, Manitoba
Residence: London, Ontario
Office: Department of **Psychology**, University of Western Ontario, London
Title: Professor
Status: Working
Degrees:
BA (Psychology), McGill University, Montreal, Quebec, 1956
MA (Experimental Psychology), McGill University, 1957
PhD (Physiological Psychology), McGill University, 1961
Awards:
Canadian Psychology Association award for Distinguished Contributions to Canadian Psychology as a Science, 1985
Canadian Association for Women in Science award for Outstanding Scientific Achievement, 1986
Fellow, American Psychological Society
Fellow, Royal Society of Canada
John Dewan Award, The Ontario Mental Health Foundation, 1992

Honorary doctorate from Simon Fraser University, 1993
Family members:
Mother: Sophia N. Hogg
Father: William J. Hogg
Children: Charlotte
Mentors: Donald O. Hebb and Brenda Milner, McGill University psychology professors who taught her to think of behaviour in terms of the **nervous system**
Favourite music: Blue Rodeo "Outskirts," R & B, Rolling Stones
Other interests: Founding president of a society for the maintenance of academic freedom. "I'm concerned about new rules in the university research environment. For instance, for politically correct reasons, certain research is now frowned upon as it might offend certain groups (like fat people or women). Also I do not like the emphasis on collaborative research. Both these trends kill the creative freedom of the individual. You just have to go ahead and find things out for yourself. This is the mark of a good scientist."
Character: Independent, non-conformist, self-assured

The Story

THE ROOM IN THE psychology building at the University of Western Ontario is dimly lit, quiet and small. There are no windows. The ventilation system is the only sound. A young male university student sits at a table ready for the test while a female graduate student gets her stopwatch ready on the other side of the table. She places a sheet of paper that contains rows and rows of little pictures in front of him and starts the stopwatch. The fellow taking the test is getting ten dollars to sit for a half hour checking off pictures that match. As soon as he finishes one page, she puts another one in front of him until two minutes are up. Then she gives him other similar tests. When he finishes, other students, both male and female, come into the room and do the tests, again for two minutes each. Later, after about a hundred people have been tested, the graduate student organizes the results to see how many rows of pictures the males matched correctly as compared to how many rows the females got right. Doreen Kimura comes in and takes a look at the results. Right away she can see that she is onto something

The Young Scientist

KIMURA GREW UP and went to school in Neudorf, a small town near the Qu'Appelle River in southern Saskatchewan. At school, Kimura was interested in writing, languages, and algebra. Facilities to do science were almost non-existent. Before finishing high school, Kimura dropped out to teach in one-room rural schoolhouses, first in Saskatchewan and then in northern Manitoba. She was 17. While in Manitoba she saw an ad in a teacher's magazine for an admission scholarship to McGill University. She applied for the scholarship just for the fun of it, and got it!

At McGill, Kimura became interested in psychology as a result of hearing Donald O. Hebb lecture in the introductory course. After she ac-quired her PhD in psychobiology, she spent two years as a post-doctoral fellow at the Montreal Neurological Institute, before working at the University of California in Los Angeles (UCLA) Medical Center and the Zurich Kantonsspital in Switzerland. She became a professor in psychology at the University of Western Ontario in 1967 and has been there ever since. She also began a small consulting business which sells **neuropsychological tests** that she developed.

The Science

BEHAVIORAL PSYCHOLOGISTS STUDY how brains work to understand how people differ from each other. One way they do this is by giving people psychological tests. For instance you might be shown a series of pictures and be told to match the ones that are the same. The test is timed, and the faster you do it, the higher your score. Kimura currently studies how male and female brains process information differently – in other words, their **cognitive functions**. She also looks at how hormones, natural chemicals in our bodies, cause different physical asymmetries in men and women. For example, she has found that, on **average**, men have larger right testicles and women have larger left breasts. With no particular practical application in mind, Kimura experiments purely for the purpose of increasing human knowledge about the differences between men and women.

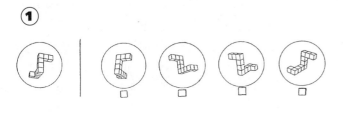

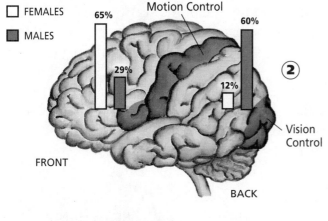

1. **Mental Rotation Test:**
In this test, you must match the object on the left with one in the group on the right. On average, men can pick out matching rotated objects like these faster than women. Women are better at matching objects based on their surroundings.

2. **Aphasia:**
Aphasias, or speech disorders, can occur when people's brains are damaged by some kind of accident or disease. In women aphasias occur when the brain damage is in the front of the brain. In men, these disorders occur when the damage is in the back of the brain.

3. **Finger Ridge Counts:**
Kimura counts the number of finger ridges between two specific points on a person's fingerprint. People with high ridge counts on the left hand are better at "feminine" tasks. On average, any **sample group** of people will have more ridges on their right hands. But Kimura has found that, on average, sample groups of women and groups of homosexual men have a higher incidence of individuals with more ridges on their left hands. Some people consider findings such as Kimura's controversial.

Activity

Object:

To study hand movements in men and women during conversation and to explain why they may be different.

You need:

- *A notebook and pencil.*
- *A watch.*
- *A person you can watch clearly for five minutes.*

What to do:

Find someone you can watch for five minutes while they are talking. They don't need to be talking to you. They could be in a restaurant or a bus or they could be talking to someone else with you. They should have nothing in their hands. The idea is to record their hand movements while they talk.

Make a table to record your **data**. The table has three columns: one for each hand, and one for both hands. It also has two rows so you can record how many times people touch themselves and how many times they move their hands in the air. Twisting a strand of hair or brushing lint off clothes would be marked as self-touching in your table. Banging a hand on a table or waving hands in the air would be marked as free movement.

After watching several different people, count up the totals of hand movements for each individual. Did you record more right hand movements or left hand movements? While people are talking, they use speech centres on the left side of the brain. Which side of the brain controls the movements of the right hand? Your experiment might help answer this question. If you pool your observations with dozens of others at your school you may have enough data to calculate a left- and right-hand movement average for men and an average for women. Scientists like Kimura study thousands of people to get better average results. Even then, it's important to realize that the results are only true for the set of people who were tested – for instance, college-age students; North Americans; people who lived in the 1990s; and so on. In your experiment, which sex did you find uses their right hand the most while they are talking? Why do you think this is? How could you use this information and how might it affect people?

	LEFT HAND	RIGHT HAND	BOTH HANDS
Self-Touching			
Free Movement			

Mystery:

KIMURA OFFERED NO mystery for future generations to solve, saying that it's the unpredictability of science that makes it interesting.

Further Reading

Kimura, D. Sex differences in the brain. *Scientific American*, September 1992.

Kimura, D. *Neuromotor Mechanisms in Human Communication*. New York, Oxford (Oxford Psychology series), 1993.

Kimura, D. and J.A. Hall. Homosexuality and Circadian Rhythms. *Neuropsychopharmacology Supplement Abstracts*, 9, 1265, 1993.

Kimura, Doreen and M.W. Carson. Cognitive pattern and finger ridge asymmetry. *Society for Neuroscience Abstracts*, 19, 560, 1993.

Charles J. Krebs
Zoologist and Ecologist

Famous for writing *Ecology*, a textbook used worldwide to teach ecology, and for his work on the Fence Effect

"We should be conservative in the ways we deal with natural systems."

The Person

Birthdate: 17 September 1936
Birthplace: St. Louis, Missouri
Residence: Vancouver, British Columbia
Office: Department of **Zoology**, University of British Columbia (UBC), Vancouver
Title: Professor of Zoology
Status: Working
Degrees:
  BSc (Biology), University of Minnesota, Minneapolis, 1957
  MA (Animal Ecology), UBC, 1959
  PhD (Animal Ecology), UBC, 1962
Awards:
  Wildlife Society, Terrestrial Publication of the Year award, 1965
  Fellow, Royal Society of Canada, 1979
  Killam Senior Fellowship, 1985
  President's Medal, University of Helsinki, 1986
  Honorary doctorate, University of Lund, 1988

Sir Frederick McMaster Senior Fellowship, CSIRO, Australia, 1992
C. Hart Merriam Award, American Society of Mammalogists, 1994
Fry Medal, Canadian Society of Zoologists, 1996
Family members:
  Father: Lawrence Krebs
  Mother: Jeanette Krebs
  Spouse: Alice J. Kenney
  Children: John and Elsie
Mentor: Dennis Chitty, a professor at UBC and world expert on **lemming** cycles
Favourite music: Beethoven's *Sixth Symphony* (Second movement)
Other interests: Photography, classical music, skiing, hiking
Character: Patient, makes lots of wisecracks, efficient, direct, organized, fair, confident, intimidating, even-keeled, fun

The Story

IT'S EARLY MAY, 1980. Charley Krebs sits at the back of the sled, tired and happy to be pulled along by the noisy snowmobile. Its high-pitched whine breaks the serenity of the frozen lake in Canada's North. But Krebs loves it: the crisp cold, the wide open whiteness. Wind and snow spray his face as the snowmobile plows through a snow drift.

Krebs thinks about the morning as the sled swooshes along over bumps and cracks in the ice. With him are four ecology students from UBC, two riding in front of him on the sled loaded with research equipment, and two up front on the snowmobile. They are returning from a six-hour session tagging snowshoe hares on a remote island in Kluane Lake in South West Yukon Territory. Working in teams, they have just finished checking live hare traps placed throughout the island. They have removed many hares from the traps, taken notes on weight, sex and health, and clipped ID tags on the hares' ears before letting them go. The teams have piles of notebooks to show for their work.

Krebs is satisfied. He's thinking about how all this new information will fit into a paper he's working on when suddenly the student driving the snowmobile yells, "Hold on, guys," and revs the engine to jump across a crack in the ice. The lake is starting to break up with the spring thaw and they have crossed a few cracks already. The snowmobile makes it across, but opens the crack too much. Before they know it, three people along with there sled and equipment are sinking fast in icy water. It doesn't help that they're all wearing winter parkas and heavy snow boots. Krebs treads water with one hand and holds the bundle of notebooks up with the other yelling, "Save the **data**! Save the data!!"

They did save the data in the notebooks – and themselves, fortunately. But his students never let Krebs forget that day. Data is hard to collect when you are a **wildlife biologist** like Krebs. He doesn't work in a laboratory. His lab is the great outdoors. Since animal life cycles take years, you need decades of observations and **data collection** to understand a particular animal.

The Young Scientist

CHARLES ("CHARLEY") KREBS grew up in a small town near St. Louis, Missouri. As a kid he remembers fishing for catfish in local rivers with his grandfather. Charley admired his grandfather and his tales of natural adventures and wildlife. In particular Krebs was drawn to the Canadian Arctic. At eight years of age he wanted to be a forest ranger. Even then, he was reading books about basic **ecology** and the science of wild animals. He was fascinated by the big mysteries of the North – did lemmings really commit mass suicide by jumping off cliffs?

All through his high school years, Krebs had an unusual summer job. He worked for a St. Louis **fur trading company** harvesting seals in the **Bering Sea**. Each summer he went by train three days to Seattle, then by boat seven days up the west coast to the northern islands. Krebs was curious about all the wildlife on the islands. It's probably because of these teenage trips that he has become one of the world experts on Northern animals like lemmings, **snowshoe hares** and **lynx**.

After getting his bachelor's degree, Krebs went to the University of British Columbia (UBC) in Vancouver, British Columbia, to study with Dennis Chitty who was (and still is) the world expert on lemmings. Krebs obtained an MA and a PhD, and then, after a two-year fellowship at Berkeley, he went back home to teach zoology at Indiana University. In 1970 Krebs returned to UBC, where he teaches and continues his work on the life cycles of lemmings, hares, and other animals.

Krebs' textbook, *Ecology,* is the standard teaching text for ecology courses worldwide. His interests have become a family affair. His wife is a research associate in ecology at UBC and often goes on field trips with him. His son works for British Columbia's ministry of the environment and his daughter is an expert on birds.

The Science

ZOOLOGY IS THE STUDY of animals. Krebs is an ecologist – a person who studies natural systems of plants and animals. His specialty is animal ecology, which is a combination of physiology – the study of the workings of an animal's body – genetics, evolution, and behaviour. One way animal ecologists conduct experiments is to mark off a section of wild country with a **grid.** The markers might be stakes in the ground, string, or coloured ribbons. By keeping logs of the numbers and behaviour of animals in different sections of the grid, animal ecologists uncover facts about animals that help us understand more about the mysteries of nature.

Krebs is still trying to unravel the mystery of lemmings and other small Northern mammals whose populations rise slowly and then fall suddenly for no apparent reason every four to ten years. Hudson's Bay Company fur trading records show these fluctuations stretching back for hundreds of years. By accident, Krebs discovered something that might help explain what's happening. In 1965 he tried a simple experiment in an Indiana pasture. He fenced in an area of grassland the size of a soccer field to see what would happen to the population of voles living inside the fence. Voles are like mice, but have shorter legs and heavier bodies. The fence extended down into the soil several inches to stop tunnelling.

Amazingly, within a year, Krebs found the population of voles had increased about five times, much more than it would have increased had the field been left unfenced. The population changes which resulted were called the **Fence Effect**. It is now also called the Krebs Effect, since Krebs was the first one to study animals this way. He has spent his working life trying to explain the Krebs Effect. He says, "You just put a fence up. You don't do anything to the animals. So what is the fence doing?" In nature you find that populations of animal species on islands are much higher than similar populations on the mainland. Is this an example of a natural Krebs Effect? According to Krebs, you have to learn a lot of details about the natural history of any animal you are trying to understand. Krebs is driven by pure curiosity – a desire to learn more and more about the natural world. His findings could ultimately be used to help manage wildlife or to design better, more sensitive methods for harvesting natural resources.

1. The Fence Effect, also known as the Krebs Effect, demonstrated here on Westham Island, British Columbia, with voles, a type of small rodent. A population explosion on the left side, the fenced-in area, has occurred and the voles have eaten everything except the thistles. After the population explosion, there's a population crash in which almost all the voles die. What interested Krebs is that these population explosions and crashes occur in lemmings and other wild animals in nature.

2. Graph showing the population explosion and crash caused by the fence. The gray line is for voles in a similar unfenced area. The black line shows the number of voles over time in the fenced area.

3. Lemmings are small rodents that look like guinea pigs. They live throughout the world in Northern latitudes. About every four years their population increases up to 500 times and then crashes to almost nothing. Even after 50 years of research, experts still don't know exactly why populations of lemmings in the North seem to disappear like this. But one thing is for sure: they do not jump off cliffs.

4. Over the years Krebs has systematically eliminated possible reasons for the Fence Effect. Food is not a factor. You can supply the fenced-in area with unlimited food, and the explosion and crash cycle still happens.

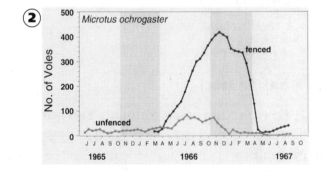

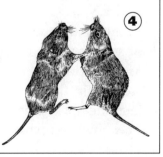

Predators are not the answer. You can make the fence low enough to let predators in but high enough to keep the voles from escaping. The Fence Effect still happens. The fence is never a deterrent for birds of prey like hawks, yet you still see the Fence Effect. Krebs now believes that the effect might be due to social behaviour among the voles and animals like them. For instance, male voles naturally migrate – that is, they move to other areas – but the fence stops them. Also, as living conditions become more crowded within the fence, aggressive voles can't leave or be kicked out, so they have more impact on other voles. According to Krebs, with voles the final crash seems to be caused by an increased tendency for mothers to kill all the babies in neighbouring mothers' nests.

Activity

Here are two projects you can try. One is better for the summer in Canada; the other is best done in winter.

Object:

To learn something about animals by following their tracks.

You need:

- *A trip to the countryside.*
- *A notebook and pencil.*
- *String and pegs.*

What to do:

1. Draw a Map of an Animal's Territory

Go to any large grassy field, such as those outside most airports, and put your nose to the ground. Part the grass and inch along, parting it in a straight line, for at least ten metres or until you find a vole runway. It will be an unmistakable tubular path about 2 or 3 cm wide like the inside of a toilet paper roll. They are like curving tubes at the bottoms of the grass stems, near where the stems join the roots. If you don't find one on the first attempt, try again, maybe in a different field. The runways curve and branch in all directions. Mark off a small area – about one square metre – with string and pegs. In your notebook try to draw a map of the vole runs in this little section of the field.

2. Record an Animal's Habits

If you are in Canada, you probably live somewhere near a spruce forest. In the winter, go cross-country skiing or hiking in the forest looking for snowshoe hare tracks. You should be able to find some without too much trouble. They look like this:

Once you learn to spot the tracks, follow a set and try to determine what the hare is eating. You can examine their droppings or look for bits of food the hare dropped while eating. Is there lots of food? Where is it located? Where do snowshoe hares like to hang out? How do they avoid predators like lynx and other wildcats? Try to write down answers to all these questions in your notebook based on what you observe.

If you are ambitious and you want to get a feeling for what real animal ecologists do, try picking a place in the woods and every winter go back to count the number of hare tracks that cross 100 metres of your path in that same part of the woods. Write this in your notebook. If you continued to do this for ten years, you would probably see a cycle begin to emerge.

ABOVE: Snowshoe hare in summer
RIGHT: Snowshoe hare in winter
PHOTOS: CHARLES KREBS

Mystery

KREBS HAS STILL NOT FIGURED OUT the mystery of the Fence Effect entirely. One thing he would like to know is the following: The Fence Effect only happens if you put up a fence. If you don't fence an area, you won't necessarily  see a population explosion and crash in that area. Yet you always see it if you fence in an area. Krebs wonders how big does a fenced-in area have to be until the Fence Effect disappears?

Further Reading

Krebs, C. J. Population cycles revisited *Journal of Mammalogy*, vol. 7, no. 1, pages 8-24, 1996.
Krebs, C. J. *Ecology*, *(4th Ed.)*. Harper-Collins, New York, 1994.
Myers, J. H. and C. J. Krebs. Population cycles in rodents. *Scientific American*, June 1974.

Julia Levy
Immunologist

Co-discovered photodynamic anti-cancer drugs

"The most important thing: Never shut off your options. You never know what the next year is going to bring, especially when you're growing up, and to cut off your options in terms of your education or where you want to go, what you want to do, and how you want to do it is the worst mistake anyone can make. It's not that you can't go back and start again, but it's very hard to retrace your steps. If you leave your options open, then when something happens you know 'That's where I want to go.' And you do it! You should never box yourself in."

The Person

Birthdate: 15 May 1934
Birthplace: Singapore
Residence: Vancouver, British Columbia
Office: QLT PhotoTherapeutics Inc., Vancouver
Title: President and Chief Executive Officer, QLT PhotoTherapeutics
Status: Working
Degrees:
   BA (Experimental Pathology), University of British Columbia, Vancouver, 1955
   PhD (**Microbiology**), University College, London, England, 1958
Awards:
   Fellow of the Royal Society of Canada, 1980
   BC Science Council Gold Medal for Medical Research, 1982
   Killam Senior Research Prize, 1986

Family members:
   Father: Guillaume Albert Coppens
   Mother: Dorothy Frances Coppens
   Spouse: Edwin Levy
   Children: two
   Grandchildren: three
Mentor: Her mother, who, in the 1940s, had to support the family while Levy's father was in a Japanese concentration camp
Favourite music: Vivaldi's flute concertos
Other interests: Piano, gardening, family and kids, tennis, cooking, writing fiction, a cedar cabin on Sonora Island
Character: Determined, impatient, shy

The Story

IT IS 1986 AND JULIA LEVY is giving a talk in Waterloo, Ontario about **photodynamic therapy**, her work on new drugs that are activated by light. She is there to meet some doctors who are trying these drugs on **cancer** patients. The doctors are very upset because Johnson & Johnson, a drug company, are closing down their **Photofrin** research program. Photofrin is one of the new photodynamic drugs and it appears to be effective against cancer. Many people are being helped by this technology but soon they will not be able to get the drug. "That was a very upsetting experience for me," says Levy now. "For the first time, I became aware that we were talking about real patients being treated for real cancer."

That night on the plane flying back to Vancouver she begins thinking, *We're in the business of photodynamic therapy. We should get into this at the first level and we should maybe start making Photofrin, at least for the Canadian investigators.* She sits pondering this all the way home and becomes very excited. She gets off the plane in Vancouver and calls her business partner, Jim Miller, and says, "We've got to do something." Levy isn't thinking about big financial takeovers. She just wants to help cancer sufferers. "Let's make the product. We know how to make it," she says. But Miller replies, "We'll take over the company." They make a deal with the pharmaceutical company American Cyanamid, raise $15 million and take over the subsidiary of Johnson & Johnson that's making Photofrin. It's a major turning point for Levy and QLT, her company.

"Being in business – in commercial science – focuses your science," says Levy. "The big difference between university and commercial science is not the quality of the research. It's your awareness that as you move a drug forward towards getting it to a patient, it's going to cost you a fortune." Perfecting a new drug treatment costs about ten times as much as inventing it in the first place, and therefore you cannot afford to make mistakes. Maybe that's why it suits Levy's personality. She likes to do things right the first time and she hates retracing her steps in any way. She says, "You can't afford too many goofs when a single experiment costs $50,000."

In April 1993, the Canadian government approved Photofrin for the treatment of bladder cancer. It can also be used to treat other cancers of the skin, lung, stomach, and cervix. In 1995 QLT and Levy received approval to treat oesophageal cancer in Canada and the USA, and they have very broad approval in Japan to treat a wide variety of cancers.

In recent years Levy has embarked on a new program to treat auto-immune diseases such as arthritis, psoriasis, and multiple sclerosis with a second-generation photodynamic drug called BPD (BenzoPorphyrin Derivative). "It's way beyond cancer," says Levy, excited about the potential to cure other diseases with this new drug. She and her team are curing arthritic mice by injecting them with BPD, then placing them into a simple box and activating the drug a few hours after the injection by flooding the box with intense red light. "We're the only people in the world doing this," says Levy.

The Young Scientist

JULIA LEVY WAS BORN IN Singapore in 1934, but when World War II came, her father was captured by the Japanese and put into a prisoner of war camp. Just before this, her mother escaped to Vancouver, Canada, with Levy and another daughter. Even after the war, when her father came back, he was a broken man and was not able to support the family. This taught Levy that you have to be self-sufficient as a woman and you should never expect to get married just to have someone who will look after you.

Even as a little girl, Levy was interested in biology, though she always felt she would grow up to be a piano teacher. On weekends she would come home from Queen's Hall boarding school in Vancouver and go for walks with her mother in the woods below 41st Avenue. Their dog would romp along collecting stray dogs who would stay at their house for several days. Sometimes Julia would take a sieve and a jar to bring back frogs' eggs. She and her sister would grow tadpoles in wash basins in the basement.

Levy enjoyed mathematics in high school, and had a particularly inspiring woman biology teacher in Grade 11. After obtaining a BA and a PhD, she became a professor of microbiology at the University of British Columbia. In the 1980s she founded her own drug company, QLT PhotoTherapeutics Inc., with several other university professors. Her husband shares her interest – he is vice-president of the company.

The Science

JULIA LEVY IS A **microbiologist** and **immunologist**, someone who studies the human immune system, the collection of molecules and **cells** that help the body fight off disease. Her company, QLT, makes a number of drugs that can be used to treat lung cancer and other types of disease. The drugs are unique in that they are **photosensitive** which means that upon being exposed to light, they change in some way that makes them toxic to cells.

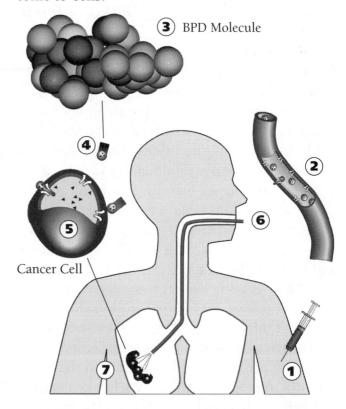

③ BPD Molecule

Cancer Cell

1. Photodynamic drug, BPD, is injected into the blood stream.

2. Lipoproteins – complex protein **molecules** that carry fatty material in blood – take the drug to all parts of the body.

3. Molecule of BPD (BenzoPorphyrin Derivative), a drug developed by Levy and other scientists at QLT.

4. BPD is brought inside cancer cell by lipoprotein.

5. Because cancer cells grow faster than normal cells, they accumulate ten times more BPD than normal cells in the body within hours of the injection.

6. Doctors use a **fibre-optic** scope to enter the lung and find the cancer tissue. Then a red laser light with the **wavelength** of 690 **nanometres** is sent down the fibre-optic probe. The light activates the BPD, which then creates free oxygen molecules. The oxygen reacts with the cancer cells and effectively "burns" them up.

7. A cancer tumour in the lung is being destroyed by photodynamic therapy.

Activity

Object:

To understand why Levy and her team use red laser light to activate their photodynamic drugs.

You need:

• *A good flashlight.*   • *A dark room.*

What to do:

Turn on the flashlight and put your hand over it, or put your mouth around the bright end. What colour is the light that you see through your hand or cheeks?

Why it works: Our bodies are mostly transparent to red light. That means red light can pass through our body's tissues. The red laser light – a 690 nanometre wavelength that Levy uses to activate photodynamic drugs – passes right through skin and flesh. Even haemoglobin, the protein that makes blood red, does not absorb red light at that wavelength.

Why do you think red light passes through our bodies? This turns out to be a handy quality because it means that many diseases can be treated by a person taking an injection of photodynamic drug, waiting a few hours, then sitting in a room with strong red light.

Mystery

LEVY SAYS THAT although researchers know a lot about the biology of cancer cells, how cancer cells develop is still one of the biggest mysteries around.

Further Reading

Levy, J. Photodynamic Therapy and Biomedical Lasers. In *Excerpta Medica, International Congress Series 1011*. Edited by Spinelli, Faute and Marchasini, 1992.

Levy, J. Proceedings of Photodynamic Therapy of Cancer II. *SPIE Proceedings Series, Vol. 2325*. Edited by Brault, Jori, Moan, Ehrenberg, 1994.

Walter Lewis and Memory Elvin-Lewis
Ethnobotanists

World experts on airborne and allergenic pollen and famous for targeting medicinal plants in the tropical rain forest. Since Walter and Memory work as a team, this chapter features both scientists.

"Do what you enjoy and go where your heart takes you."

– Walter

"Remember to have patience for technology to catch up to you and your discovery."

– Memory

The Person, Walter H. Lewis

Birthdate: 26 June 1930
Birthplace: Near Ottawa, Ontario, but grew up in Victoria, British Columbia
Residence: St. Louis, Missouri
Office: Biology Department, Washington University, St. Louis, Missouri
Title: Professor of Biology, Washington University; Senior Botanist, Missouri Botanical Garden
Status: Working
Degrees:
  BA (Honours), University of British Columbia (UBC), Vancouver, 1951
  MSc (Botany and Biology), UBC, 1954
  PhD (Biology), University of Virginia, Charlottesville, 1957
  Post doctoral work at Kew Gardens, London, and at the Swedish Academy of Sciences, Stockholm

Awards:
  Guggenheim Fellowship, 1963
  DuPont Fellowship, 1953
  Fellow of the Linnean Society of London, 1983
  Fellow of the Royal Geographical Society, London, 1987
Family members:
  Father: John Wilfred
  Mother: Florence
  Spouse: Memory Elvin-Lewis
  Children: Memoria; Walter H., Jr.
Mentor: Walter H. Flory, his PhD thesis advisor
Favourite music: Andean flute music
Other interests: Gardening, antiques, family, travel
Character: Congenial, determined

The Person, Memory Elvin-Lewis

Birthdate: 20 May 1933
Birthplace: Vancouver, British Columbia
Residence: St. Louis, Missouri
Office: Biology Department, Washington University, St. Louis, Missouri
Title: Professor of Ethnobotany and Microbiology in Medicine.
Status: Working
Degrees:
BA, UBC, 1952
Medical Technologist, Pearson TB Hospital, Vancouver, British Columbia, 1954-1955
MSc (Medical microbiology), University of Pennsylvania School of Medicine, Philadelphia, 1957
MSc (Virology and Epidemiology), Baylor School of Medicine, Houston, Texas, 1960

PhD (Medical microbiology), University of Leeds, Yorkshire, England ,1966
Awards:
Fellow of the Linnean Society of London, 1995
Family members:
Father: Richard James Elvin
Mother: May Winnefred Foster
Spouse: Walter Lewis
Children: Memoria; Walter H., Jr.
Mentor: Her father, who encouraged her to understand science and medicine
Favourite music: American folk music
Other interests: Gardening, antiques, family, travel, gourmet cooking
Character: Sociable, patient, stolid, forthright

The Story

HOLDING HIS HALF-FULL GOURD of **chicha**, Walter Lewis smiles, wishing he didn't have to drink another drop. It tastes sour, like a combination of yogurt, warm beer, and mashed potatoes. But the headman – the *apu* of the Achuar Jivura village in the **Peruvian Amazon** jungle – is looking him right in the eye. To refuse this friendship-ceremony drink would be an insult to his hosts.

Lewis takes another look at the yellowish liquid in his gourd. He knows that Achuar women make chicha by chewing a kind of **cassava root** and spitting it into a huge bowl. Then they let it stand for a while to **ferment**. The air in the open hut is wet and hot. Lewis feels his shirt stick to the sweat on his back as he turns to glance at his wife sitting among the women just outside the men's circle. A smoldering cooking fire gives everything the smell of smoked fish. The forest outside is alive with shrieking jungle birds, while inside the hut, pet parrots, monkeys, and dogs squawk and bark. A crowd of gawking naked children surrounds Lewis and his wife Memory Elvin-Lewis. *We are the zoo*, thinks Lewis, as he takes a final sip of the sour-tasting brew like a good **ethnobotanist**.

The Lewises have traveled to the Peruvian jungle in search of new **medicinal plants** that might yield new drugs. The Lewises are ethnobotanists and they specialize in communicating with native peoples around the world to learn about their traditional medicines. Mariano, the headman, is telling Walter Lewis about the healing powers of a certain plant whose roots are used to help women through the final stages of childbirth.

While Walter is talking to the headman, Memory notices a big grin on the face of an old woman in the back row. In Achuar **culture** women do not sit with the men, but have their own special area within the hut. Memory quietly goes to talk to the old woman, who turns out to be Mariano's aunt. She takes Memory outside to show her the plant Mariano is talking about, all the while telling her how men don't know much about this medicine, since it's strictly used by women. When Memory sees the plant she learns that it's not the root the Achuar use, but rather the leaf. On closer inspection later, Walter discovers that it's not the leaf that has the medicinal quality, but a **fungus** called ergot which grows on the topmost leaves of the plant.

The Lewises credit many of their discoveries to the way they work as a team. If Walter had been in the jungle on his own perhaps he never would have discovered this medicine. As a man, he would probably not have talked to the women of the tribe, and he would have embarked on a futile search, looking for the active ingredient in the roots of the plant.

The Young Scientists

Walter Lewis

WHEN WALTER WAS 12 his dad asked him what he wanted for his birthday. The Lewis family lived in Victoria, British Columbia, and Walter was fascinated by an uncle who had a plant **nursery** in the countryside. Walter told his dad he'd like a greenhouse for his birthday and his father gave him one. It was made of wood and glass and was about 3 metres long and 2 metres wide with planting benches on each long wall. Walter's uncle taught him how to grow roses from cuttings. The next summer Walter began selling his roses in Victoria.

His mom and dad wanted him to become a dentist. Walter went to Victoria College (which later became the University of Victoria) to study towards dentistry, but he took extra botany courses on the side to satisfy his curiosity about plants. After his second year of university, he announced to his parents that he would become a botanist, not a dentist.

Memory Elvin-Lewis

WHEN MEMORY WAS A GIRL, her father, who was a physician, took her with him on his house calls, and as a teenager she helped in his office. She was fascinated by all things scientific and her father encouraged her by helping her understand what he did. She was not like other girls at Queens Hall school for girls and wanted to go to public school (Prince of Wales) where she believed she would get a better education. In high school she always topped the class in science. As a teenager she volunteered in the St. John Ambulance Brigade and became a sergeant.

At UBC, when she took her first microbiology course, she remembers thinking, *This is it!*

In the mid-1960s, Memory and her co-workers recorded a case of a young boy dying of strange natural causes. Nobody could understand the boy's case history or figure out why he died, so blood specimens were put away and frozen. Twenty years later when the disease of **AIDS** was characterized, Memory recognized the symptoms and had the boy's frozen blood analysed. The case is now recognized as the first recorded case of AIDS in America.

The Science

ETHNOBOTANY IS THE STUDY of plants by obtaining information from people around the world. The Lewises specialize in discovering new drugs from plants used in **folk medicine** by native tribes in South America and other tropical parts of the world. The Lewises are considered world experts on **airborne** and **allergenic pollen.**

Three quarters of all modern drugs come directly or indirectly from plants used in folk medicine. The Lewises are trying desperately to catalogue the wide variety of plants used by tropical **rain forest** cultures before the forests are chopped down. They have collected thousands of plants and found dozens of traditional medicines. These include a wound-healing sap that makes cuts and scrapes heal 30 percent faster, various anti-malarial plants, anti-arthritis plants, and more. The tropical jungles where most of these plants grow are disappearing. At the same time, the people who know how to use these plants are becoming more **Americanized** and are losing their traditional culture and knowledge of the forest. The Lewises and people like them are trying to talk with these people before it is too late. After testing with modern medical and chemical methods, some of the plants they discover may become the widely used miracle drugs of the future.

1. An Achuar Elder
Now dead, this wise elder taught the Lewises much about the medicinal plants of the Achuar.

2. The Hut

The Achuar hut sits in a clearing in the forest. The hut is about 12 metres long and 7 metres wide. Several families live together inside. Unmarried and widowed women live at one end. Meetings are held at the other end around a Snake Stool where the headman or *apu* sits. Open fires burn on the floor and the smoke goes out a hole in the roof.

3. Gourd with Holly leaves

Each morning before dawn the Achuar men drink guayus, a very strong pleasant-tasting caffeine drink made from holly leaves. Each man usually drinks about a litre (4 cups). Within 45 minutes they vomit about half of it back up. The vomiting is not caused by the guayus but is a custom of the tribe. When boys reach maturity they join the men in the morning ritual of drinking and regurgitating guayus. The Lewises do not know why the tribe has developed this custom. Perhaps vomiting every morning is a healthy ritual in a jungle environment where many deadly parasites thrive.

4. Methylergonovine

When Walter Lewis returns from the jungle to his university laboratory he uses chemical identification techniques to determine the molecular structure of the active ingredients in the medicinal plants he brings back. This is a typical diagram of a **molecule** similar to the active ingredient in the ergot fungus the Lewises found growing on a plant used by Achuar women to aid in childbirth.

Activity 1

Object:

To be an ethnobotanist in your own home town.

You need:

• *Six objects made of wood from around your house or classroom.*

What to do:

To get a feeling for what it's like to be an ethnobotanist, try to identify what type of wood was used for each object. Where did the wood come from? How was it made into the final product?

Can you ask your **tribal elders** (your parents or teachers) if they know where the wood came from? What does the origin of the wood tell you about you and your family?

Activity 2

Another place to be an ethnobotanist is in the grocery store. Ethnic grocery stores like Chinese, East Indian, or West Indian ones are good places to look. See if you can find an unfamiliar fruit or vegetable. Ask someone in the store where the fruit or vegetable comes from and find out how to prepare it. Remember to watch the facial expressions of the people you talk to. The Lewises have found over and over again that a slight grin or twinkle in the eyes means there's more to the story. It's important to ask more questions when you see something like this or you might miss an important step in the food's preparation. Ask where the vegetable grows. How is it used? We depend on people from cultures around the world because the knowledge they have about preparing foods and medicines enriches our lives at home every day.

Mystery

IN THE PERUVIAN JUNGLE the Achuar have shown the Lewises a plant they use to treat "the frightened people." The Lewises do not know what

the Achuar people mean by this, but they feel that if this mystery could be solved then a new drug for anxiety or mental illness might be discovered.

Further Reading

Lewis, W., et al. *Medicinal Plants and Chemistry of South America (3 Volumes)*. Chapman & Hall, London, (in press 1997).

Lewis, W. and M. Elvin-Lewis. Medicinal plants as sources of new therapeutics, *Annals of the Missouri Botanical Gardens*, vol. 82, 1995.

Lewis, W., et al. Ritualistic use of the holly Ilex Guayusa by Amazonian Jivaro Indians. *Journal of Ethnopharmacology*, 33, pages 25-30, Elsevier Scientific Publishers, Ireland, 1991.

Lewis, W. and M. Elvin-Lewis. *Medical botany: Plants Affecting Human Health*. John Wiley & Sons, New York, 1977.

Tak Wah Mak

Immunologist

Discovered the T-Cell receptor, a key to the human immune system

"Don't be afraid to tackle science if you enjoy it."

The Person

Birthdate: 4 October 1946

Birthplace: China

Residence: Toronto, Ontario

Office: Department of Immunology, University of Toronto, Ontario

Title: Professor of Immunology at the University of Toronto; Senior Scientist, Ontario Cancer Institute in Toronto; Director, Amgen Institute, Toronto

Status: Working

Degrees:

BSc (Biochemistry), University of Wisconsin, Madison, 1967

MSc (Biophysics), University of Wisconsin, 1968

PhD (Biochemistry), University of Alberta, Edmonton, 1971

Awards:

E.W.R. Steacie Award, National Sciences and Engineering Research Council, Ottawa, 1984

Ayerst Award, Canadian Biochemical Society, 1985

Merit Award, Federation of Chinese Professionals of Canada, 1985

Stacie Prize, Stacie Trust Foundation, 1986

Fellow of the Royal Society of Canada, 1986

Canadian Association of Manufacturers of Medical Devices Award, 1988

Emil von Behring Prize, Phillips-Universitat Marburg, West Germany, 1988

U. of Alberta 75th Anniversary Distinguished Scientist Award, 1989

Gairdner International Award, Gairdner Foundation, 1989

McLaughlin Medal, Royal Society of Canada, 1990

Canadian Foundation for AIDS Research Award, 1991

Cinader Award, 1994

Royal Society of London, 1994

Family members:

Father: Kent Mak

Mother: Shu-tak (Chan)

Spouse: Shirley (*née* Suet-Wan Lau)

Children: Shi-Lan, Shi-Yen

Mentors: Professor Howard Temin at the University of Wisconsin; Ernest McCulloch, Director, Ontario Cancer Institute 1983-1992; Roland R. Ruekert, Director, Virology, University of Wisconsin

Favourite music: Mozart's *Piano Sonata No. 331*

Other interests: Tennis, golf

Character: Absent-minded, impulsive, driven, too gentle, never loses temper

The Story

TAK MAK IS A VERY imaginative fellow. When asked to describe his work as an **immunologist**, instead of telling a story about himself, he came up with the following tale concerning the life of an imaginary T-Cell:

Tommy T-Cell is a biodetective. His job is to patrol the human body investigating suspicious characters. Think of the **cells** in the human body as shops on a city street. Billions and trillions of police detectives like Tommy T-Cell are driving by all the time looking in all the shop windows for something unusual going on. Each T-Cell is trained to find one and only one type of criminal. Tommy is also known as a **Helper T-Cell**, part of the body's **immune system**, but you can think of him as a cop.

As Tommy cruises through blood and tissue he meets a **macrophage** – a specialized cell that's like a garbage truck in the body. Macrophages go around collecting bits of your own living and dead cells. They find parts of invading **viruses** and **bacteria**, dust, pollen, and any junk that's floating around. They stick pieces of this garbage on their outside surfaces in special places where detectives like Tommy can see them. Tommy has uniquely shaped spikes all over his surface, called receptor sites, that recognize one kind of garbage. (In 1983, Tak Mak discovered these **T-Cell receptors**.) Tommy's got about 5000 receptor sites and each one is exactly the same. No other T-Cell has spikes like Tommy's. His are specially designed to fit a tiny bit of **protein** from a virus that causes colds. Tommy tries his re-

ceptors on the macrophage, but nothing happens, so he moves on. The whole thing takes less than a second.

As Tommy floats along he remembers his days years ago at the body's Police Academy, the **thymus**, where he learned how to tell foreign invaders from good cells that belong to the body. The thymus is a fist-sized gland located just above the heart. It is bigger and more active in babies than in adults. In the first years of life, the thymus gives all the T-Cell detectives in the body their life-long assignments. T-Cells start out in the thymus as police cadets. They get trained by special macrophages that show new T-cells every possible little bit of garbage that a normal healthy body produces. These bits are called "self." T-Cells whose receptors recognize "self" are killed in the thymus before they can leave. If they ever got out they would become bad cops that attack good cells instead of invaders.

Tommy finally cruises up to a macrophage that shows him a piece of a cold virus. He checks it with his receptors. It's a match. Right away Tommy leaps into action. The virus has only been in the body for five minutes. First Tommy sends out chemicals that signal regular police officers in the body – **B cells** – to make **antibodies**. Antibodies are like heat-seeking missiles that zero in on a particular virus and kill it. Tommy also calls in a SWAT team of **killer T-Cells** and together they go out in search of the invader. They also start dividing rapidly, doubling in number about every six hours. It takes four days before millions of T-Cells, B-Cells and Killer T-

Cells are mobilized to kill all the virus in the body. Immune system cells are some of the fastest dividing cells in the body.

One day Tommy is cruising the body on his usual rounds when he meets a thug in a black leather jacket, an **AIDS** virus. He decides to check him out with his receptors, but before he can do anything, the little creep gets right inside Tommy through a tiny hole near the handle that Tommy uses when he visits macrophages. Viruses don't usually attack T-Cells but AIDS does. That's what makes AIDS so bad. Now that Tommy has the AIDS virus, little bits of AIDS proteins will appear on his surface. This makes Tommy look very bad to other cells in the immune system. Tommy sees a Killer T-Cell coming and says his prayers. Tommy knows that a Killer T-Cell is trained to kill anything that looks foreign. The Killer T-Cell sees that bit of AIDS on Tommy and without a second thought kills his boss. That's the end of Tommy.

The tragedy of AIDS is that T-Cells are the mastermind detectives of the body's defense system, the ones who organize the other cops. Once AIDS is inside T-Cells, they look like spies to the rest of the immune system. So the body kills off its best cops, which then makes it harder to fight AIDS and any other infection. Most people with AIDS actually die of a common disease that would never kill someone with a healthy immune system.

The Young Scientist

TAK MAK'S FATHER was a successful businessman and the family home was in a predominantly white, upper middle-class district of Hong Kong. They lived next door to the consulates of Norway and Denmark. Mak was the only Oriental kid in his neighbourhood, but like all the other boys, he liked to play marbles in the dirt and kick soccer balls around.

He wasn't particularly interested in school but his mother insisted that he do well and study hard. It helped that at school he was in a very bright group of about 20 kids. Most of them went to universities all over the world. Mak went to the University of Wisconsin in Madison. In the early 1970s, after he received his PhD, Mak began his research at the Ontario Cancer Institute in Toronto and is still there today. Since then, he has become a professor at the University of Toronto and the director of the Amgen Research Institute in Toronto, which develops, patents and markets transgenic mice – animals who carry immune system genes transferred from human beings.

The Science

MAK IS AN IMMUNOLOGIST and a **molecular biologist**. He examines the structure and function of **molecules** and cells in the human immune system, which protects the body from dirt and disease. His research may lead to cures for many auto-immune diseases where the body's immune system malfunctions – diseases like diabetes, multiple sclerosis, rheumatoid arthritis, lupus, myasthenia gravis, and others.

Ever since Mak discovered the genes for the T-Cell receptor, he has used this knowledge to create knockout mice. These are mice with missing DNA (DeoxyriboNucleic Acid) instructions for making just one protein in the immune system.

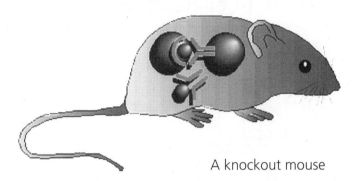

A knockout mouse

To Mak, the immune system is like a huge company that's so big and complicated you can't tell how it functions. But there is a systematic way to find out. One day you take "John Smith" out of the company building and see what stops functioning. Maybe the mailroom grinds to a halt. Now you know what John Smith does. Then you put John Smith back and you try the same thing with another person. Eventually you find out how the whole company works. Along with many other researchers around the world, Mak is using a similar process to understand how the immune system works. They knock out certain genes in mice and then they see what part is missing in the immune systems of those mice.

The human immune system is very complicated and the following is just a very simple explanation of one major part.

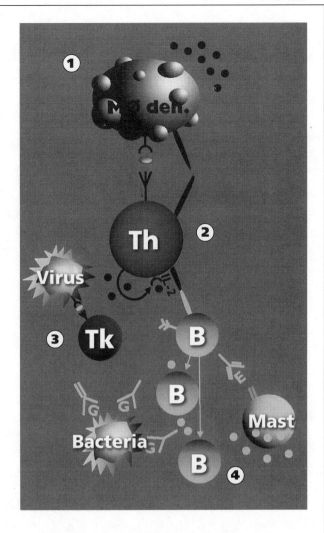

1. **Macrophages** are like garbage collectors. They get bits of molecules from invaders and present them to T-Cells for identification.

2. **Helper T-Cells** (Th) are the masterminds of the immune system. They use their receptors to identify invaders and send signals to B-Cells (B) and Killer T-Cells (Tk) to start the attack. Each T-Cell receptor recognizes one short piece of a protein molecule about eight **amino acids** long. There are trillions of unique T-Cells in a healthy body. Enough to recognize any foreign molecule that enters the body.

3. **Killer T-Cells** are best at killing viruses. They can recognize a virus and then release a **toxin**, or poison, that kills it and any others in the vicinity.

4. **B-Cells** are particularly good at destroying bacteria. They make antibodies (G) which glom onto bacteria and make them easy to kill. B-Cells can also trigger **mast cells** which act as a kind of long term memory for the immune system so a defence can be mounted faster the next time the body is attacked.

Activity

One of the greatest mysteries of the human immune system is how our 100,000 genes can contain enough instructions to create not only us, but also several trillion different T-Cells. In just the last ten years researchers have discovered the clever way it works.

Object:

To calculate the number of possible different T-cell receptors that your body's immune system can make from just the few hundred protein chains encoded in your immune system DNA.

You Need:

• *A calculator and these facts:*

T-cell receptors consist of two proteins called alpha and beta. All proteins are made of chains of amino acids. Each T-Cell receptor protein chain has a bottom part that is constant like the trunk of a tree and a top part that is divided into three major sections called Variable, Diversity, and Joining. Human DNA has the genetic code to make 109 different protein segments for the variable portion of the Alpha chain. Similarly there are 61 different possible Joining segments. The Alpha chain has no Diversity segment. It has only one constant trunk segment, so to calculate the number of possible different Alpha chains just multiply 109 x 61 x 1 = 6649

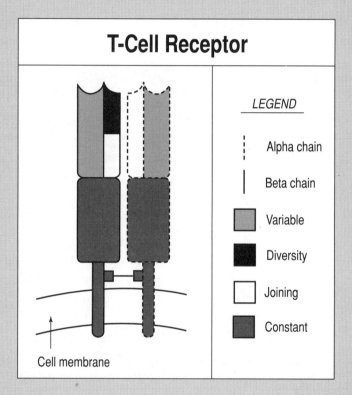

T-Cell Receptor

LEGEND

- - - Alpha chain

| Beta chain

■ Variable

■ Diversity

□ Joining

■ Constant

Cell membrane

Here is a table to help you:

	Variable	Diversity	Joining	Constant
Alpha	109	0	61	1
Beta	64	2	13	2

What to do:

Try to calculate the total possible number of T-Cell receptors that your immune system can make. (Hint: multiply everything together.) How big is your number? Is it in the millions, billions, or trillions?

Now add this fact. A special enzyme puts a few extra amino acids between the Variable and Diversity chains. These are chosen randomly from our 21 amino acids, so you need to multiply again by 21, three or four times for each chain. Now how many possibilities are there?

Mystery

MAK BELIEVES THAT in the future, scientists will use the immune system to clean out leftover cancer cells after tumours are removed surgically or killed with chemotherapy. He also believes that much better vaccines can be developed for malaria and other diseases that are currently difficult to control. He also thinks that a cure will be found for juvenile diabetes.

But for Mak the biggest unsolved mystery of all is the way the immune system distinguishes between foreign invaders and "self." He says the thymus is only half the story because many new **antigens** (or foreign molecules) attack our bodies long after the thymus has finished the bulk of its work training T-Cells.

Further Reading

Mak, T.W., editor. *The T-Cell Receptor*. Plenum Press, New York, 1988.

Mak, T.W. and H. Wigzell, editors. AIDS: Ten years later. *FASEB Journal*, July 1991.

Mak, T.W. and D. E. Bergsagel. *Molecular Mechanisms and Their Clinical Application in Malignancies*. Academic Press, New York, 1991.

Janeway, C. A., Jr. How the immune system recognizes invaders. *Scientific American*, September 1993.

Mak, T.W., et al. Irf-1 is an essential transcription factor for antiviral response to interferons. *Science*, 1994.

Mak, T.W., et al. T-Cell development and function in gene-knockout mice. *Current Opinions in Immunology 6*, 298-307, 1994.

John Charles Polanyi
Chemist

Won the 1986 Nobel Prize for Chemistry for using chemiluminescence of molecules to explain energy relationships in chemical reactions

"The most exciting thing in the twentieth century is science. Young people ask me whether this country is serious about science. They aren't thinking about the passport that they will hold, but the country that they must rely on for support and encouragement."

The Person

Birthdate: 23 January 1929
Birthplace: Berlin, Germany, but grew up in Manchester, England
Residence: Toronto, Ontario
Office: Department of **Chemistry**, University of Toronto, Ontario
Title: Professor of Chemistry
Status: Working
Degrees:
  BSc, Manchester University, Manchester, England 1949
  MSc, Manchester University, 1950
  PhD, Manchester University, 1952
Awards:
  Marlow Medal of the Faraday Society, 1962
  Steacie Prize for Natural Sciences, 1965
  Henry Marshall Tory Medal, Royal Society of Canada, 1977
  Wolf Prize, 1982
  Nobel Prize for Chemistry, 1986
  Izaak Walton Killam Memorial Prize, 1988
  Royal Medal of the Royal Society of London, 1989

Officer of the Order of Canada, 1974
Companion of the Order of Canada, 1979
Fellow of Royal Society of Canada, 1966
Royal Society of London, 1971
Royal Society of Edinburgh, 1988
Foreign Member of American Academy of Arts and Sciences, 1976
Foreign Associate of the US National Academy of Sciences, 1978
Member of the Pontifical Academy, Rome, 1986
Family members:
  Father: Michael Polanyi
  Mother: Magda Elizabeth (Kemeny)
  Spouse: Anne (Sue) Ferrar Davidson
  Children: Michael and Margaret
Mentors: His father; also E.W.R. Steacie, a Canadian pioneer in chemistry
Favourite music: Tchaikovsky
Other interests: Skiing, walking, art, literature, poetry, peace activism
Character: Busy, boyish, enthusiastic, helpful

The Story

AT ABOUT EIGHT O'CLOCK on a Thursday night, John Polanyi walks into the janitorial closet he calls a laboratory. The year is 1956. The young University of Toronto lecturer can't expect to have much lab space. He isn't even an assistant professor yet. Polanyi's graduate student, Ken Cashion, who is wearing one of his many short-sleeved Hawaiian shirts, says, "Well, I think we're ready for another run."

"Did you check the seals on the 'Stokes'?" asks Polanyi, glancing at the giant vacuum pump thwapping away in the corner.

"Yes. They're not great, but I think they'll hold for one more experiment," says Cashion.

The fresh-air scent of **ozone** catches Polanyi's nose as Cashion opens the hydrogen valve and flicks a switch. For this experiment they need **hydrogen** gas as single **atoms**. (Hydrogen occurs naturally in pairs of hydrogen atoms.) Ken has scrounged the electrical discharge unit from a **neon** sign. By jolting the flow of hydrogen with 6000 volts of electricity, Polanyi and Cashion break the gas into single hydrogen atoms. Polanyi likes the soft pinky neon glow hydrogen makes but he worries about its explosive power. Some hasty calculations they made the day before show the lab probably won't blow up, but they aren't entirely sure.

As it turned out, the experiment was a success and Polanyi and Cashion recorded something that no one had ever seen before – a tiny amount of light produced by the reaction of hydrogen with chlorine. This light was **chemiluminescence**. Because Polanyi understood the source of the feeble light emissions in his experiment, he was able to predict exactly what kind of energy had to be applied to make this chemical reaction take place. Over the years he expanded his theories for other **chemical reactions**. This understanding eventually resulted in Polanyi's Nobel Prize.

The Young Scientist

WHEN POLANYI WAS 11 years old, his father, who was a chemistry professor at the University of Manchester in England, sent him to Canada so that he would not be hurt during World War II bombings in England. Polanyi stayed with a family in Toronto for three years. He remembers going on a bicycle camping trip and reading the *Count of Monte Cristo* and *War and Peace*. He was not interested in science as much as in sociology and literature.

In school Polanyi thought it was sort of dumb just to follow instructions for a chemistry experiment and get the "right" result. He would always fool around and try to vary things just to see what would happen. He was very curious. The problem was that he would always get the "wrong" result. This would get him in trouble and his teachers often said he lacked the discipline to learn. He kept at it, however, and eventually got very interested in science. But he likes to tell kids that a life-long commitment to something need not start out with a love affair.

After the war, Polanyi went back to Manchester where he obtained his university education, including a PhD in chemistry. He came back to Canada after that, first for a job at the National Research Council where he worked for a while with Gerhard Herzberg, who was studying **energy** states of **molecules**. After a stint at Princeton University in New Jersey, in 1956 Polanyi got a job lecturing at the University of Toronto.

The Science

JOHN POLANYI IS A **physical chemist**. He studies the physics of chemical reactions – the energy states and the movements of molecules during the moment of reaction. This field of chemistry is called **reaction dynamics**. His work has helped answer the question: How do you get a chemical reaction to go? Do you tickle the molecules or do you slam them together? It turns out that in some cases tickling works, while in others you just have to slam molecules against each other. As Polanyi says, "The importance of this work is that we have a picture of reacting atoms in the transition state."

The transition state of a chemical reaction is the brief period, often only millionths of a second long, when the starting materials have combined together but have not yet completely transformed themselves into the products of the reaction. This knowledge of reaction dynamics has allowed chemists to fine-tune reaction conditions to improve yields in chemical processes. An unexpected result of Polanyi's work has been the understanding and development of powerful new lasers.

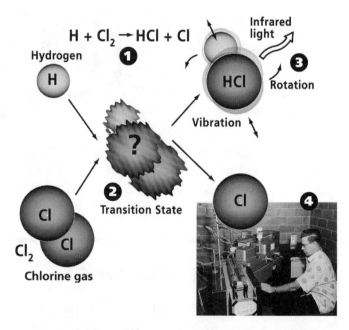

$$H + Cl_2 \rightarrow HCl + Cl$$

1. The Nobel Prize-Winning Experiment

A lot of energy is given off when hydrogen and chlorine react to form hydrogen chloride, but nobody knew much about this energy when Polanyi arrived at the University of Toronto in 1956 and decided to study it. Little did Polanyi realize that this simple reaction would lead to a Nobel Prize 30 years later.

2. Transition State

For a brief instant at the moment of reaction, the molecules are in a transition state as they turn into new chemicals. Polanyi's experiments led to a picture of the arrangement of atoms in the transition state. At the time it was known that molecules had three kinds of motion: spinning or **rotational energy**, buzzing or **vibrational energy**, and the energy of movement from one point to another or **translational energy**. What was entirely unknown was how the energy during a reaction was divided up among these three types of energy. Polanyi's experiments began a new field of chemistry called reaction dynamics, the prediction of the pattern of the motion of molecules in a chemical reaction.

3. Chemiluminescence

Polanyi used an **infrared spectrometer** to measure the light energy emitted by the new-born products of the chemical reaction. The product molecules emit a very feeble light called chemiluminescence, which Polanyi recorded. He used this information to distinguish between vibrational and rotational energies in the molecule. His understanding of light emitted by chemical reactions later allowed him to propose vibrational and chemical lasers, the most powerful sources of infrared radiation ever developed.

4. The Lab

Polanyi's graduate student assistant Ken Cashion set up the Nobel Prize-winning apparatus and was the first to see the result of the experiment. The two researchers had to borrow the spectrometer from others who would have been furious if they had realized how the spectrometer had been dismantled and modified for the experiment.

Mystery

POLYANI BELIEVES THAT one of the great mysteries is the molecular basis of life. He believes that in the future we will have devices that operate in the 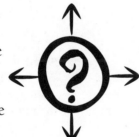 molecular dimension, allowing observations of chemical reactions under much more widely varying conditions than currently possible.

Further Reading

Stevenson, R, and J. Polanyi. Seeking order out of chaos. *Chemistry in Britain*, October 1987.
Polanyi, J. The dangers of nuclear war. *Pugwash Symposium in Toronto*, May 1978

William Ricker

Fisheries Biologist

Inventor of the Ricker Curve for describing fish population dynamics

"Try and arrange your work so that you're doing something that you're interested in. There's quite a bit of routine in research work but I've never worked on a project that I wasn't very interested in."

The Person

Birthdate: 11 August 1908
Birthplace: Waterdown, Ontario
Residence: Nanaimo, British Columbia
Office: Nanaimo Biological Station, Canadian Department of Fisheries and Oceans
Title: Retired Chief Scientist, Fisheries Board of Canada
Status: Retired
Degrees:
  BA, University of Toronto, Ontario, 1930
  MA, University of Toronto, 1931
  PhD, University of Toronto, 1936
Awards:
  Eminent Ecologist, Ecological Society of America, 1990
  Order of Canada, 1986
  Fry Medal, Canadian Society of Zoologists 1983
  Flavelle Medal, Royal Society of Canada, 1970
  Award of Excellence, American Fisheries Society, 1969
  Gold Medal, Professional Institute of Public Service of Canada, 1966
  Fellow of the American Association for the Advancement of Science, 1960
  Fellow of the Royal Society of Canada, 1956
Family members:
  Mother: Rebecca Rouse
  Father: Harry Edwin Ricker
  Spouse: Marion (Caldwell)
  Children: four sons
  Grandchildren: three
Mentors: Professors Dymond, Walker, Coventry and Harkness, University of Toronto; W. A. Clemens and R. E. Foerster, Pacific Biological Station; F.I. Baranov for his 1918 monograph about fish; R. A. Fisher for his book, *The Genetical Theory of Natural Selection*
Favourite music: Bach, especially *The Brandenburg Concertos*; Handel; Mozart
Other interests: Plants, birds, geology, insect classification, bass viol, Canadian history, languages, archaeology
Character: Generous, modest, self-effacing, quiet

The Story

STANDING ON A THIN LEDGE of rock, just below **Hell's Gate Falls** on the Fraser River, William Ricker dips his net into the eddy at his feet. He brings up a six-pound **sockeye salmon** for tagging. This one is fresh and strong, not like the tired ones who are having trouble with the rapids. Again and again the weak ones find their way into his net. From a pocket, Ricker pulls out two little red and white metal disks and a 5 cm pin. He wipes his brow and waves to his partner who is also tagging fish a few metres away. The sun is hot. A steady hot wind blows up the narrow canyon. There is no road down to where they are, only a steep trail.

Ricker is 30. It is the summer of 1938, the first time he has worked on the big river and he's enjoying himself. It's also the first year of the Canadian Salmon Commission's study of Fraser sockeye. Nobody really knows yet how or why salmon return after years in the sea to mate and lay eggs in the very same creek where they were born.

While his partner holds the fish down, Ricker uses a pair of pliers to attach the bright tag through the fish's body just below the dorsal fin. Then he throws the wild sockeye back into the water to fight its way upriver in the roaring rapids. The team of four men catches and tags up to 20 fish per hour – several thousand in all, enough to accomplish the goals of the study, which are to find what fraction of the fish go to each of a dozen or so **spawning grounds** to mate and lay eggs at different seasons. Spawning grounds are the shallow creek beds where female salmon lay eggs which male salmon then fertilize. Observers in those regions are on the lookout for the salmon and are making estimates of the numbers on each spawning ground.

The Young Scientist

WHEN HE WAS 11 YEARS OLD, William Ricker began studying his dad's star charts. His father was science master at North Bay Normal School. Eventually Ricker could name all the constellations and the brightest stars. Each spring, all through high school, Ricker would get up most mornings at five. For three hours before breakfast he would ride his bike into the woods or along the shoreline near North Bay, Ontario, looking for birds. While he was at university he would get summer jobs at the Ontario Fisheries Research Laboratory, mainly working on trout in the Great Lakes. After a job studying salmon life history and enhancement at Cultus Lake, British Columbia, he became a professor of zoology at Indiana State University, where he taught about birds and fish from 1939 to 1950. Then he went back to Canada to work as editor of publications for the Fisheries Research Board of Canada. In 1964 he moved to Nanaimo to become Chief Scientist of the Fisheries Research Board of Canada. Since 1973 he has continued to work on a voluntary basis on the history of Fraser River salmon fisheries and other projects.

During his life he has identified 90 new species of stoneflies and written a Russian/English dictionary of fisheries terms, among many other activities. He is currently working on a history book about early travel on the Fraser River canyon.

The Science

Fisheries biology is the study of fish habitat and population. Knowing the number of **spawners** in a given year is crucial for predicting how many fish will be available for future harvest. Ricker knows salmon runs like some people know World Series baseball statistics. He has kept track of the Canadian Salmon Commission's estimates of the Fraser River sockeye ever since 1938.

Each year different numbers of salmon return to spawn, depending on the species. Different salmon species go through different cycles. For example, the big sockeye run of 1997 is the same "line" or "cycle" as the record-breaking run of 1913 which included about 100 million fish. For sockeye, such huge numbers occur only every four years. So the next big run should be 2001. Other years are one tenth as numerous or less.

Ricker was the first to suggest several possible reasons for the cyclic variation in returning salmon stocks. Biologists are still collecting evidence to determine the correct explanation. The Fraser sockeye are on a four-year cycle possibly because most of the fish mature at four years of age. Farther North, five-year cycles are also common. **Pink** salmon have a two-year life cycle. For **cohos** it's usually three years, while **chinook** or spring salmon return at any age from two to seven years. Chinook are the largest and most powerful of all salmon. In fact, the largest salmon ever caught in the world was a chinook weighing in at over 57 kg.

Ricker is famous for his mathematical model of **fish population dynamics**, now called the **Ricker Curve**. He first described this model in a book he wrote in the 1950s on the computation of fish population statistics. The book is now known throughout the world as the **Green Book**.

Ocean Sockeye Salmon

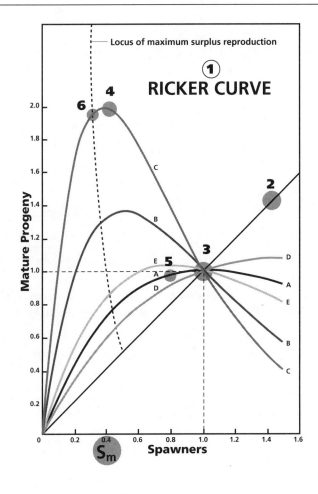

Locus of maximum surplus reproduction

① **RICKER CURVE**

Mature Progeny

Spawners

S$_m$

1. **The Ricker Curve** is still used all over the world to determine average maximum catches for regional fisheries. Each curve represents a different type of fish population. This is what governments use to decide how many days commercial fishers can be allowed to fish for salmon or cod so that there are enough fish left to more than reproduce themselves next year.

2. **Line of natural replacement**. Along this line, spawners (adult fish who lay eggs or fertilize them) are replaced by an equal number of progeny (fish who grow up to be adults).

3. **Natural Equilibrium**. At this point, spawners equal progeny. If there was no commercial fishery, this is where the fish population would naturally tend to stay. In nature fish don't go much beyond this level because they get too crowded. Spawning beds get messed up and many eggs die.

4. Salmon are interesting because their Ricker Curve looks more like this. At this point at the top of the curve, the population is reduced to 40 percent of the natural equilibrium by fishing, but some fish, like salmon, produce many more mature progeny when their spawning grounds are less crowded.

5. For a fish species that followed Ricker Curve A, if commercial fishers were allowed to catch 20 percent of the mature spawners, the fish population would be at this point. There would be less progeny, but enough to sustain the catch – a 20 percent surplus.

6. The point of **maximum sustainable catch** on any Ricker Curve is shown by the curving dotted line. (S$_m$ shows the maximum point for salmon.) Note that it's actually a bit to the left of the peak of a curve. This is because the distance between the curve and the natural replacement line is greatest at this point. Anywhere to the left of this line you are overfishing and will reduce the next generation's harvest.

Spawning Sockeye Salmon

95

Activity

Object:

To tell the difference between many different varieties of fish.

You need:

- *A library book with good pictures and descriptions of fish local to your area. Try cod, trout, or salmon, but any fish will do.*
- *A trip to a big fish market or your favourite fishing spot.*

What to do:

At the market:

- Take your book to the fish market and try to find the distinguishing feature of each type of trout, salmon, or cod that is available.

- Write down their proper Latin names.
- See if you can find any fish that are mislabelled in the market.

If you go fishing:

Try to identify everything you catch. Keep track of the size and number of fish you catch. Write down the depth, water temperature, and time of day.

Keeping records like this is not only scientific, it will help you catch more fish. You'll be able to check your records and know where and how to catch more fish the next time you go to a particular spot.

Further Reading

Ricker, W. Russian-English dictionary for students of fisheries and aquatic biology. *Bulletin of the Fisheries Research Board of Canada* 183: 1-428, 1973.

Ricker, W. Computation and interpretation of biological statistics of fish populations. *Bulletin of the Fisheries Research Board of Canada* 191: 1-382, 1975. (This is The Green Book discussed above.)

Ricker, W. Stock and recruitment. *Journal of the Fisheries Research Board of Canada*, 11(5): 559-623, 1954.

Ricker, W. Back-calculation of fish lengths based on proportionality between scale and length increments. *Canadian Journal of Fisheries Aquatic Sciences*, 49(5): 1018-1026, 1992.

Michael Smith

Biochemist, Molecular Biologist

Won the 1993 Nobel Prize for Chemistry for discovering site-directed mutagenesis

"In research you really have to love and be committed to your work because things have more of a chance of going wrong than right. But when things go right, there is nothing more exciting."

The Person

Birthdate: 26 April 1932
Birthplace: Blackpool, England
Residence: Vancouver, British Columbia
Office: Biotechnology Laboratory, Faculty of Medicine, University of British Columbia (UBC), Vancouver
Title: University Killam Professor, Peter Wall Distinguished Professor of Biotechnology
Status: Working
Degrees:
  BSc (Honours Chemistry), University of Manchester, England, 1953
  PhD (Chemistry), University of Manchester, 1956
Awards:
  Jacob Biely Faculty Research Prize, UBC, 1977
  Fellow, Royal Society of Canada, 1981
  Boehringer Mannheim Prize of the Canadian Biochemical Society, 1981
  Gold Medal, Science Council of BC, 1984
  Fellow, Royal Society (London), 1986
  Gairdner Foundation International Award, 1986
  Killam Research Prize, UBC, 1986

Award of Excellence, Genetics Society of Canada, 1988
G. Malcolm Brown Award, Canadian Federation of Biological Societies, 1989
Flavelle Medal, Royal Society of Canada, 1992
Nobel Prize for Chemistry, 1993
Manning Award, 1995
Laureate of the Canadian Medical Hall of Fame
Family members:
  Father: Rowland Smith
  Mother: Mary Agnes Armstead
  Children: Tom, Ian, Wendy
Mentor: Har Gobind Khorana, Nobel Prize-winning chemist who taught him the organic chemistry of biological **molecules** which make up **DNA**
Favourite music: Sibelius's *Second Symphony* (slow movement)
Other interests: Philanthropy, scouts, camping, hiking, sailing, skiing, reading the *New Yorker* and the *Manchester Guardian*
Character: Shy, caring, busy, focused, generous, a procrastinator

The Story:

MICHAEL SMITH ARRIVES in his office wearing his usual shabby old sweater and trousers that long ago should have been sent to a charity like the Salvation Army. You would never guess that just a few days before he had been awarded half a million dollars, his share of the 1993 Nobel Prize for Chemistry. Smith passes by a wall of shallow shelves jammed full of medals, awards and plaques for prizes he has won. The office is modestly furnished with a cluttered, lived-in look. A beautiful picture-window looks out onto the treed UBC campus and the coast mountains in the distance. Smith picks up the telegram from Sweden to take another look at the Nobel announcement.

"Darlene?" he calls out the door to his administrator, Darlene Crowe, who is sitting at her desk.

"Yes, Mike," she calls cheerily. Everyone's in a good mood because of the prize.

"If you ever see my behaviour start to change and I get a swelled head with all this attention, I want you to give me a good swift kick," says Smith.

Crowe remembers only one occasion on which she had to "kick him." Mostly, he behaves himself. Smith relies heavily on people like Crowe. "He's a bit like the rabbit in *Alice in Wonderland*," she says fondly of her boss, who often runs late. Smith rewards his co-workers generously. He took 12 colleagues to Stockholm with him, mostly graduate students and research assistants, all expenses paid, to share in the glory of the Nobel awards ceremony.

Smith didn't keep the Nobel Prize money. He gave half of it to researchers working on the genetics of schizophrenia, a widespread mental disorder for which research money is scarce. The other half he gave to Science World BC and to the Society for Canadian Women in Science and Technology.

Certainly Smith could afford it. He had made a small fortune in 1988 when he sold his share of Zymogenetics Inc., a Seattle-based biotechnology company that he co-founded in 1981. Even before he won the Nobel Prize, his award-winning **genetic engineering** techniques were used by Zymogenetics to develop a strain of yeast implanted with the human **gene** for insulin. With the drug company, Novo-Nordisk, Zymogenetics commercialized a process that used yeast to produce human insulin.

The original idea for **site-directed mutagenesis** came to Smith while talking with an American scientist named Clyde Hutchison over coffee in an English research institute. Every seven years, university professors get one year off, with pay, to travel anywhere in the world to do research. This is called a sabbatical. It was 1976 and Smith was spending a sabbatical year in Fred Sanger's lab, part of the famous institute in Cambridge, England, where DNA (DeoxyriboNucleic Acid) was first explained by Watson and Crick. Smith was there to learn how to sequence genes – in other words, how to determine the order of the thousands of links that make up a chain of DNA.

He was in the cafeteria explaining to Hutchison how he was making short chains of **nucleotides** – the chain links in DNA – for use in the separation and purification of DNA fragments. His technique was based on the natural affinity of one DNA chain to link up with its mirror image. It didn't take much of a leap to realize that the same method might be used to induce **mutations** – new qualities or traits in offspring not found in their parents – but this meant changing directions again, and not for the first time. It took Smith and his team several more years to perfect the method. At first it didn't work at all, but Smith kept at it. Eventually the technique became so well-known and useful it ended up winning the Nobel Prize.

Smith didn't become successful by accident. He's a very hard worker – some say a workaholic. Things were not always easy for him. When he submitted his first article on site-directed mutagenesis for publication in *Cell*, a leading academic journal, it was rejected. The editors said that the article was not of general interest. Smith never stopped working on his idea. Above all, he was always prepared to do what he calls "follow-your-nose research" – repeatedly changing directions to explore new ideas even if it means learning entirely different processes and techniques.

The Young Scientist

MICHAEL SMITH WAS BORN into a working-class family in Blackpool, England. His mother and father both had to work from their early teens onward, she in the holiday boarding house of her mother and he in his father's market garden. Smith was seven when World War II broke out. Though his family lived pretty far north in England, he does remember one time when his mom and dad were not home and German bombs fell on either side of their house, just barely missing him and his brother, Robin.

In those days, English working-class school children who were 11 years old had to take an exam called the Eleven-Plus to see if they would go on to a private school (and probably university) or just continue in the public school system where they would learn a trade and finish at the age of 16. Smith did very well in his Eleven-Plus and was offered a scholarship to a local private school called Arnold School. He didn't want to go, however, because the students there were considered snobs and he thought his friends would make fun of him. Luckily, his mother insisted that he go.

Going to Arnold School was not a very happy time in Smith's life. He lost most of his old friends. He had homework to do every night and they didn't. He did not like the food at Arnold School but was forced to eat it by strict teachers. He was not very good at sports, which were very important in English private schools. He had few friends at the new school. His big front teeth stuck out so he was teased by his schoolmates. Fortunately he was sent to a dentist to see about his overbite and the dentist introduced him to the world of Boy Scouts, where he made friends and learned about camping and the outdoors. It's partly because of this love of nature and camping that Smith later decided to settle in Vancouver, Canada.

Smith did not go to a prestigious English university like Oxford, but did get into the honours chemistry program at Manchester University. He hoped to get all A's, but alas, he was a B student. He was very disappointed, but he still got a state scholarship and managed to complete a PhD.

Smith wanted to do post-doctorate research on the west coast of the USA, and he wrote to many universities, but was rejected by them all. Then in 1956 he heard of a young scientist in Vancouver, British Columbia, Gobind Khorana, who had a position available to work on biologically important molecules. This was not the chemistry in which Smith had been trained, but he went to Vancouver anyway. It turned out to be a very good decision, because in Khorana's lab Smith began learning the chemistry that would lead to his Nobel Prize. Khorana himself received a Nobel Prize in 1968 for work on the **genetic code** – research that Smith was involved in during the late 1950s at UBC.

For years Smith worked at the Fisheries Research Board of Canada Laboratory in Vancouver, and published many papers about crabs, salmon, and marine mollusks, but he managed to sustain his research in DNA chemistry with grants he obtained on his own, outside of his fisheries-related work. The lab was located on the UBC campus, and because he was collaborating so much with professors in **biochemistry** and medicine, in 1966 he was appointed a UBC professor of biochemistry in the Faculty of Medicine, where he remains today.

The Science

MOLECULAR BIOLOGY IS THE STUDY of biological systems at the level of individual **chemicals** and molecules. Michael Smith is an expert on the chemistry of DNA – the molecule that makes up genes, the instructions required to create every part of an organism. DNA is a large molecule that is like a twisting chain. Actually it is two chains twisted together. Smith works on **genomics** – the sequencing of the DNA of an organism to understand how it works.

What Smith developed that won him fame and fortune was a new way of creating mutations in living organisms. Plant and animal breeders rely on naturally occurring beneficial mutations that result in improved plants and animals. Conversely, unwanted natural mutations can cause diseases like cystic fibrosis or sickle-cell anemia. Smith found a way to create a specific mutation by precisely changing any particular part of the DNA in an organism. This has allowed countless researchers around the world to develop special bacteria, plants, and animals with new desirable qualities or abilities that either do not occur naturally or that would take years and years of trial and error breeding to achieve. With further research, his technique might even be used to correct bad mutations that cause disease.

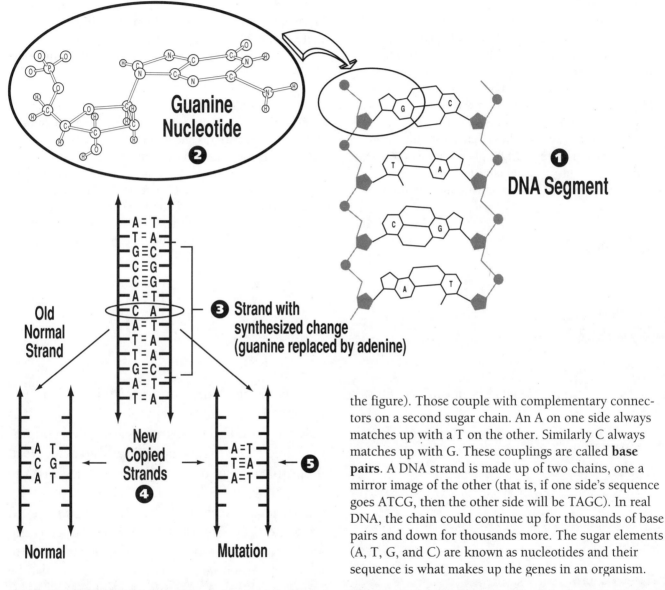

1. A small portion of a long DNA molecule showing the backbone (in light gray) made of **deoxyribose**, a type of sugar. The backbone sugar segments are all the same but they can have one of four different basic connectors: Adenine, Thymine, Cytosine and Guanine (A, T, C, G in the figure). Those couple with complementary connectors on a second sugar chain. An A on one side always matches up with a T on the other. Similarly C always matches up with G. These couplings are called **base pairs**. A DNA strand is made up of two chains, one a mirror image of the other (that is, if one side's sequence goes ATCG, then the other side will be TAGC). In real DNA, the chain could continue up for thousands of base pairs and down for thousands more. The sugar elements (A, T, G, and C) are known as nucleotides and their sequence is what makes up the genes in an organism.

2. The nucleotide Guanine. The phosphate sugar is on the left and the basic group is on the right. Note the two hydrogen atoms and one oxygen atom poking out on the extreme right. They form the bond with Cytosine on the sister chain.

3. The idea for which Smith won the Nobel Prize was to slip a **synthetic** stretch of nucleotides – called an **oligonucleotide** – into one DNA chain. "Synthetic" means the nucleotide was created in a test tube, not by nature. The synthetic segment is added to normal DNA using standard chemicals for breaking and reforming DNA chains. But there is one thing wrong with this synthetic oligonucleotide: it has an Adenine where there should be a Guanine. This is done on purpose to create a mutation. (Remember, A normally combines with T, and G goes with C.) The four nucleotides below and above the Adenine act as a kind of address that causes this stretch of DNA to match up to the right place on the other DNA strand. (In humans you need only 17 nucleotides to define a unique match somewhere among our 100,000 genes.)

4. When this new altered DNA is put back into an organism, say a **bacterium**, and it divides in the normal process of growth and reproduction, one half of the DNA will recombine normally and will produce a correct copy of the original gene – a normal bacterium. The other side with the synthetic oligonucleotide will create a mutation because a Thymine is sitting where there should be a Cytosine. The resulting mutant bacterium might have some new appearance or function that it never had before.

5. With Smith's technique, geneticists can **mutate** a gene by precise substitution of one or more nucleotides in a DNA sequence (as shown here). They can also delete nucleotides or add extra nucleotides to the sequence. Before Smith's technique there was no way to create specific mutations. Geneticists had to expose a bunch of organisms to radiation or chemicals that would result in all sorts of mutants, then select the one that they wanted. It was all by random chance, and it could

Activity

Object:

To design your own oligonucleotide and see if it's part of a real gene.

You need:

- *A pad and paper.*
- *A computer connected to the Internet.*
- *The table, at the top of the next page, showing the genetic code.*

What to do:

Using the four basic nucleotides of the DNA chain (A, C, G, T) make up a DNA chain by randomly choosing about 20 or 30 units- AACTGCTTCGGATATCGCAGC, for example.

Now take the chain you made and divide it into groups of three units each: AAC TGC TTC GGA TAT CGC AGC. These groups are called codons. Each one codes for one specific **amino acid**. Next, look up each codon in the table on page 103 to find out what amino acids they represent. For example, AAC would be Asparagine, TGC Cysteine, TTC Phenylalanine, GGA Glycine and so on. Next you convert this amino acid chain to a row of capital letters. These letters can also be found in the table, beside the abbreviation for each amino acid. For instance, Cysteine or Cys = C. Our **protein chain** would now look like this: NCFGYRS. This string of letters can now be checked on a computer run by the National

		Second Position				
		T	C	A	G	
First Position	T	TTT Phe (F) TTC " TTA Leu (L) TTG "	TCT Ser (S) TCC " TCA " TCG "	TAT Tyr (Y) TAC TAA Stop TAG Stop	TGT Cys (C) TGC TGA Stop TGG Trp (W)	T C A G
	C	CTT Leu (L) CTC " CTA " CTG "	CCT Pro (P) CCC " CCA " CCG "	CAT His (H) CAC " CAA Gln (Q) CAG "	CGT Arg (R) CGC " CGA " CGG "	T C A G
	A	ATT Ile (I) ATC " ATA " ATG Met (M)	ACT Thr (T) ACC " ACA " ACG "	AAT Asn (N) AAC " AAA Lys (K) AAG "	AGT Ser (S) AGC " AGA ARG (R) AGG "	T C A G
	G	GTT Val (V) GTC " GTA " GTG "	GCT Ala (A) GCC " GCA " GCG "	GAT Asp (D) GAC " GAA Glu (E) GAG "	GGT Gly (G) GGC " GGA " GGG "	T C A G

Third Position

NOTE: Capital letters in parentheses beside the amino acid name abbreviations are code letters for amino acid sequencing that you send to the WWW search engine. "Stop" is a special signal to the cell's protein-making system to stop transcribing. It marks the end of a protein chain, not an amino acid.

Center for Biotechnology Information at the US National Library of Medicine in Bethesda, Maryland. The table on page 104 shows the allowable letters you can submit for a computer search.

Try making up your own DNA sequence and protein chain by following the steps above. When you are ready, point your Internet web browser to http://www.ncbi.nlm.nih.gov/BLAST. When you are there, click on Advanced BLAST search which takes you to a page where you pick the blastp Program. You can leave Database as nr. Now enter your string of letters into the search box (for example, NCFGYRS). Below this, set Expect to 1000. Everything else can be left as is. Click the submit button and in a moment an automated system will show you the probable gene matches – if there are any – for that oligonucleotide.

If you get a match, you will see a list of possible

proteins that your gene might code for. By clicking on items in this list you can find out more about the protein and its genetic code. Did you get a match? The string NCFGYRS in the example above turns out to match a type of antibiotic found in the white blood cells of chickens. What protein does your gene represent? If your sequence was not part of a gene, try again until you find one.

FASTA TABLE OF AMINO ACID LETTER CODES

A	alanine	K	lysine	U	selenocysteine
B	aspartate or asparagine	L	leucine	V	valine
C	cystine	M	methionine	W	tryptophan
D	aspartate	N	asparagine	Y	tyrosine
E	glutamate	P	proline	Z	glutamate or glutamine
F	phenylalanine	Q	glutamine	X	any
G	glycine	R	arginine	*	translation stop
H	histidine	S	serine	-	gap of indeterminate length
I	isoleucine	T	threonine		

Mystery

SMITH BELIEVES A CHANGE is coming in how people do biological research. Soon the total sequence of the DNA in all the genes for a human being – the human **genome** – will be known. Those genes have the code or "recipe" for each of the 100,000 **proteins** that make up a person, but we currently understand only about 5,000 of them. The hard part will be discovering what part of the human genome does what, picking out what is crucial, and learning how to recognize the most important bits of DNA from the rest.

Further Reading

Smith, M. Site-directed Mutagenesis and Protein Engineering. In *Proteins: Form and Function*, Edited by Bradshaw, R.A. and Purton, M. Elsevier, Cambridge, 1990.

Smith, M., et al. A method for introducing random single point deletions in specific DNA target sequences using oligonucleotides. *Nucleic Acids Research* 17, 4015-4023, 1989.

Watson, J. D., et al. *Recombinant DNA (2nd Ed.)*. Scientific American Books, New York, New York, 1993.

Lap-Chee Tsui
Molecular Geneticist

Found the gene that causes cystic fibrosis

"Knowing science can enrich your life. Basically, science is a foundation for genuine common sense."

The Person

Birthdate: 21 December 1950
Birthplace: Shanghai, China
Residence: Toronto, Ontario
Office: Hospital for Sick Children, Toronto, Ontario
Titles: Senior Scientist and Sellers Chair of Cystic Fibrosis Research in the Department of Genetics at the Research Institute of the Hospital for Sick Children, Toronto; Professor of Molecular and Medical Genetics at the University of Toronto
Status: Working
Degrees:
BSc (Biology), The Chinese University of Hong Kong, 1972
MPhil (Biology), The Chinese University of Hong Kong, 1974
PhD (Biological Sciences), University of Pittsburgh, Pennsylvania, 1979
Awards:
The Paul di Sant'Agnese Distinguished Scientific Achievement Award, The Cystic Fibrosis Foundation (USA), 1989
Gold Medal of Honor, Pharmaceutical Manufacturers Association of Canada, 1989
Royal Society of Canada Centennial Award, 1989

Fellow of the Royal Society of Canada, 1990
Award of Excellence, Genetic Society of Canada, 1990
Courvoisier Leadership Award, 1990
Gairdner International Award, 1990
Fellow of the Royal Society of London, 1991
Doris Tulcin Cystic Fibrosis Research Achievement Award, The Cystic Fibrosis Foundation (USA), 1991
Officer of the Order of Canada, 1991
The Cresson Medal, Franklin Institute, 1992
The Mead Johnson Award, 1992
Distinguished Scientist Award, The Canadian Society of Clinical Investigators, 1992
Sarstedt Research Prize, 1993
XII Sanremo International Award for Genetic Research, 1993
J.P. Lecocq Prize, Academie des Sciences, Institut de France, 1994
Henry Friesen Award, The Canadian Society for Clinical Investigation and the Royal College of Physicians and Surgeons of Canada, 1995
Medal of Honour, Canadian Medical Association, 1996
Family members:
Father: Jing-Lue
Mother: Hui-Ching (Wang) Hsue

Spouse: Lan Fong Ng
Children: Eugene and Felix
Mentors: K. K. Mark, who taught him how to concentrate on a single thing, and be good at it; Roger Hendricks, who taught him how to encourage independent thinking and not to tell students what to do; Manuel Buchwald, who taught him how to be critical and look at the broad perspective; and Han Chang who taught him how to be flexible and adaptive, and to understand the Western (American) way of thinking.
Favourite music: Puccini's opera, *Turandot*, end of Act I
Other interests: Travelling, food, basketball, drawing
Character: Shy, positive, laughs a lot

The Story

RICHARD ROZMAHEL PASSES THE TIME by reading the bulletin board hanging above the wheezing printer attached to the **DNA** sequencer. There's an ad from a company selling genetic research chemicals. They're offering a free T-shirt sporting the words: "Ultra Pure Human Being." At the bottom he reads, "Send six peel-off seals from any GIBCO BRL Enzymes and receive an *I Make My Living Manipulating DNA* briefcase free."

Ain't it the truth, thinks Rozmahel to himself as he pulls yet another variation of the same tedious experiment from the printer. He looks at the printout absently as he makes his way back to his desk in the corner of the crowded genetics lab. People and equipment take up every possible space. Shelves groan with bottles, dishes, and jars. He passes a friend staring into a **microscope**. A big humming refrigerator juts out into the passageway. Another student wears gloves while she puts hundreds of precisely measured portions of various liquids into tiny test tubes.

Rozmahel stops suddenly just before he gets to his desk. Something is unusual about this printout. There it is: a three-**base pair deletion** —

a type of genetic **mutation** in a sequence of DNA (DeoxyriboNucleic Acid). DNA molecules are long chains of instructions for making **proteins**, which themselves are long chains of connected molecules called **amino acids**. Each DNA instruction comes in a three-piece unit called a three-base pair, and each one stands for a particular amino acid needed in the construction of a protein. To Rozmahel, this three-base pair deletion is as if one bead had vanished from a precious necklace. A mutation such as this might cause something as simple as a change in eye colour or as complex as a deadly disease.

Instead of sitting down at his desk, Rozmahel rushes to show his supervisor, Dr. Tsui (pronounced "Choy"). It's almost six o'clock and most people have left for the night, but Tsui is still working.

Tsui's office is small. When Rozmahel arrives, Tsui is hunched over the desk poring over some other experimental results. The shelves are loaded with books. Piles of paper cover every horizontal surface. Rozmahel looks at the shabby green rug while he waits.

"What is it, Richard?" asks Tsui with a smile.

"I'm pretty sure I've found a three-base pair deletion. Look here." Rozmahel indicates the two DNA sequences. One is from a normal person's **genes** and one is from a person with cystic fibrosis (CF) – a fatal disease that kills about one out of every 2000 Canadians, mostly children. Cystic fibrosis is the most common genetic disease among white people. Kids who have cystic fibrosis are born with it. Half of them will die before they are 25 and few make it past 30. It affects all the parts of the body that secrete mucous – places like the lungs, the stomach, the nose, and mouth. The mucous of kids with cystic fibrosis is so thick that sometimes they cannot breathe.

Tsui looks at the printout and says, "This is very good, Richard. Now show me that it's real." Tsui doesn't seem excited at all but he knows this is a solid clue, a major hint that they have found what they are looking for: the gene for cystic fibrosis, and the cause of that terrible disease. But he has had false hopes before, so he is not going to celebrate until they check this out carefully. Maybe the difference between the two gene sequences is just a normal variation between individuals. If you take any two normal people and compare 1000 DNA bases, you have a good chance of finding the same thing Rozmahel just found. There are plenty of little variations between individuals.

Tsui remembers that day, 9 May 1989, as the day they discovered the gene for cystic fibrosis. He and his team spent the next five months making sure that their discovery was real, doing tests over and over to see whether the results would be the same. They identified a signature pattern of DNA on either side of the base pair deletion, and using that as a marker they compared 100 normal people's genes with the identical DNA sequence from 100 cystic fibrosis patients. By September 1989 they were sure they had the cystic fibrosis gene.

The Young Scientist

LAP-CHEE TSUI GREW UP in Dai Goon Yu, a little village on the Kowloon side of Hong Kong near the Kai Tak airport. He would hang out with a group of kids, mostly boys, and they would go exploring in ponds, catching tadpoles and fish to do simple experiments.

One favourite project was to go to the market and buy silkworms. They would bring home the silkworms and pick leaves off the mulberry bushes to feed them. Tsui remembers that one day he and his friends picked almost all the leaves off a mulberry bush in a neighbour's yard. The furious fellow came out and chased the kids away.

As a boy Tsui dreamed of being an architect and still draws all his own diagrams and slides. He did not take up genetics until after his PhD. He was more interested in studying the nature of diseases.

The Science

MOLECULAR GENETICISTS TRY to understand the structure and function of genes. Lap-Chee Tsui is particularly interested in the gene for cystic fibrosis and other genes on human **chromosome** number 7. Chromosomes are threadlike strands found in the nuclei of animal and plant **cells**. Chromosomes carry hereditary information about the organism in DNA molecules.

After Tsui found the CF gene in 1989, he had to figure out exactly what that gene did. Over the years, Tsui and his team have discovered that the DNA sequence with the mutation was part of the instructions for making a special protein called CFTR (Cystic Fibrosis Transmembrane conductance Regulator), a part of the cell membrane in certain special **epithelial** (surface) cells that generate mucous. These special cells might line the airways of the nose and lungs or the stomach wall.

The CFTR protein regulates a channel through the cell wall for **chloride ions**, which, through a process called **osmosis,** adjusts the wateriness of fluids secreted by the cell. Proteins are made of long chains of amino acids. The CFTR protein has 1480 amino acids. Kids with cystic fibrosis are missing one single amino acid in their CFTR. Because of this, their mucous ends up being too thick and all sorts of things become difficult for them. Thanks to Tsui's research, scientists now have a much better idea of how the disease works and can easily predict when a couple will produce

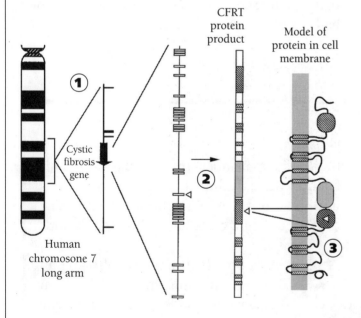

1. Human chromosome 7
The cystic fibrosis gene sits on the long arm of chromosome 7. One out of every 25 people in the Caucasian

population carries the genetic mutation for CF in this gene. Chromosome 7 has 150,000,000 base pairs or units of DNA.

2. The cystic fibrosis gene
Using **microbiological** techniques, Tsui first localized the CF gene to a region of the chromosome. The region has 230,000 DNA base pairs which spell out a series of 1480 amino acids that curl up to make the Cystic Fibrosis Transmembrane conductance Regulator (CFTR) protein. The little triangle shows the location of the three-base pair deletion mutation that Tsui discovered.

3. Model of CFTR protein in cell membrane
A normal gene makes CFTR, which regulates the passage of chloride ions and hence the secretion of mucous in epithelial (surface) cells lining the gut, lungs, and so on. One missing amino acid at this spot causes the majority of cases of CF. The remainder are caused by about 700 other kinds of mutations of the CFTR gene, each accounting for a small percentage of cases.

a child with cystic fibrosis. With increasing understanding, scientists may also be able to devise improved treatments for children born with the disease.

Why do one in 25 Caucasians carry the mutation for CF? Tsui thinks that people who carry it may also have linked beneficial mutations that might, for instance, give them more resistance to diarrhoea-like diseases. It's not uncommon in nature to find the "good" linked together with the "bad."

Activity

Object:

*To identify your own **blood type** based on your parents' blood types.*

You need:

- *Your mom's blood type (A, B, AB, or O).*
- *Your dad's blood type (A, B, AB, or O).*

(Note: if you cannot find out both your parents' blood type, just pick two of the four possible blood types and do the activity for fun.)

What to do:

Knowing that you get one chromosome from your mom and one from your dad, can you figure out what your possible blood type is? You need to know that people with blood type A can have either two A chromosomes (AA), or one A and one O chromosome (AO). Similarly people with type B blood have chromosomes in the form of BB or BO. Type AB people have one A and one B chromosome (AB) and type O people must have two O chromosomes (OO). So, for example, if a type AA person is the mother and the father is type BO, there are two chances for an AB child and two chances for an AO child. Try to figure out what blood type you (and any of your brothers or sisters) probably have.

Blood Type	A	B	AB	O
Possible Blood Chromosomes	AA or AO	BB or BO	AB	OO

Possible blood chromosomes for children from AA type mother and BO type father:

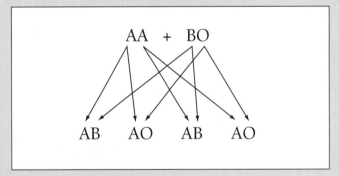

Which means the couple has a 50/50 chance of having either AB type children or AO type children. Use the same type of reasoning to figure out your own family's combinations.

Mystery

THE GENES OF A MONKEY and a human are almost identical, varying by only about 2 percent. How can such a small difference result in such different animals? Why do humans develop into humans and monkeys into monkeys? It has to do with the way in which an organism controls which genetic instructions are read from its DNA. This control system is called the regulation of gene expression and is still very poorly understood. Tsui likens the situation with monkeys and humans to two orchestras, each having exactly the same instruments, and the same music to play. Yet the two orchestras can sound entirely different if they have different conductors. The greatest mystery to Tsui is identifying and characterizing the "conductor" in the human genetic system.

Further Reading

Buchwald, M. and Lap Chee Tsui. Isolation of the Cystic Fibrosis Gene. In *Canadians for Health Research*, Box 126, Westmount, Quebec H3Z 2T1, 1992.

Balkwill, F. and M. Rolph. *Amazing Schemes Within Your Genes*. Cold Spring Harbor Laboratory Press, Plainview, New York, 1994.

Endel Tulving
Cognitive Psychologist

World expert on human memory function

"Don't listen to authorities. Find out what the problem is, find out the facts, and make up your own mind. Use the scientific method to work things out. There's no reason why the scientific method should stay in the lab. It can solve many problems and I wish more people would adopt the experimental method: 'Let's try this and see if it works.' There's no reason to expect this to be the right answer. Trust your feelings and try out various things. Use trial and error, objectivity and plenty of alternatives."

The Person

Birthdate: 26 May 1927
Birthplace: Estonia
Residence: Toronto, Ontario
Office: Rotman Research Institute, Baycrest Centre, North York, Ontario
Status: Retired, but still working on several projects
Degrees:
  BA (Honours Psychology), University of Toronto, Ontario, 1953
  MA (Psychology), University of Toronto, 1954
  PhD (Experimental Psychology), Harvard University, Cambridge, Massachusetts, 1957
Awards:
  Fellow, Center for Advanced Study in Behavioural Sciences, Stanford, California, 1972
  Senior Research Fellowship, National Research Council, 1964-65
  Izaak Walton Killam Memorial Scholarship, Canada Council, 1976
  Howard Crosby Warren Medal, Society of Experimental

Psychologists, 1982
Distinguished Scientific Achievement Award, American Psychology Association, 1983
Foreign Honorary Member of the American Academy of Arts and Sciences, 1986
Guggenheim Fellowship, 1987
Foreign Associate, US National Academy of Science 1988
William James Fellow, American Psychological Society, 1990
Foreign Member, Royal Swedish Academy of Sciences, 1991
Fellow, Royal Society of London, 1992
Killam Prize, Canada Council, 1994
Gold Medal Award for Lifetime Achievement, American Psychological Foundation, 1994
Family members:
Father: Juhan
Mother: Linda

Spouse: Hilda Mikkelsaar
Children: Elo Ann and Linda
Mentors: not available
Favourite music: Dvorak's *New World Symphony*, opening movement; anything by Sibelius

Other interests: Tennis, walking, chess, history of science
Character: Creative, impatient, positive, optimistic

The Story

ENDEL TULVING IS STANDING at the blackboard before a fourth-year **cognitive psychology** class at the University of Toronto. They're on the fourth floor of the newly built Sidney Smith building. It's a long unfriendly room with no windows. A blackboard stretches the length of one wall. Everyone is sitting around a big table. There's a smell of fresh paint. Tulving is explaining his theory that **memory** is a two-part process – that laying down memories and retrieving them are separate functions.

"Just because a person cannot recall a word seen only a minute ago does not mean that the word is not in the memory," says Tulving.

A student says, "Well, do you have any evidence for this?"

Tulving says, "But this is self evident." Nevertheless he notes the doubtful expression on the student's face. They break for coffee and Tulving goes to his office around the corner. Deep in thought and troubled about the situation in the classroom, he comes up with an experiment to demonstrate his point to the class. Later, he conducts the experiment, using the class as **psychological subjects**. He tells everyone to concentrate and listen carefully while he says about twenty words: "Yellow," "Rifle," "Beethoven," "Violin," and so on. After he is

finished he asks the class to write down as many words as they can remember. Most can get about eight or ten. After they are done he picks up a student's paper and notices that she did not remember the word "Yellow." He says, "Do you remember a colour?" Instantly the student remembers "Yellow." He repeats this for the other missed words with the same miraculous result. Finally, the student who doubted that words not recalled were actually in memory, reluctantly admits, "Perhaps you have a point."

The Young Scientist

THE SON OF A JUDGE, Endel Tulving grew up in urban Estonia, but enjoyed summers at the family farm. Tulving was a good student, but spent most of his time pursuing sports, especially track and field. His friends were fascinated by crystal radios, which were the great new invention of the day, but he was not interested. He was concentrating on trying to run one hundred metres in under 12 seconds. Tulving built himself a track on the family farm and practiced everything there, from the 100 metre dash to javelin throwing.

He went to gymnasium, a type of high school in Estonia. He was not at all interested in science, although some of his teenage thoughts were: *When did time begin? What was there before time? Where does the universe end? Is ESP possible?* The only subject he found interesting was psychology, the study of behaviour and thinking, because Tulving felt it was a totally incomplete science. He thought everything else in science was already known, and found it boring that things could be so predictable.

Tulving left Estonia when he was 17 and finished gymnasium in Germany when he was 19. Because of World War II and the Soviet occupation of his country, Tulving was separated from his parents for the next 20 years without knowing what had happened to them. After the war ended, he worked for the Americans as a translator in Germany and spent one year as a medical student in Heidelberg, Germany.

Tulving came to Canada in the early 1950s to go to the University of Toronto. After obtaining a BA and an MA there, he went to Harvard University for his PhD. In 1956 he returned to teach psychology at the University of Toronto.

The Science

COGNITIVE PSYCHOLOGISTS STUDY the human mind. They ask, "How do we know anything?" or "What is a memory?" To Tulving, the human mind is the biggest unsolved mystery in the universe. In recent experiments to figure out how memory works, Tulving employed machines that use **X-rays** and other forms of **radiation** to obtain images of the working brain.

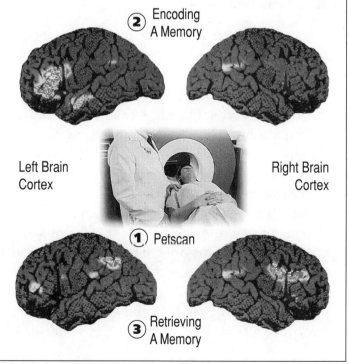

② Encoding A Memory

Left Brain Cortex

Right Brain Cortex

① Petscan

③ Retrieving A Memory

1. A **PET scanner** is a machine that shows what parts of your brain are especially active while you are doing or thinking something. PET stands for Positron Emission Tomography.

2. **Encoding** or recording memories. Tulving showed that memory is a two-stage process. First, memories are laid down. The front left part of the brain plays an important role in laying down memories for specific events which occur only once. This is called episodic memory.

3. **Retrieving memories.** In the second stage of memory according to Tulving, memories are retrieved. The right front and rear of the brain appear to be important for the retrieval of episodic memories. Scientists don't know why some parts of the brain encode memories and other parts retrieve them.

Activity

Object:

To show that retrieving information from memory is separate from laying down memories.

You need:

- *A friend to listen, remember, and answer questions for a few minutes.*
- *A watch with a second hand to time your friend.*

What to do:

Ask a friend to name all the months of the year and time the response. Most people can do this in about eight seconds. Now ask the person to name them in alphabetical order. Almost no one can do this correctly in less than two minutes. Both questions ask you to use your memory to retrieve something from your mind that you already know. Why do you think one way is faster than the other?

You can also conduct the experiment that Tulving tried with his class. See the list for some words and their categories. Then ask your friend to listen carefully as you slowly read out the words in the first column, taking two or three seconds per word. Your friend should try very hard to remember all the words. When you have finished,

Word	Category
granite	rock
France	country
Jupiter	planet
poodle	dog
Einstein	scientist
soccer	sports
lion	cat
tyrannosaurus	dinosaur
hour	unit of time
pansy	flower

ask your friend to write down all the words he or she can remember. Do not help or give any hints. Now check the list and note which ones your friend could not remember. Look in the table and say the category words as hints for the words missed. Can your friend now remember the words that he or she forgot? What does this tell you about how human memory works?

Mystery

HUMAN MEMORY IS STILL a big mystery to Tulving. For instance, how do we travel back into our own pasts using only our minds?

Further Reading

Tulving, E., and D. Schacter. Priming and human memory systems. *Science*, vol. 247, January 1990.

Interview with Endel Tulving. *Journal of Cognitive Neuroscience*, vol. 3, no. 1, Massachusetts Institute of Technology, 1991.

Tulving, E. and D. Schacter, editors. What Are the Memory Systems of 1994? In *Memory Systems*, MIT Press, Cambridge, Massachusetts, 1994.

Tulving, E., et al. Hemispheric encoding/retrieval asymmetry in episodic memory: Positron emission tomography findings. *Proceedings of the National Academy of Sciences, USA* 91, pages 2016-2020, 1994.

Irene Ayako Uchida

Cytogeneticist

World-famous Down syndrome researcher

*"Do your best, no matter what you do –
even if it's a menial job."*

The Person

Birthdate: 8 April 1917
Birthplace: Vancouver, British Columbia
Residence: Burlington, Ontario
Office: Department of Pediatrics, McMaster University, Hamilton, Ontario
Title: Professor **Emeritus**, Departments of Pediatrics and Pathology, McMaster University; Director of Cytogenetics, Oshawa General Hospital
Status: Retired, but still interested in the effect of radiation on chromosome division as shown in Down syndrome, spontaneous abortions and other syndromes resulting from having the wrong number of chromosomes
Degrees:
BA, University of Toronto, Ontario, 1946
PhD, University of Toronto, 1951
Awards:
Ramsay Wright Scholar, University of Toronto, 1947
Woman of the Century, National Council of Jewish Women, 1967

Manitoba Annual Queen Elizabeth II Lectures, Canadian Pediatric Society, first invited speaker, Children's Hospital, Winnipeg, 1967
Named one of 25 Outstanding Women, International Women's Year, Ontario, 1975
1000 Canadian Women of Note 1867-1967, Media club of Canada and Women's Press Club of Toronto,1983
Officer of the Order of Canada, 1993
Founder's Award Canadian College of Medical Genetcists, 1994
Family members:
Father: Sentaro
Mother: Shizuko
Mentors: Curt Stern, geneticist, and Bruce Chown, blood group specialist
Favourite music: Beethoven's *Violin Concerto*
Other interests: Violin, piano, art, photography
Character: Hard worker, feisty, jovial, gracious

The Story

IRENE UCHIDA HAS BEEN ASKED to join the morning hospital rounds at Children's Hospital in Winnipeg, Manitoba. It's 1960. She's talking about patients who have the symptoms of **trisomy** of chromosome 18 – having three number 18 chromosomes instead of the normal two. A doctor named Jack Sinclair raises his hand and says, "Hey, I think we have one of those on the fourth floor."

He takes her up to the ward right away. They get a blood sample from the patient and add some anticlotting agent. Uchida immediately goes to work to identify the chromosomes. Diagnosing trisomy by actually looking at a patient's chromosomes is something very new, and has never been done by anybody in Winnipeg.

She takes the blood to the cytology lab, a place in the hospital for examining **cells**. The lab has the vinegary smell of **acetic acid solution**. Low tables by the windows have lots of **microscopes** with technicians in white lab coats seated at most of them. Along the opposite wall, a few people are preparing samples and slides.

First Uchida lets the red blood cells settle in the vial, then she takes the white blood cells off the top with a pipette, a long glass tube that is used to suck up small amounts of liquid. She transfers the cells to a small glass container containing a medium where they grow and multiply for three days inside an **incubator**. Then she takes out the liquid and centrifuges it down. A **centrifuge** is a device that spins **test tubes** around super fast to force all the heavy stuff to the bottom, leaving lighter cells and liquid at the top. She fixes the cells with acetic acid solution, and drops them onto a **glass slide** so that the cells break and spill out their chromosomes. She stains the material on the slide with a **dye**, puts it under the microscope and looks for the chromosomes – long twisty banded strands of protein and **DNA**. She finally does find three number 18 chromosomes instead of the normal two, confirming the **diagnosis**. This cytogenetic analysis is a first for Winnipeg and Canada.

The Young Scientist

AS A YOUNG GIRL, Irene Uchida joined Canadian Girls in Training at the Powell Street United Church in Vancouver. She also served as an organist for services and choir work, and was in demand as a pianist for meetings because she could play any request by ear.

Later, at the University of British Columbia (UBC), she was a member of the Japanese Students Club and the Cosmopolitan Club, and was a violinist in the UBC orchestra. She also served as a reporter for *The New Canadian*, a weekly Japanese Canadian newspaper in Vancouver. During World War II, she was very active in the Japanese Canadian Citizens for Democracy, which played a vital role for Canada's Japanese community. Because Canada was at war with Japan, it was a period of great anxiety for all the Japanese people of Canada. Many were uprooted from their homes by an Order-in-Council of the Federal Government in 1942.

Uchida was forced to stop her education at UBC and leave her comfortable home in Vancouver. She and her family were taken to Christina Lake, a self-supporting centre for the Japanese, but she was called shortly afterward to act as principal of the largest Japanese camp school at Lemon Creek in the Kootenays. She became known for her creative ideas for unusual programs and extracurricular activities.

Two years later she was allowed to continue her education at Victoria College in the University of Toronto, graduating in 1946 with a BA and also winning the Ramsay Wright Scholarship. She planned to take up social work, but one of her professors persuaded her to enter the field of genetics.

In 1951 Uchida received her PhD in zoology and began her career as a Research Associate at the Hospital for Sick Children in Toronto. Her work in genetics focused on the study of twins, children with **congenital** heart diseases and those with a variety of other abnormalities such as mongolism – now known as **Down syndrome**.

In 1959, while working with *Drosophila* (fruit fly) chromosomes at the University of Wisconsin on a Rockefeller Fellowship, Uchida turned her attention to human chromosomes. When scientists in France discovered that Down syndrome patients had an extra chromosome (47 instead of 46), Uchida decided to try to learn the cause of the extra chromosome. She continued her research in Winnipeg when she was appointed Director of the Department of Medical Genetics at the Children's Hospital there in 1960. In her first study of human chromosomes, Uchida found that there appeared to be an association between pregnant women who received **X-rays** and the occurrence of Down syndrome in their babies.

In 1969, armed with a Medical Research Council grant, she went as a visiting scientist to the University of London and Harwell, England, to study a technique for analyzing the chromosomes of mouse **ova**, or eggs.

After returning to Canada, Uchida continued her research on the effects of **radiation** on humans and mice at the McMaster University Medical Centre in Hamilton, Ontario, as well as carrying out her teaching duties as a professor. She also initiated a Genetic Counselling Program at the McMaster Medical Centre. As Director of the Cytogenetics Laboratory in Oshawa, Ontario, her responsibilities included the diagnosis of chromosome abnormalities in patients with congenital abnormalities, mental retardation, and other genetic diseases. In addition, Uchida helped **diagnose** irregularities in the chromosomes of **fetuses**. She has been invited to speak in many countries and is a member of various provincial, national, and international scientific organizations.

The Science

CYTOGENETICS IS THE study of chromosomes in cells. It concentrates on the behaviour and identification of chromosomes. By knowing the state of the chromosomes and especially the genes within them, scientists can now predict many genetic disorders. Uchida was the first person to bring the cytogenetic technique to Canada. One of the many practical applications of cytogenetics is the ability to diagnose genetic diseases in unborn fetuses, thus preparing many pregnant mothers and their spouses for the birth of an abnormal child, or giving them the choice to terminate the pregnancy.

1. In humans, 23 pairs of chromosomes have tens of thousands of genes that carry the information needed to create a unique person. For each pair, one comes from the father, the other from the mother. The bands indicate different types of DNA (DeoxyriboNucleic Acid – the molecule that contains genetic information). Cytogeneticists use the bands to help match the pairs.

2. These are the chromosomes of Jodi Kaczur, a Special Olympics champion and actor, who happens to have Down syndrome. You can tell by Jodi's two X chromosomes that she is a girl. Boys have one X and one Y chromosome.

3. About one child in 700 is born with Down syndrome. Down syndrome is caused by the accidental tripling of chromosome number 21 during conception. Other genetic diseases are caused by tripling of chromosomes number 13 or 18. The tripling is called trisomy. People with trisomy of chromosomes 13 or 18 usually die as fetuses, and are miscarried. Those who are born alive do not usually live more than a year.

4. Jodi with actor Arnold Schwarzenegger. Down syndrome people are not so handicapped as you might think. According to Uchida, who has known hundreds of them, "They are very happy, generally affectionate and always nice people." Unfortunately, because of their disease, they do not often live beyond their forties. New education and training programs are helping Down syndrome people live happy productive lives just like anyone else.

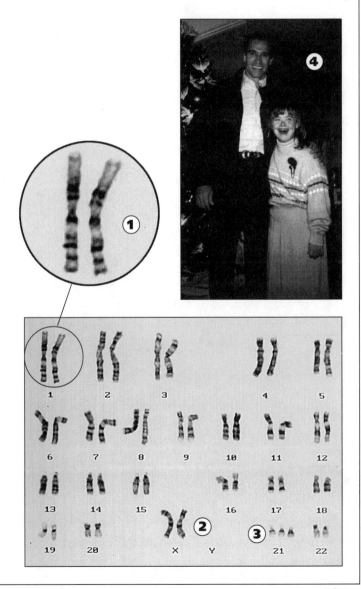

119

Activity

Object:

To sort chromosomes.

You need:

- A photocopier.
- Scissors.
- A typical chromosome set like the one below. A complete set of chromosomes like this is called a chromosome spread or **karyotype**.

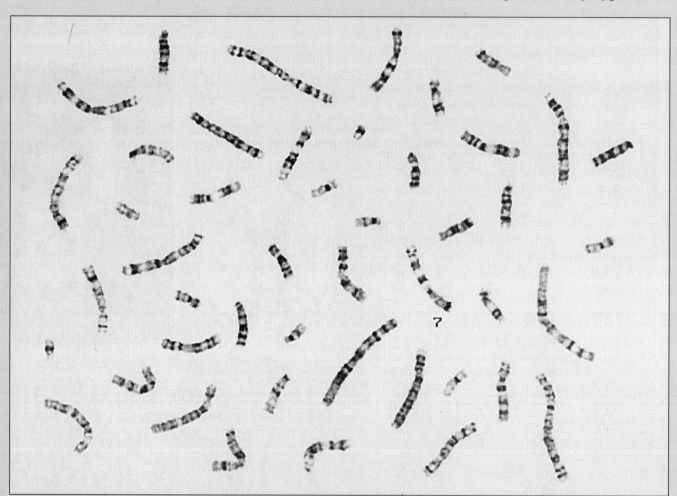

What to do:

Photocopy this page on a good quality photocopier, then cut out the chromosomes in the figure above. Now try to sort them into pairs by carefully looking at the patterns of banding on each chromosome and the lengths of the two arms on each chromosome. See if you can discover if this person has Down Syndrome or some other form of trisomy.

Mystery

UCHIDA BELIEVES GENETICISTS may be able to find out how to deactivate one of the chromosomes in an individual with trisomy. This happens naturally during the embryonic development of all women – one of their X chromosomes is always  deactivated. If geneticists can find a technique to deactivate certain chromosomes such as the extra number 21, number 13, or number 18, the related genetic diseases may be cured at an early embryonic stage.

Further Reading

Field, D. Down's Syndrome and Radiation: The Work of Dr. Irene Uchida. In *Science, Process and Discovery*. Edited by D. Field. Addison-Wesley, Don Mills, 1985.

Short Biographies

Short Biographies

HERE ARE BRIEF DESCRIPTIONS of the lives and work of over one hundred more great Canadian scientists. The reasons why they were not included in the long profiles section are many. Some may not have held Canadian citizenship during their greatest work. Some may not be alive today. Some did not have time to be interviewed or were otherwise unavailable. Others have already been described extensively by many other writers. If there is a scientist you would like to see profiled, and she or he is not included in the profile section or this longer list, please email, phone, mail, or fax your suggestion. For addresses and numbers see page 198 at the back of this book on the Great Canadian Scientists Project Website and CD-ROM. I will try to add him or her to the next edition of *Great Canadian Scientists*.

Abbreviations

Degrees

BEng	Bachelor of Engineering
BSc	Bachelor of Science
BA	Bachelor of Arts
BASc	Bachelor of Applied Science
LittB	Bachelor of Literature
MSc	Master of Science
MA	Master of Arts
MD	Medical Doctor
MEng	Master of Engineering
PhD	Doctor of Philosophy

Other

b.	born
ca.	circa or around
d.	died
IEEE	Institute of Electrical and Electronic Engineers
MIT	Massachusetts Institute of Technology, Cambridge, Massachusetts
MRC	Medical Research Council, Ottawa, Ontario
NRC	National Research Council, Ottawa, Ontario
NSERC	Natural Sciences and Engineering Research Council
UBC	University of British Columbia, Vancouver, British Columbia
UNESCO	United Nations Educational, Scientific, and Cultural Organization
UWO	University of Western Ontario, London, Ontario

Icons

♂	Female	♀	Male
	Biology		Physics
	Chemistry		Other Sciences
	Medicine		
Ⓝ	Nobel Laureate		

Abbott, Maude ♀ ⚕

b. 18 March 1869, St. Andrew's East, Quebec; d. 2 September 1940
Pathologist
Developed a classification system for congenital heart diseases

Abbott won a scholarship to McGill University, Montreal in her senior year of high school. She earned her BA and then decided to study medicine. McGill at that time did not allow women to enter its medical program, so Abbott attended Bishop's College and received her medical degree in 1894. In 1897, she wrote a successful paper on heart murmurs, but a male friend had to present it for her since women were not admitted to the Montreal medical society where she was to read the paper. In 1898 she was appointed curator of McGill's Medical Museum. Here she began cataloguing specimens and became interested in pathology, the study of disease. She focused her studies on heart disease and began work on her book, *The Atlas of Congenital Cardiac Disease*, in which she described her new classification system for congenital heart diseases. In 1923 she became Chief of Pathology at a woman's medical college in Pennsylvania. In 1926 Abbott returned to McGill in Canada, where she pioneered the use of museum exhibits as teaching aids. She also wrote a history of nursing which was later used in nursing schools across the country. In 1936 her atlas was published and was praised as an important addition to medical knowledge. She was also made an honorary member of the all-male Osler Society, which was named after Sir William Osler, a famous pathologist who had encouraged Abbott in her studies.

Sources: *Legendary Canadian Women*, 1983; *Despite the Odds*, 1990; Canadian Science and Engineering Hall of Fame

Affleck, Ian Keith ♂

b. 2 July 1952, Vancouver, British Columbia
Physicist; Professor of Physics, UBC
Researches the theory of elementary particles, condensed matter, and cosmology

Affleck was educated at Trent University in Peterborough, Ontario (BSc, 1975) and at Harvard University in Cambridge, Massachusetts (PhD, 1977). He is an expert on the theory of elementary particles. He is currently working on theories that bridge those for elementary particles – neutrons, protons, quarks, and so on – and those for condensed matter solids like crystals, semiconductors, metals, gems, and so on. He received the Governor General's Medal in 1975, the Herzberg Medal in 1990, the Rutherford Medal, and the UBC Killam Prize in 1991.

Source: *Canadian Who's Who*, 1993

Aguayo, Albert Juan ♂

b. 16 July 1934, Argentina
Neurophysiologist; Professor of Neurology and Physiology, and Director of the Centre for Research in Neuro-
    science, McGill University, Montreal, Quebec
Studies regeneration of neurons in the brain and spinal cord

Aguayo received his MD at the University of Cordoba, Argentina in 1959. He proved that damaged nerve cells in animals can regenerate and form new connections, which was regarded as impossible before his revolutionary 1980 experiment on severed nerve fibres in the rodent brain. He discovered that nerve cells do not die immediately when damaged, but may survive for months. This survival provides opportunity for healing, under the right conditions, such as the enveloping presence of Schwann cells – support cells that provide structure and insulation for nerve fibres. Although actual cures of serious nerve injuries have not yet been achieved, more recent research with damaged optic nerves indicates they can sometimes recover to some extent. He is head of a national research group studying regeneration of neurons in the brain. Aguayo is a recipient of the Gairdner Award, and in 1991 received the W. H. Helmerich III Award for Outstanding Achievement in retina research.

Sources: *Who's Who in America*, 1994; *Newsweek*, 7 October 1985; *Boston Globe*, 19 October 1992

Alcock, Alfred John ♂ ✳

b. 3 February1938, Glasgow, Scotland
Physicist
Expert in laser and plasma physics

Alcock has been head of Advanced Laser Techniques and Applications at the Institute for Microstructural Sciences, National Research Council of Canada, since 1991. He was educated at the   University of Toronto in Ontario (BSc, 1959) and Oxford University in England (PhD, 1965). He is an expert in laser and plasma physics – a phase of matter beyond solids, liquids, and gasses that consists of highly ionized particles and is typically super hot. He received the Herzberg Medal in 1975.

Source: *Canadian Who's Who*, 1993

Altman, Sidney ♂

Molecular biologist; won the 1989 Nobel Prize for Chemistry for discovery of catalytic RNA

See the detailed profile in the Profiles section.

Armstrong, Robin Louis ♂ ✳

b. 14 May 1935, Galt, Ontario
Physicist
Researches condensed matter physics

Armstrong has been President of the University of New Brunswick in Fredericton since 1990. He was educated at the University of Toronto in Ontario (Msc, 1959; PhD, 1961). He studies electromagnetic interactions, radiology, and other aspects of physics. He received the Herzberg Medal in 1973.

Source: *Canadian Who's Who*, 1993

Atwood, Harold Leslie ♂ ⚕

b. 15 February 1937, Montreal, Quebec
Physiologist
Studies mechanisms of synaptic transmission

Atwood is Professor of Physiology and Director of the Medical Research Council Group in Nerve Cells and Synapses at the University of Toronto in Ontario. He has studied biology in Canada, America and Scotland, and taught in Israel. He is a Fellow of the Royal Society of Canada.

Source: *Canadian Who's Who*, 1993

Bancroft, George Michael ♂ ✳

b. 3 April 1942, Saskatoon, Saskatchewan
Chemical physicist; Professor at UWO
Developed Mössbauer spectroscopy

Bancroft received his BSc and MSc at the University of Manitoba in Winnipeg and his PhD at Cambridge University in England (1967). He has made important contributions to electron spectroscopy and radiation studies, and has served as the driving force behind the development of a Canadian synchrotron radiation facility. He won the Rutherford Memorial Medal in 1980, and the Herzberg Award in 1991.

Source: *Who's Who in America*, 1994

Banting, Sir Frederick Grant ♂ ⚕ Ⓝ

b. 14 November 1891, Alliston, Ontario; d. 21 February 1941
Medical Doctor
Successfully isolated insulin and received the Nobel Prize

Banting studied medicine at the University of Toronto, obtained his medical degree in 1916, and served for the remainder of World War I as a medical officer overseas. He was awarded the Military Cross for heroism under fire. Banting later became interested in diabetes mellitus, a disease which at that time meant a slow but certain death. He and his colleague, Charles Best, discovered a hormone called insulin that helped people suffering from diabetes to live normal lives. In 1923 Banting was awarded the Nobel Prize for this work. Outraged that his co-worker had not also been awarded the prize, he gave half his share to Best. The Banting Research Foundation was established by Canadian Parliament that same year. With the coming of World War II, Banting was again involved with medical war work and died in a plane crash over Newfoundland.

Sources: *Asimov's Biographical Encyclopedia of Science and Technology*, 1982; Canadian Science and Engineering Hall of Fame

Barr, Murray Llewellyn ♂ ◖

b. 20 June 1908, Belmont, Ontario
Professor Emeritus of Anatomy, UWO
Discovered sex chromatin

Barr's main interest has been cytological research as it applies to sex anomalies and mental retardation. He is author of numerous publications in the field of cytology (the study of the structure and function of cells), principally the cytology of the nervous system and human cytogenetics. He received his BA from UWO in London, Ontario in 1930, his MD in 1933, and his MSc in 1938. He discovered sex chromatin in 1949, a substance made of DNA and protein which made it possible to determine the cellular sex of an individual. He has received numerous awards, including the Flavelle Medal of the Royal Society of Canada, the Ortho Medal from the American Society for the Study of Sterility, the Award of Merit from the Gairdner Foundation, and the Maurice Goldblatt Award from the International Academy of Cytology.

Source: *Canadian Who's Who*, 1993

Bell, Alexander Graham ♂ ⌁

b. 1874, Edinburgh, Scotland; d. 1922
Invented the telephone

Bell was not a Canadian citizen but he did much of his most distinguished work in Canada. Throughout his life Bell was interested in the education of deaf people. Among his most famous students was Helen Keller. His work with hearing and speech led to his most famous invention, the telephone, in 1876. Although the first phone conversation took place in the USA, Bell said he developed the idea in

1875 in Brantford, Ontario. It is certain that many of his early experiments were conducted there, including the first long distance telephone call, between Brantford and Paris, Ontario. He also invented the microphone. The Bell Telephone Company and other related businesses made Bell a wealthy man, and he was able to pursue a wide range of scientific interests. He spent his winters in the US on business, and hissummers in Cape Breton Island, Nova Scotia working on scientific research, which ranged from the genetics of sheep breeding to aviation. His Silver Dart aircraft was the first to fly in Canada, in 1909, and his hydrofoil speed boats held the world record for more than ten years. Bell died of diabetes in 1922, ironically the same year that Banting discovered insulin.

Source: Canadian Science and Engineering Hall of Fame

Belyea, Helen

b. not available; d. 1986
Geologist
The only female geologist allowed to work in the field by the Geological Survey until 1970

Belyea was an award-winning geologist who studied at Dalhousie University in Halifax, Nova Scotia and earned her PhD from Northwestern University in Evanston, Illinois in 1939. She became a teacher, and later served in the Canadian Navy. In 1945, Belyea was hired as a technologist by the Canadian Geological Survey and was promoted to geologist in 1947. After oil was struck at Leduc, Alberta, she was one of two geologists sent in 1950 to monitor the discovery. Belyea received many awards for her work, including the Barlow Memorial Award from the Canadian Institute of Mining and Metallurgy, and was granted honorary doctorates from two universities. In 1976 she was made an Officer of the Order of Canada.

Source: *Despite the Odds*, 1990

Berkely, Edith

b. 1875; d. 1963, Vancouver, British Columbia
Biologist
Expert in the field of polychaete taxonomy

Berkely published 46 scientific papers, many about polychaete marine worms, both alone and with her husband, an agricultural chemist. She also had several organisms named for her. Berkely's achievements were recognized by UBC, which established the Edith Berkely Memorial Lectures in 1969.

Source: *Despite the Odds*, 1990

Best, Charles Herbert ♂ ⚕

b. 27 February 1899, West Pembroke, Maine; d. 1978
Biochemist; Professor
Co-discoverer of insulin

Best was educated in Toronto, Ontario and London, England (DSc, University of London, 1928). After graduating in physiology and biochemistry, Best started to work with Frederick Banting on the problem of diabetes. They discovered insulin four months later. Best developed a method of drying and storing blood serum for military use and received military honours for this in 1944. His name is also associated with such drugs as histamine, heparin, and choline. He received the Flavelle Medal in 1950, and was the first winner of the Pan American Prizefrom the Sao Paulo Biennial Foundation of Brazil.

Source: *Encyclopedia Canadiana*, 1971

Bienenstock, John ♂ ⚕

b. 6 October 1936, Budapest, Hungary
Medical Doctor; Dean of Health Sciences, McMaster University
Developed the concept of the common mucosal system

Bienenstock was educated in England. He became a physician and later a university professor. He studied at Harvard Medical School in Cambridge, Massachusetts, but joined McMaster University in Hamilton, Ontario in 1968. His work involves studying how the lungs and respiratory system protect themselves from disease. He was awarded the Order of the Red Cross in 1990.

Source: *Canadian Who's Who*, 1993

Black, Davidson ♂ Ⓝ

b. 25 July 1884, Toronto, Ontario; d. 15 March 1934, Beijing, China
Anthropologist
Identified a new species of ancient human, Peking Man

Black became a professor of anatomy and anthropology, receiving his MD at the University of Toronto in 1906. While head of the department of anatomy and honorary co-director of the Cenozoic Research Lab of Peking Medical Union College, Black identified a new species of ancient human, *Sinanthropus pekinensis* (Peking Man), from fossils found at Chou Kou Tien (Zhoukoudian) near Beijing, China. His research on Peking Man became the basis for contemporary knowledge about human evolution. He was former Professor and Head of the Department of Anatomy, and co-director of the Cenozoic Research Laboratory, at the Peking Medical Union College in Beijing, China.

Sources: *The Canadian Encyclopedia*, 1988; *Encyclopedia Canadiana*, 1977

Bolton, James Robert ♂

b. 24 June 1937, Swift Current, Saskatchewan
Chemist; Professor, Department of Chemistry, UWO
Studies photochemistry and the photodegradation of pollutants

Bolton received his degrees in Canada (BA, University of Saskatchewan, Saskatoon, 1958; MA, 1960) and England (PhD, Cambridge University, England, 1963). He studies how ultraviolet light (and even sunlight) causes the destruction of organic pollutants in contaminated waters, working both at UWO and at Solarchem Environmental Systems in Markham, Ontario, a company that designs and sells equipment for the treatment of wastewater contaminated with organic pollutants. He has patented inventions, has served as a consultant to many different firms and government agencies, and has long been interested in the use of solar energy. He has written many books and papers on photochemistry.

Source: *Canadian Who's Who*, 1993

Bondar, Roberta Lynn ♀

b. 4 December 1945, Sault St. Marie, Ontario
Neurobiologist; Astronaut, Canadian Space Agency
First Canadian woman astronaut in space

When Bondar was young she would gaze up at the clear night skies of Northern Ontario and pretend to be Flash Gordon on an asteroid in search of Ming the Merciless. She made models of rockets, collected posters and badges from NASA, and played with crystal radio sets, hoping to make first contact with alien beings. She took physics and mathematics courses in high school, received university degrees in zoology and biology (BSc, University of Guelph, Ontario, 1968; MSc, UWO, 1971; PhD, University of Toronto, Ontario, 1974), and became a doctor specializing in neurology (MD, McMaster University, Hamilton, Ontario, 1977). She also acquired a private pilot's license. Then she was accepted into the Canadian Space Program and trained in the USA for three full years to do science in space. In January 1992, she became the first Canadian woman in space when she flew on the space shuttle *Discovery* as a payload specialist on the first International Microgravity Laboratory Mission.

Sources: Roberta Bondar, personal communication; Canadian Space Agency

Boyd, Gladys ♀

b. ca. 1895; d. 1970
Medical Doctor
One of the first doctors to treat diabetic children with insulin

Boyd received her medical degree from the University of Toronto in 1918. She became one of the pioneers in the treatment of juvenile diabetes and an internationally recognized expert on childhood nephritis, or inflammation of the kidneys. From 1921 until 1950, she was head of the Endocrine Service at the Hospital for Sick Children in Toronto. She directed research into diabetes, nephritis, and tuberculosis. Boyd was elected president of the Federation of Medical Women of Canada in 1932.

Source: *The Indomitable Lady Doctors*, 1974

Boyle, Willard ♂ ✳

b. 19 August 1924, Amherst, Nova Scotia
Physicist; Retired former Executive Director of Research, Communications Sciences Division, Bell Labs in New Jersey
Invented the Charge Coupled Device

Boyle's family moved to Quebec, where he grew up in a log cabin. He received no formal education until high school but went on to earn a PhD in physics from McGill University in Montreal, Quebec, in 1950. Three years later, he joined Bell Laboratories. Boyle's major contributions include the first continuously operating ruby laser, which he invented with Don Nelson in 1962, and the first patent (with David Thomas) proposing a semiconductor injection laser. Also in 1962 he became Director of Space Science and Exploratory Studies at Bellcomm, a Bell subsidiary providing technological support for the Apollo space program. In 1964 he returned to Bell Labs, switching from research to the development of electronic devices, particularly integrated circuits, which are now essential building blocks in telecommunications and electronics in general. In 1969, Boyle and George Smith invented the Charge-Coupled Device (CCD). CCDs are used as imaging devices, memories, filters, and signal processors. They have revolutionized astronomy (the Hubble Space Telescope uses CCDs at its prime focus) and created entirely new industries (e.g. video cameras and camcorders). For this invention, Boyle and Smith were joint recipients of the Franklin Institute's Stuart Ballantine Medal in 1973, and of IEEE's 1974 Morris Liebmann Award. In 1975, Boyle returned to research as Executive Director of Research for Bell Labs, where he was in charge of four laboratories until his retirement in 1979.

Source: Willard Boyle, personal communication

Brimacombe, J. Keith ♂ 〽

b. 7 December 1943, Windsor, Nova Scotia
Metallurgist; Engineer; Alcan Chair in Materials Process Engineering, UBC
Solves problems in the metals processing industry

Brimacombe received an honours BASc from UBC (1966) and a PhD from Imperial College, University of London, England (1970). As Director of the Centre for Metallurgical Process Engineering at

UBC, his research focuses on the industrial production of metal, including such processes as continuous casting of steel, flash smelting of lead, and copper converting. He performs computer-aided analysis based on knowledge derived from plant and laboratory measurements. Brimacombe's work has resulted in nine patents and two books. He is the recipient of the BC Science Council Gold Medal in 1985 and the Manning Award in 1987, as well as many metallurgical society awards.

Sources: The Manning Awards Committee; Keith Brimacombe, personal communication

Brockhouse, Bertram Neville

Nuclear physicist; won the 1994 Nobel Prize for Physics for designing the Triple-Axis Neutron Spectroscope and using it to investigate condensed matter

See the detailed profile in the Profiles section.

Brooks, Harriet

b. 1876, Exeter, Ontario; d. 1933
Physicist
Canada's first female nuclear physicist

Brooks graduated from McGill University, Montreal, Quebec, in 1898, with a BA in mathematics and natural philosophy. In 1899, she began research with Ernest Rutherford, the famous English physicist. He encouraged her and, in 1901, she became the first woman to study at the Cavendish Laboratory at Cambridge University, England, where she earned her MA. For a brief period she also worked at Marie Curie's lab in France. A year later, Brooks returned to McGill to continue her research with Rutherford. She was the first person to realize that one element can change into another. She was also among the early discoverers of radon, and the first researcher to attempt to determine its atomic mass.

Sources: *Bridges*, June/July 1989; *Women in Science*, 1986

Bruton, Len ♂ 〽

b. not available
Electrical Engineer; Professor of Electrical and Computer Engineering, Calgary, Alberta
Designed and developed electronic filters

Bruton has done extensive research in the field of real-time analog and digital signal processing. His research interests include multidimensional signal processing, sub band filtering of images, and image and audio compression. One of the most common uses of Bruton filters is in the touch-tone telephone. He is Coordinator of the Calgary Centre of the Canadian MICRONET Network of Centres of Excellence. Recipient of the 1991 Manning Award.

Sources: The Manning Awards; Len Bruton's homepage

Bull, Gerald ♂ ⌁

b. 1928, North Bay, Ontario; d. 22 March 1990
Aerophysicist; artillery designer; ballistics expert
Designed the supergun, the GC-45 howitzer

Bull was a brilliant but controversial expert in ballistics and gunnery. He studied aerophysics at the University of Toronto, Ontario (PhD, 1951). From 1961 to 1967, he co-directed McGill University's High Altitude Research Projectile (HARP) program in Montreal, Quebec. While testing missiles for a government project called Velvet Glove, he realized that scientific instruments could also be fired from a gun and survive, if put in a proper casing. This led to his great dream to build a supergun that could launch objects like satellites into space for less cost than rockets could. He was sentenced and jailed for one year in 1980 for illegally selling weapons to South Africa. Later, Saddam Hussein, leader of Iraq, offered Bull a chance to build his gun, but Bull's research ended when he was killed by assassins in 1990.

Source: *Maclean's*, 22 April 1991

Buyers, William James Leslie ♂ ⚛

b. 10 April 1937, Aboyne, Scotland
Senior Scientist, Atomic Energy of Canada Ltd. (AECL) Research, Chalk River Nuclear Laboratories
Researched magnetic excitations and structures of solids and liquids

Buyers went to grammar school in Aberdeen, Scotland, and studied physics at university there (PhD, 1963). He received the Rutherford Medal from the Royal Society of Canada in December 1986 for his work in magnetic excitations and lattice vibrations in ordered and disordered materials, and for his determination of the structures of solids and liquids. Buyers was manager of the Neutron and Solid State Physics Branch, AECL Chalk River, until 1991.

Source: *Canadian Who's Who*, 1993

Chang, Thomas Ming Swi ♂ ◊

b. ca. 1924, Swatow, China
Physiologist; Director, Artificial Cells and Organs Research Centre, McGill University, Montreal, Quebec
Invented the artificial cell

In 1957, while still an undergraduate at McGill University in Montreal, Chang invented the world's first artificial cell. His idea was to make tiny, ultrathin plastic microcapsules that could hold biological agents such as enzymes. If he could control the permeability of the plastic membrane, he could control what passed through the wall of his artificial cell, and thus mimic many of the functions of real cells. After earning his PhD in physiology, Chang developed the first artificial blood and a new cellular-based approach to an artificial kidney, liver, and pancreas. While various drawbacks persist, Chang's inventions have proved useful as temporary measures for clearing toxic substances from liver and kidney failure patients' blood streams. Chang is a recipient of the Order of Canada.

Source: McGill University Office of Media and Public Relations

Chapman, John Herbert ♂ ⚛

b. 28 August 1921, London, Ontario; d. 28 September 1979, Vancouver, British Columbia
Physicist; Space scientist; Administrator
Builder of the Canadian space program

From 1949 to 1968, Chapman was scientist, superintendent, and deputy chief superintendent in the Defense Research Telecommunications Establishment in Ottawa, and then assistant deputy minister for research in the federal Department of Communications. From 1958 to 1971, Chapman played a key role in initiating and directing the successful Alouette/IS scientific Earth satellite program. In 1966, he was appointed chairman of a government study group to examine the upper atmosphere and space programs in Canada. The resulting report was a landmark contribution to space policies and plans in Canada and led to the redirection of Canada's space program from scientific to applications satellites. Chapman was also the prime mover behind Canada's co-operative program with NASA and the European Space Agency to design, build and demonstrate the Hermes Communications Technology Satellite.

Source: Canadian Space Agency

Chitty, Dennis Hubert ♂ 🍃

b. 18 September 1912, Bristol, England
Professor Emeritus of Zoology, UBC
One of the first animal ecologists in the world

Chitty came to Canada in 1930. He was educated in Canada and England (BA, University of Toronto, Ontario, 1935; MA, 1947 and PhD, 1949, from Oxford University, England). He is the author of various scientific papers on the changes in natural populations of animals, especially small mammals. Chitty's studies are cited in all ecological textbooks and he has inspired a large number of experimental ecologists. He has studied wild animal population cycles for more than 60 years and is regarded as a world expert on lemmings. He won a Master Teacher Award in 1973, and the Fry Medal in 1988.

Source: *Canadian Who's Who,* 1993

Chiu, Ray Chu-Jeng ♂ ⚕

b. 13 March 1934, Tokyo, Japan
Medical Doctor; Professor, and cardiovascular and thoracic surgeon, Montreal General Hospital Research Institute, Montreal, Quebec
Pioneered surgical technique of cardiomyoplasty for failing hearts

Chiu received his MD from National Taiwan University, and his PhD in experimental surgery from McGill University, Montreal, in 1970. He pioneered a new type of experimental surgery that removes some of a heart patient's back muscle, attaches it to the ribs, and wraps it around the heart. A specially designed pacemaker contracts the back muscle in time with the heart's own contractions, thus helping a weak heart to function. Chiu was the first to overcome the physiological obstacles to using other types of muscles to assist the heart's function. Heart muscle is the only kind that can contract regularly without tiring; other muscles require periods of rest. Thus the physiological and chemical factors of the back muscle have to be modified to become more like the heart. Collaborating with David Inuzzo, a biochemist from York University, Chiu subjected the back muscle to four to six weeks of constant low frequency electrical stimulation, after which it came to resemble heart muscle. The stimulation alters the expression of certain genes in the muscle cells. The process was actually discovered by biochemists in the late 1960s, but was not applied to heart surgery until Chiu and researchers like him began to work on the problem.

Source: *McGill News,* Fall 1990

Clark, Colin Whitcomb ♂ 📈

b. 18 June 1931, Vancouver, British Columbia
Mathematician; Professor of Mathematics, UBC
Invented mathematical bioeconomics

Clark received his mathematics degrees from UBC (BA, 1953) and the University of Washington (PhD, 1958). He applied his mathematical knowledge to accurately identify and analyze renewable resources like fisheries, and how to manage them so that that some of the resource is used, but enough is left to reproduce for future harvests. His book, *Mathematical Bioeconomics,* explains his approach. He received Killam Sr. Research Fellowships twice, and the Biely Faculty Research Prize in 1978.

Source: *Canadian Who's Who,* 1993

Collip, James Bertram ♂ ⚘

b. 20 November 1892, Belleville, Ontario; d. 19 June 1965, London, Ontario
Medical Doctor; Biochemist; Dean of Medicine, UWO
One of the original patentees of insulin, and one of first to isolate parathyroid hormone

Collip became a medical researcher after obtaining his PhD from the University of Toronto, Ontario. At Banting's request, Collip was asked to join the team investigating the internal secretion of the pancreas. A skilful biochemist, he produced the first insulin suitable for use on human beings. With Best and Banting, he was one of the original patentees of insulin, and in 1923 received a one-quarter share of the Nobel Prize money awarded to Banting and J. J. R. MacLeod. He contributed to endocrinological research, and was one of the first to isolate the parathyroid hormone. In 1928, he became a professor of biochemistry at McGill University in Montreal, where for the next decade he and his students were leaders in endocrinology, pioneering the isolation and study of the ovarian and gonadotrophic hormones.

Source: *The Canadian Encyclopedia*, 1988

Conway, Brian Evans ♂ ⚗

b. 26 January 1927, London, England
Chemist; Professor of Chemistry, University of Ottawa, Ontario
A leader in the field of electrochemistry

After receiving a BSc (1946) at Imperial College of Science and Technology, London, England, and a PhD (1949) and DSc (1961) at the University of London, England, Conway became an expert in electrochemistry. He has contributed much to the understanding of electrode kinetics, particularly those of the hydrogen evolution and the very earliest stages of metal oxidation. He has also served as a consultant to chemical research labs. He has received the Noranda Award and Medal, the Palladium Medal in 1989, and both the Linford Medal and the Kendall Award in 1984.

Source: *Canadian Who's Who*, 1993

Copp, D. Harold ♂ ⚘ ⚘

b. 16 January 1915, Toronto, Ontario
Biochemist; Former head of physiology department, UBC
Discovered and named the protein calcitonin, for use in the treatment of bone disease

Copp decided to enter medicine when his brother died after being shot by a burglar. Copp earned his MD in 1939 at the University of Toronto, Ontario, graduating with a gold medal, and received his PhD in biochemistry in 1943 at the University of California at Berkeley. After he joined UBC's physiology department he investigated the regulation of calcium in the body, and discovered calcitonin, a hormone that inhibits the release of calcium from the bones. Copp is famous all over the world for his discovery, which is used in synthetic form to treat osteoporosis, a bone disease, and other diseases such as Paget's disease, hypercalcemia, and rheumatoid arthritis. He was inaugurated into the Canadian Medical Hall of Fame by the Medical Research Council in May 1994.

Source: *Georgia Straight*, 1 July 1994

Costerton, J. William ♂ ◊

b. 21 July 1934, Vernon, British Columbia
Microbiologist; Director of the Centre For Biofilm Engineering, National Science Foundation Engineering Research Center and the University of Calgary, Alberta
Pioneered biofilm microbiology

Costerton became an expert in microbiology and electron microscopy after receiving degrees from UBC (BA, 1955; MA, 1956) and UWO (PhD, 1960). In 1978, when he was a University of Calgary postdoctoral student, Costerton shook up the established science of microbiology with a new view of bacterial life. He and his team worked out a way to see the structure of the slimy substance that seemed to anchor bacteria to surfaces in cattle stomachs. When they took the bacteria into the lab and purified them, however, they became just like ordinary bacteria. It became obvious that test-tube bacteria are not the same as naturally occuring bacteria. Natural bacterial colonies were creating their own microhabitat, sticking to surfaces and covering themselves with a slimy layer of protective molecules. Costerton named these molecules biofilms. The researchers found that biofilm bacteria were often team players – different species working in physiological co-operation. Costerton and his team have applied their knowledge to developing new technologies in areas ranging from oil production to bacteria-resistant medical devices. He holds several biological patents and is president of the Microbios company. He received the Haultain Prize in 1984 and the Izaak Walton Killam Memorial Prize in 1989, and holds a NSERC industrial research chair.

Sources: *Canadian Who's Who*, 1993; NSERC

Coxeter, Donald H. S. M. ♂ ∿

Mathematician; world's Greatest Classical Geometer

See the detailed profile in the Profiles section.

Daley, Roger ♂

Meteorologist; principal constructor of the Canadian numerical weather forecasting system

See the detailed profile in the Profiles section.

Dansereau, Pierre ♂

b. 5 October 1911, Montreal, Quebec
Ecologist and botanist, Université du Québec à Montréal
Popularized environmental issues

Pierre Dansereau received degrees in botany and agriculture at College St.-Marie (BA, 1931), Institute Agricole d'Oka (BSc, 1936) and Université de Genève (DSc, 1939). He worked in the Montreal and the New York Botanical Gardens, and has directed ecological research centres. He has written many books on ecology and the urban environment, and is the author of a series of TV films on the environment. He has won numerous awards, including the Fermat medal; the Massey Medal; Prix Esdras-Minville; Prix Marie-Victorin; the Killam Prize; the Lawson Medal; and the Lifetime Achievement Award from Environment Canada in 1989.

Source: *Canadian Who's Who*, 1993

de Bold, Adolfo J. ♂

b. ca. 1945, Paran, Argentina
Biochemist; Professor of Pathology and Physiology, and Director, Cardiac Cell and Molecular Biology Laboratory, University of Ottawa Heart Institute, Ottawa, Ontario
Discovered that the heart produces a hormone, the Atrial Natriuretic Factor (ANF)

As an undergraduate, de Bold studied at the National University of Cordoba, Argentina. In 1968, he came to Canada, where he received his MSc and PhD in pathology at Queen's University in Kingston, Ontario. In 1973, he was appointed Assistant Professor of Pathology at Queen's. Although de Bold trained primarily in biochemistry, he also studied experimental pathology. He used his combined skills to look at the cell biology of the mammalian atrial cardiocyte (heart muscle cell) which culminated in 1980 with the discovery of Atrial Natriuretic Factor (ANF), a polypeptide hormone produced by the cardiac muscle cell of the heart atrium. He thus demonstrated that the heart has an endocrine function and opened a field of research that has led to many new insights in biology. De Bold has won the Gairdner Foundation International Award, The Ernest C. Manning Principal Award, and the CIBA Award in Hypertension Research. He was also nominated for a Nobel Prize.

Source: Adolfo de Bold, personal communication

Derick, Carrie

b. 1862, Clarenceville, Quebec; d. 1941
Geneticist
Pioneered work in heredity

Derick received her BA from McGill University, Montreal, Quebec, in 1890, earning the highest marks and winning several prizes. The following year, she became the first female instructor at McGill University. In 1896, she earned her MA and, after a long struggle, was made a lecturer. Five years later, she was appointed acting chairperson of the botany department, a position she held for nearly three years. But when the university finally filled the position permanently, it passed over Derick, and hired a man. Derick eventually became the first woman ever appointed to a full professorship at a Canadian university. Her research on heredity was read by scientists around the world and paved the way for the future study of genetics. She was one of the few women listed in *American Men of Science* (1910). McGill awarded her the honorary title of Professor Emerita.

Source: *Despite the Odds*, 1990

Deslongchamps, Pierre ♂ ⚗

b. 8 May 1938, Saint-Lin, Quebec
Chemist; Professor of Chemistry, University of Sherbrooke, Quebec
Pioneered the synthesis of organic molecules

Deslongchamps received his BSc in Chemistry from the University of Montreal, Quebec, in 1959. After completing his doctoral studies at the University of New Brunswick (1964), he worked at Harvard University in Cambridge, Massachusetts, in the laboratories of Nobel prize-winner R. B. Woodward, who was trying to synthesize Vitamin B-12. After Deslongchamps moved to the University of Sherbrooke, he pioneered advances in the fabrication of complex organic chemicals, a key contribution to many areas of science, as well as to the search for more effective drugs. At the age of 26 he synthesized ryanodol, a very complex molecule. He also synthesized the twistane molecule and accomplished the total synthesis of agarofuran, hinesol, and occidentalol, all during a four-year period. His discovery of the role of stereoelectronic effects in controlling certain organic reactions has become a fundamental concept of organic chemistry, actually changing the way scientists look at molecules. He has won many awards, including a Steacie Fellowship, the Canada Gold Medal (from NSERC) and the Prix Marie-Victorin.

Sources: Robert M. Cory, personal communication; *Contact* (NSERC newsletter), Spring 1993; *Canadian Who's Who*, 1993

Dow, Jean ♀ ⚕

b. not available; d. 1927, Peking, China
Medical Doctor
One of first researchers to isolate the organism which causes kala-azar disease

Dow earned her medical degree from the University of Toronto, Ontario in 1895. Later that year, she traveled to China, where she would spend the rest of her life. Dow was a surgeon in China for over 30 years. For 20 years, she was the only woman doctor at the Canadian Presbyterian Mission in Honan. There, she did research into the organism which causes kala-azar, a wasting disease that is prevalent in Africa, Asia, and the Middle East. Her work paved the way for the development of treatment for this illness, which previously had a fatality rate of 70 percent. Dow received a medal from the Chinese government for her service during the great famine of 1920.

Source: *The Indomitable Lady Doctors*, 1974

Duckworth, Henry Edmison ♂ ⚛

b. 1 November 1915, Brandon, Manitoba
Physicist; former Chancellor and Professor Emeritus of Physics, University of Manitoba, Winnipeg
Determined precise atomic mass by greatly increasing resolution of the mass spectrometer

Duckworth started out studying English as well as mathematics. He became interested in physics by teaching it in a high school and went back to university to study physics in depth, receiving his BA and BSc in botany at the University of Manitoba (1935, 1937) and his PhD in Physics from the University of Chicago, Illinois (1942). He was able to determine precise atomic mass by using mass spectrometers with greatly improved resolution, providing evidence for sudden changes in nuclear stability corresponding to modern nuclear shell theory. This was fundamental for understanding nuclear chemistry and the transmutation of the elements. He is the author of important books, notably *Mass Spectroscopy* (1958), and *Electricity and Magnetism* (1960). He received the Tory Medal from the Royal Society of Canada in 1965, became an officer of the Order of Canada in 1976, and was awarded the SUNAMCO Medal of International Union of Pure and Applied Physics in 1992.

Sources: *Modern Men of Science*, 1966-68; *Canadian Who's Who*, 1993

Fallis, (Albert) Murray ♂ 🍃

b. 2 January 1907, Minto Township, Ontario
Biologist; former Professor, Department of Zoology, University of Toronto, Ontario
Father of Canadian parasitology

Fallis studied biology at the University of Toronto (BA, 1932; PhD 1937) and became an expert in parasitology, the study of parasites. He has directed the departments of parasitology at the Ontario Research Foundation and the School of Hygiene at the University of Toronto, has served as a consultant for the World Health Organization, and is emeritus member of various scientific societies of parasitology.

Source: *Canadian Who's Who*, 1993

Fedoruk, Sylvia ♀ ⚕

Saskatchewan
Medical physicist
Member of the team that developed the first Cobalt 60 units for cancer treatment

Fedoruk grew up in rural Saskatchewan, and was taught by her father in a one-room schoolhouse. Later, while living in Windsor, Ontario during World War II, she was encouraged to go into science by her English teacher and she entered the University of Saskatchewan's medical program in Winnipeg. Fedoruk graduated in physics in 1951, and for 35 years she was chief medical physicist for the Saskatchewan Cancer Foundation. During this time, Fedoruk was involved in the development of both the Cobalt 60 unit, and one of the first nuclear scanning machines. She was also involved in athletics all through school, and, in 1986, she was inducted into the Canadian Curling Hall of Fame. In 1986, she was named Woman of the Year by the YWCA. In 1988, Fedoruk became Lieutenant-Governor of Saskatchewan.

Source: *Claiming The Future*, 1991

Fenerty, Charles ♂ ⟋

b. January 1821, Upper Sackville, Nova Scotia; d. 10 June 1892, Lower Sackville, Nova Scotia
Inventor
First person to make newsprint from wood pulp

Fenerty was concerned about the difficulty a local paper mill was having in obtaining an adequate supply of rags to make quality paper. He succeeded in making paper from wood pulp as early as 1841 but neglected to publicize his discovery until 1844, by which time others had patented a paper-making process based on wood fibre.

Source: *The Canadian Encyclopedia*, 1988

Fessenden, Reginald A. ♂ 〰

b. 6 October 1866, East Bolton, Quebec; d. 22 July 1932
Chemist; inventor
Made first radio broadcast and scores of other inventions

Fessenden was a child prodigy, learning Greek, Latin, and French at an early age. Later, he turned to science and worked as chief chemist for Thomas Edison during the 1880s, then briefly for Westinghouse. With millionaire backers, he formed his own company and developed his most remarkable invention, the modulation of radio waves. Fessenden's technology – called the heterodyne principle – has remained fundamental to radio to this day, allowing reception and transmission on the same aerial without interference. On Christmas Eve 1906, ships off the Atlantic coast with Fessenden-designed equipment received the first radio broadcast. Fessenden eventually held 500 patents. One, in 1929, was for the fathometre, which could determine the depth of water under a ship.

Sources: *Asimov's Biographical Encyclopedia of Science and Technology*, 1982; NRC Hall of Fame

Fibiger, Hans Christian ♂ ⚕

b. ca. 1942, Denmark
Leader in brain research, and in the causes and treatments of clinical depression

Fibiger earned his BSc at the University of Victoria, British Columbia, in 1966, and his PhD at Princeton, New Jersey, in 1970. He went to UBC in 1972, where he conducted research into the causes of "anhedonia," or depression. His work shows that a complex of neurons in the midbrain contains the neurotransmitter dopamine, which is an essential part of the electrochemical process that we experience as pleasure or "reward." His laboratory was the first in the world to show that dopamine neurons are associated with the feeling of pleasure that cocaine, d-amphetamine and other drugs provide. This knowledge is the basis for the treatment of depression by drugs that attempt to balance dopamine levels in the midbrain. According to international citation indexes, Fibiger is among the 200 most-frequently quoted scientists in the world, in any field. He received the 1993 BC Science and Engineering Gold Medal Award in Health Sciences.

Source: Science Council of British Columbia

Filipovic, Dusanka ♀

b. date not available, Toronto, Ontario
Engineer
Developed method to reclaim Chlorinated FlouroCarbons (CFC) refrigerants

Filipovic is Deputy Chairman of Halozone Technologies Inc., a Mississauga, Ontario company that helps people safely deal with halogenated hydrocarbon compounds, such as refrigerants, CFCs, methyl bromide fumigants, and other toxic substances. She developed and patented the "Blue Bottle" technology that makes this possible. A single CFC molecule can destroy 100,000 ozone layer molecules. Filipovic's company received US Environmental Protection Agency certification in 1994. Filipovic received the 1993 Manning Principal Award.

Source: The Manning Awards

Franklin, Ursula

b. 16 September 1921, Munich, Germany
Physicist; metallurgist; Professor Emeritus of Metallurgy and Materials Science, and Director of Collegium
  Archaeometricum, University of Toronto, Ontario
Pioneered the physics of ancient archeological materials

Franklin acquired her PhD in experimental physics from Technical University in Berlin, Germany, then joined the Ontario Research Foundation as a senior scientist. She has taught and researched extensively in the field of materials science, and in the area of the social impact of technology. Much of her work has been done in conjunction with archaeologists on ancient materials; she pioneered the development of archaeometry, which applies the modern technique of materials analysis to archaeology. To determine the effect of fallout from testing nuclear weapons, she worked on gathering and analysing data on the strontium-90 accumulation in the teeth of children in Canada. Franklin is a former member of the Science Council of Canada, and an officer of the Order of Canada. In 1984 Franklin became the first woman to be named a University Professor at the University of Toronto. She received the Governor-General's Award in Commemoration of the Person's Case in 1991, and was made a Companion of the Order of Canada in 1992.

Sources: *Canadian Who's Who*, 1994; *The Canadian Encyclopedia*, 1988

Frappier, Armand ♂

b. 26 November 1904, Salaberry-de-Valleyfield, Quebec
Microbiologist; Professor of Bacteriology and Chief of Laboratories (Hôpital St.-Luc), University of Montreal,
  Quebec
Researched BCG vaccine for tuberculosis and infant leukemia

After receiving his MD (1930) and MSc (1931) at the University of Montreal, Frappier studied tuberculosis and BCG (bacille Calmette-Guérin) vaccine. He was one of the first North Americans to confirm the safety and efficacy of BCG as a vaccine for tuberculosis and to develop ways to study and use it. He showed it also had preventative effects in cases of infant leukemia. In addition, he studied the mechanisms of infection and of resistance to certain infections. Frappier was the founder of the Institut de microbiologie et d'hygiène de Montréal, which was renamed Institut Armand-Frappier in 1975.

Source: *The Canadian Encyclopedia*, 1988

Fyfe, William S. ♂ ⚗

b. 4 June 1927, Ashburn, New Zealand
Geochemist; Professor Emeritus, Department of Geology, UWO
Father of modern geochemistry and global change

Fyfe was the first student from his one-room school to attend university. He received his BSc in 1948 from Otago University, New Zealand, followed by his MSc in 1949 and PhD in 1952. Early in his career, he made important contributions to the knowledge of isomorphism, studying the behaviour of rock-forming minerals under high temperature and stress. His investigation of metamorphism – the chemical and physical transformation of rocks under pressure and stress at the base of mountain systems – revolutionized the field of metamorphic petrology. While Dean of Science at UWO (1986-90), he established the Interface Science Research Centre. Fyfe's Canadian research effort focused on the role of fluids and tectonics in creating deposits of precious metals, particularly gold. He did research on a range of biosphere-geosphere interactions, including the role of micro-organisms in concentrating metals and the role of geothermal systems in creating ocean nutrients. Concerned with the environmental implications of human energy consumption, Fyfe conducted research into problems associated with burning coal. His knowledge of the geology of ancient rocks and the movement of fluids in the earth's crust were key to research into the possibility of safe geological disposal of high-level nuclear waste. He was also involved in soil erosion studies and prevention. He led the establishment of the Global Change program, a comprehensive international investigation of the earth's life-support systems. He was awarded the Canada Gold Medal for Science and Engineering, NSERC, in 1991.

Sources: *Canadian Who's Who*, 1993; NSERC

Galdikas, Biruté ♀ ◊

Physical Anthropologist; world's foremost expert on Orangutans

See the detailed profile in the Profiles section.

Geist, Valerius ♂ ◌

b. 2 February 1938, Nikolajew, USSR
Wildlife biologist; Professor of Environmental Sciences, University of Calgary
Expert in wildlife biology and environmental design

Geist received a BSc in 1960 and a PhD in 1966, both from UBC, and became a wildlife biologist. He proposed game ranching as a way to be able to use wild animals while preserving them, but later turned against the idea and now crusades against game farms. He believes that legalizing the sale of wild game will create an open market on all animals that live in the wild. He is known for his studies of ungulates like mountain sheep, elk, and mule deer.

Sources: *Canadian Who's Who*, 1993; *Nature Canada*, Spring 1987

Gesner, Abraham ♂ ◌

b. 2 May 1797, Cornwallis, Nova Scotia; d. 29 April 1864, Halifax, Nova Scotia
Physician; geologist; chemist; inventor; professor; author
Invented kerosene oil and founded the modern petroleum industry

Gesner became a medical student in London, England, and graduated as a physician and surgeon. He then became the first government geologist in a British colony. He studied, described and mapped the distribution of rock formations in Nova Scotia, New Brunswick, and Prince Edward Island. Beginning in about 1846, he developed experiments for distilling coal oil from solid hydrocarbons. Gesner coined the name "kerosene" for the lamp oil he perfected by 1853, and patented his processes in 1854. His other inventions include a wood preservative, a process of asphalt paving for highways, briquettes made from compressed coal dust, and a machine for insulating electric wire. After overseeing the setup of a factory in the USA, he sold his patents in 1863, and returned to Halifax and a professorship at Dalhousie University.

Source: *The Canadian Encyclopedia*, 1988

Gillespie, Ronald James ♂ ◌

b. 21 August 1924, London, England
Chemist; Professor Emeritus, Department of Chemistry, McMaster University, Hamilton, Ontario
Developed VSEPR (Valence Shell Electron Pair Repulsion) Theory

Gillespie studied chemistry (BSc, University College, London, 1944; PhD, 1949) and became an expert in molecular chemistry, particularly the geometric properties of molecules. He is the author of *Molecular Geometry* (1972), *Chemistry* (1986; 2nd edition in 1989) and *The VSEPR Model of Molecular Geometry* (1991). VSEPR can be used to describe and predict the shapes of molecules (e.g. linear, cubical, pyramidal, etc.) based on the number of electron pairs in the outer shells. He has received numerous honorary degrees and awards, including the Izaak Walton Killam Memorial Prize, the Tory Medal from the Royal Society of Canada, and the Noranda Award.

Source: *Canadian Who's Who*, 1993

Gold, Phil ♂ 🍃

b. 17 September 1936, Montreal, Quebec
Medical Doctor; oncologist; professor; Executive Director of the Montreal General Hospital
Developed the first and still most widely used blood test for certain types of cancer

After Gold received his BSc (1957), MSc (1961) and PhD (1965) from McGill University in Montreal, he and Samuel Freedman discovered a carcinoembryonic antigen (CEA) produced during growth of cancer cells of the digestive system. This antigen is produced in tumors and fetal embryonic gut, pancreas, and liver cells, but not by normal adult cells. A blood test was developed that can indicate the presence, spread, or reoccurrence of cancer. The CEA test has proved useful in assessing the extent of a cancer, its growth rate and response to treatment, but it is not reliable in testing for the presence of tumors, since early tumors do not produce enough CEA to be detected. The discovery of CEA opened the new field of onco-fetal antigens. Recently, the CEA gene was cloned and its functional activity is under investigation. Gold won the Gairdner Award in 1978, the 1982 Manning Award, the F.N.G Starr Award of the Canadian Medical Association in 1983, and the Izaak Walton Killam Award in 1985. He became a Companion of the Order of Canada in 1986 and an Officer of the Order of Quebec in 1990.

Sources: The Manning Awards; *McGill Communiqué*; Phil Gold, personal communication

Gosling, James ♂ 📈

b. 19 May 1956, Calgary, Alberta
Software Engineer, Sun Microsystems, Inc.
Created the Java programming language

At the age of 13, Gosling discovered computers at the University of Calgary, where he later received a BSc in Computer Science (in 1977). In 1983 he received a PhD in Computer Science from Carnegie-Mellon University in Pittsburgh, Pennsylvania. After Gosling joined Sun Microsystems in 1984, he developed a project called NEWS (Network Extensible Windowing System), a PostScript-interpreter-based system of distributing computer-processing power across a network. In 1991, Gosling began working on Java, a new programming language, as a secret project. The results were released in 1995, adding a new dimension to Internet capabilities. Java allows small programs, or applets, to be distributed over a network and safely used by client software on potentially any platform. Gosling also wrote the first version of Emacs for UNIX. Other accomplishments include: a multiprocessor version of UNIX; several compilers; mail systems and window managers; and a satellite data acquisition system.

Sources: *Globe and Mail*, 17 October 1995; Sun Microsystems

Grafstein, Bernice ♂ ◊

b. ca. 1920
Professor of Physiology and Biophysics, Department of Physiology, Cornell University Medical College, New
  York, New York
World expert on nerve cells

Grafstein received her BA from the University of Toronto, Ontario, in 1951, and her PhD from McGill University, Montreal, in 1954. She is famous for studying the transport of materials down the axons of nerves the long connecting arms that nerve cells use to communicate with other cells. She was the Vincent and Brooke Astor Distinguished Professor in Neuroscience at Cornell University and was the first woman president of the American Society for Neuroscience.

Source: *Who's Who in America*, 1994

Gray, Joseph Alexander ♂ ✳

b. 7 February 1884, Melbourne, Australia; d. 5 March 1966, London, England
Physicist; research professor, Queen's University, Kingston, Ontario
Early pioneer of nuclear physics

After graduating from Melbourne University in 1907, Gray worked in Ernest Rutherford's lab in Manchester, England, studying the interaction of electrons and X-rays with atoms. In 1912 he went to McGill University in Montreal, Quebec, and after World War I returned there. From 1924 until retiring, he was a research professor at Queen's University in Kingston, Ontario. His discoveries regarding the breadth of the energy spectrum of electrons and the scattering of X-rays were important contributions to the development of the new theory of the atom. His work foreshadowed the Compton Effect (for which A.H. Compton received the Nobel Prize). Gray received the first Gold Medal of the Canadian Association of Physicists in 1956. An international unit of radiation measurement (the GRAY) is named after him.

Source: *The Canadian Encyclopedia*, 1988

Gros, Philippe ♂

b. not available
Biochemist; Director of biochemistry lab, McIntyre Medical Sciences Building, McGill University, Montreal, Quebec
Cloned the Nramp gene and the mdr gene

Working with Emile Skamene (McGill Centre for the Study of Host Resistance), Erwin Schurr, and Ken Morgan (Epidemiology and Biostatistics), Philippe Gros cloned the BCG gene in mice and then identified the equivalent gene in humans, called Nramp. Mutations in the Nramp gene create vulnerability to several infectious diseases, including tuberculosis, leprosy, salmonellosis (typhoid fever), and leishmaniasis. Gros and his team also researched the mechanism by which this gene controls susceptibility to these infectious diseases. Gros's other major breakthrough is the cloning of the mdr (multidrug resistance) gene family, which controls resistance to drugs used in anticancer chemotherapy. Gros is the recipient of the first Michael Smith Award of Excellence and an MRC Senior Scientist Award in 1995 (both awards from the Medical Research Council of Canada).

Sources: *McGill Reporter*, 3 March 1995; *MRC Communiqué*

Hardy, John Christopher ♂

b. 10 July 1941, Montreal, Quebec
Nuclear physicist; Director, TASCC (Tandem Accelerator Superconducting Cyclotron) Division, Atomic Energy of
  Canada, Chalk River, Ontario
Studies atomic energy and nuclear physics

Hardy was educated at McGill University, Montreal (BSc, 1961; MSc, 1963; PhD, 1965). He worked at the Lawrence Radiation Laboratory in Berkeley, California, at Atomic Energy of Canada, Chalk River, and at CERN in Geneva, Switzerland. He was head of the Nuclear Physics Branch at Chalk River from 1983 to 1986. He received the Herzberg Medal in 1976, and the Rutherford Medal in Physics in 1981.

Source: *Canadian Who's Who*, 1993

Hare, Frederick Kenneth ♂

b. 5 February 1919, Wylye, England
Geographer; Professor Emeritus; Chancellor, Trent University, Peterborough, Ontario
Internationally famous environmentalist and meteorologist

Hare received his BSc from the University of London, England, in 1939 and his PhD (Geography) from the University of Montreal, Quebec, in 1950. He has been director of various research institutes and was awarded the Patterson Medal from the Canadian Meteorological Service in 1973, the Massey

Medal from the Royal Canadian Geographical Society in 1974 and the IMO Prize from the World Meteorological Organization in 1988.

Source: *Canadian Who's Who*, 1993

Harrison, Jed ♂ ⚗

b. 16 December 1954, Vancouver, British Columbia
Chemist; Professor, Department of Chemistry, University of Alberta, Edmonton
Applied microchip technology to chemical analysis

Harrison received his BSc from Simon Fraser University, Burnaby, British Columbia (1980) and his PhD from MIT (1984). He joined the Analytical Chemistry division at the University of Alberta as a faculty member in 1984. He is a leader in the development of miniature analytical systems, whereby micromachining techniques are used to fabricate tiny three-dimensional structures that can carry out chemical analyses on a piece of silicon or glass a couple of centimetres square. The result is a "lab-on-a-chip," useful for immunological tests for hormones and drug abuse, DNA diagnostics, tests for soil and water contamination, and detection of biological warfare agents on the battlefield. Their small size makes test kits portable and inexpensive. As well, chemical analyses can be completed in seconds. A lab-on-a-chip also requires only a minute volume of test material – about one billionth of a millilitre. Perhaps most amazing are the detection limits of these devices. They are capable of detecting picomolar concentrations – that's like one Tylenol tablet dissolved in 12 Olympic-sized swimming pools. Harrison received a 1996 Steacie Memorial Fellowship.

Source: NSERC

Hebb, Donald O. ♂ 📈

b. 1904, Chester, Nova Scotia; d. 1985, Halifax, Nova Scotia
Psychologist; Chairman and Chancellor, Psychology Department, McGill University, Montreal, Quebec
Developed Hebb synapse and cell assembly theory

Hebb began his adult life intending to be a novelist, and decided that his calling required an understanding of psychology. He received his BA from Dalhousie University, Nova Scotia (1925), his MA in psychology from McGill University, Montreal and his PhD from Harvard University, Cambridge, Massachusetts (1936). Hebb spent two decades working with researchers like Penfield and Lashley, culminating in 1949 with the publication of *The Organization of Behaviour*, a keystone of modern neuroscience. In it, Hebb proposed neural structures, called cell assemblies, which were formed through the action of feedback loops, or what is now called the Hebb synapse. The cell-assembly theory guided Hebb's landmark experiments on the influence of early environment on adult intelligence and foreshadowed neural network theory, an active line of research in artificial intelligence.

Source: *Scientific American*, January 1993

Herzberg, Gerhard ♂ ✳ Ⓝ

Physicist; 1971 Nobel Prize winner for Chemistry, for Molecular Spectroscopy

See full profile in the Profiles section.

Hill, Kenneth ♂ ✳

b. not available
Electrical Engineer
Pioneered work in optical fibre communications

In 1978, Hill discovered that irradiating optical fibre with a laser permanently changes the refractive index of the fibre's core, an effect he called photosensitivity. Direct results of his work are the development of low cost/high performance devices such as wavelength filters, multiplexers and laser frequency stabilizers, important for telecommunications. Optical sensors for measuring temperature and strain are also beneficial outcomes for the construction industry. Hill is a 1995 Manning Award recipient.

Source: The Manning Awards

Hillier, James ♂ ✳

b. 22 August 1915, Brantford, Ontario
Physicist; head of electron microscope research, RCA Labs, Princeton, New Jersey
Co-designed the first commercially available electron microscope in North America

While studying at the University of Toronto, Ontario (BA, 1937; MA, 1938; PhD, 1941), Hillier and his colleague, A. Prebus, constructed an improved electron microscope which produced resolutions usable in a lab. Hillier also discovered the principle of the stigmator for correcting astigmatism of electron microscope objective lenses. He invented the electron microprobe microanalyser, and was the first to picture tobacco mosaic viruses and an ultra-thin section of a single bacterium. He became an American citizen in 1945, was inducted into the National Inventors Hall of Fame in 1980, and received the Albert Lasker Award in 1960 as well as the Commonwealth Award in 1980.

Sources: *Who's Who in America*, 1994; *Asimov's Biographical Encyclopedia of Science and Technology*, 1982

Hogg-Priestley, Helen Battles ♀

b. 1 August 1905, Lowell, Massachusetts; d. 1993
Astronomer; Professor Emeritus, University of Toronto, Ontario
Researched globular star clusters and popularized astronomy

Helen Battles Hogg-Priestley (née Sawyer) began her research in the field of globular star clusters and their variable stars while working towards her PhD in astronomy (Radcliffe, 1931). She worked with major telescopes in Victoria, British Columbia, Tucson, Arizona, and Richmond Hill, Ontario. Well known for her lectures and her radio and television shows, Hogg published numerous scholarly articles and the popular book, *The Stars Belong to Everyone*. She was awarded the Sandford Fleming Medal from the Royal Canadian Institute in 1985. The minor Planet No. 2917 was named Sawyer Hogg.

Source: *The Canadian Encyclopedia*, 1988

Holling, Crawford S. ♂

b. 6 December 1930, Theresa, New York
Zoologist; Professor, Department of Zoology, University of Florida, Gainesville
Studied natural systems and the response of predators to prey

Holling came to Canada at age five. He became a zoologist and ecologist after receiving degrees from the University of Toronto, Ontario (BA, 1952; MA, 1954), and UBC (PhD in zoology, 1957). His work emphasizes the resilience of natural systems and how they maintain their structure in the face of disturbances, rather than requiring human intervention to control things. He received the Mercer Award and the Austrian Cross of Honour for Sciences and Art.

Sources: *Canadian Who's Who*, 1993; *Journal of Business Administration*, Fall-Winter 1990

Hubel, David ♂

b. 1926, Montreal, Quebec
Physicist; medical doctor; Professor, Department of Neurobiology, Harvard Medical School, Cambridge, Massachusetts
Mapped the visual cortex

Hubel majored in physics at McGill University in Montreal, Quebec, and then became interested in the medical world. He enrolled in McGill's medical school, without ever having taken a biology course. In 1958, Hubel moved to Johns Hopkins University, Baltimore, Maryland, and teamed up with Torsten Wiesel, a researcher from Sweden. The pair almost immediately began to make key discoveries about the part of the brain involved in vision – the visual cortex. A year later they moved to Harvard Medical School, continuing their experiments. Throughout the 1960s and 1970s, Hubel and Wiesel co-authored a series of ground-breaking papers on the visual cortex. They used microelectrodes and modern electronics to detect the activity of individual neurons, using cats as their subjects. (The cats were not harmed by these experiments; indeed, their purring created vibration problems.) Thanks to the work of Hubel and Wiesel, the visual cortex has become the best-known part of the brain. Hubel and Wiesel shared the Nobel Prize for Medicine in 1981.

Sources: Interview in *Omni Magazine*, February 1990; *Chambers Concise Dictionary of Scientists*, 1989

Hutchinson, Richard William ♂

b. 17 November 1928, London, Ontario
Geologist; Professor, Colorado School of Mines, Golden, Colorado
Developed the concept of exhalative ore deposits

Hutchinson received a BSc at UWO in 1950, an MSc at the University of Wisconsin, Madison, in 1951, and a PhD in 1954. He is responsible for the concept of exhalative ore deposits, which became a successful model in exploring massive sulphide deposits in rock strata around the world. The model indirectly but correctly predicts that massive sulphides should be found around hot fluid vents on the sea floor. He has won numerous awards and medals.

Sources: *Who's Who in America*, 1994

Isgur, Nathan ♂

b. 25 May 1947, Houston, Texas
Particle Physicist; Theory Group Leader, CEBAF (Continuous Electron Beam Accelerator Facility), Virginia
Developed theory for the 3-quark model

Isgur received a BSc from the California Institute of Technology in Pasadena (1968), and a PhD from the University of Toronto, Ontario (1974). He and co-workers studied strongly interacting subnuclear particles and showed that quantum chromo-dynamic forces are crucial to understanding quarks. In 1978, he and Gabriel Karl proposed the 3-quark model that is now the standard model of the proton and the neutron. He received the Steacie Prize (1986), the Herzberg Medal (1984), and the Rutherford Medal (1989).

Sources: *Canadian Who's Who*, 1993; *Physics Today*, November 1983

Israel, Werner ♂

Cosmologist; co-discoverer of Black Hole Theory

See full profile in the Profiles section.

Iverson, Kenneth ♂

b. not available
Computer scientist, I.P. Sharp Associates, Toronto, Ontario
Invented the APL computer programming language

In 1954, Iverson received his PhD at Harvard University, Cambridge, Massachusetts, where he was Assistant Professor of Applied Mathematics from 1955 to 1960. He developed a new notation for operations on numeric arrays, and IBM created an interpreter to execute expressions in Iverson's notation. He joined IBM and in 1962 published a description of his notation in *A Programming Language* (APL). This language challenges conventional algebraic syntax but is compact, simple, and easy to learn. In 1970, Iverson was named an IBM Fellow. He won the Turing Award in 1980.

Source: *Best's Review*, May 1990

Jackson, John David ♂ ✳

b. 19 January 1925, London, Ontario
Physicist; researcher, Berkeley Lab, SSC Central Design Group, Berkeley, California
Author of *Classical Electrodynamics*

Jackson received his BSc in physics and mathematics at UWO (1946) and his PhD in physics from MIT (1949). He was head of the theory group at Fermilab in Batavia, Illinois, and later was head of the physics division at the Lawrence Berkeley Lab. Jackson was the first person to calculate and remark upon the astoundingly small width of the J/psi resonance. He is the author of two classic textbooks, *Physics of Elementary Particles* (1958), and *Classical Electrodynamics* (1962).

Source: *Who's Who in America*, 1994

Jasper, Herbert Henry ♂ 🍂

b. 27 July 1906, La Grande, Oregon
Neurophysiologist; Professor Emeritus, Department of Physiology, University of Montreal, Quebec
Noted for studies on electrical activity in human and animal brains

Jasper earned his MD at McGill University, Montreal, in 1943, not because he wanted to be a doctor but to get access to patients to study. Today he is recognized as one of the world's leading neurophysiologists. Jasper conducted the first electroencephalograph (EEG) in the US in 1935. He led the Montreal Neurological Institute's neurophysiology and EEG labs from 1939 to 1961, at the request of Wilder Penfield, the Institute's founder. He had impressed Penfield with his EEG skills on the exposed human brain while Penfield operated. Jasper also co-wrote an important text on epilepsy with Penfield.

Among many other awards, he received the Albert Einstein Prize from the World Cultural Council in 1996.

Source: *The McGill Reporter*, 25 January 1996

Johns, Harold Elford ♂ ⚛

b. 4 July 1915, Chengtu, West China
Biophysicist; Professor of Medical Biophysics, University of Toronto, Ontario
Designed Cobalt 60 units for treatment of cancer

Johns was educated at McMaster University, Hamilton, Ontario (BA, 1936), and the University of Toronto (MA, 1937; PhD, 1939). He wrote *The Physics of Radiation Therapy* in 1953, and *The Physics of Radiology* in 1961 (4th edition, 1983). He received the Roentgen Award of the British Institute of Radiology in 1953; the Gairdner International Award in 1973; and the W.B. Lewis Award of the Canadian Nuclear Society in 1985. He holds a number of patents for the design of Cobalt 60 units for treatment of cancer, a standard device for radiation therapy.

Source: *Canadian Who's Who*, 1993

Jonas, John ♂

b. not available
Metallurgist; Chair (until 1995), Canadian Steel Industry Research Association, McGill University, Montreal, Quebec
Developed steel alloys that don't crack in the cold of Canada's Far North

Jonas graduated from McGill University in 1954 and earned his PhD in mechanical sciences at Cambridge University, England, after working in the mills of the Steel Company of Wales for a year. He contributed to advances in steel rolling techniques, which differ with each alloy, and has five patents for the process that produces the niobium-laced steel used in Canada's far north. The steel doesn't crack in extreme cold, and thus keeps oil in the pipelines off the tundra and out of the sea. Among numerous other awards, Jonas received the Grande Médaille of the Société Française de Métallurgie et de Matériaux, the first Canadian to be so honored.

Sources: *Westmount Examiner*, 21 November 1991; *The McGill Reporter*, 7 December 1995

Kallin, Catherine ♀

b. not available
Physicist; Professor, Department of Physics, McMaster University, Hamilton, Ontario
Contributed to the theory of high temperature superconductors

It was only by chance that Kallin, now recognized as one of the top condensed matter theorists in the world, got into physics. In high school she dropped physics after Grade 10. A community college course in physics for poets piqued her interest in the subject and led her to the honours physics program at UBC. Kallin and her collaborators made microwave measurements on high-temperature superconductors, determining their electrical and magnetic properties to understand why the materials are superconductors at all. When superconductors were discovered in 1911, it was thought that superconductivity wouldn't exist above -243 degrees Celsius. But high-temperature superconductivity (above -243) was discovered in 1986, and in subsequent years the temperature rose to the present record of -113 degrees Celsius. Kallin and others are trying to discover whether proposed electron-electron interactions are the cause of high-temperature superconductivity. Kallin received a Steacie Memorial Fellowship in 1996.

Source: NSERC

Kamen, Martin David ♂ ⚗

b. 27 August 1913, Toronto, Ontario
Biochemist
First isolated Carbon-14

Kamen received a PhD in 1936 from the University of Chicago, Illinois. He was interested in the isotopes of light elements such as oxygen, nitrogen, and carbon. In 1940, he isolated carbon-14, which turned out to have a half life of 5,700 years. It quickly became, and has remained, the most useful of all isotopes in biochemical research. The technique of carbon-14 dating has been used to work out the age of artifacts in countless historical and archeological studies. Kamen also worked with oxygen-18, a stable but rare isotope connected with photosynthesis.

Source: *Asimov's Biographical Encyclopedia of Science and Technology*, 1982

Kebarle, Paul ♂ ⚗

b. not available
Chemist; Professor, University of Alberta, Edmonton
Pioneered the measurements of gas-phase ion-molecule equilibria using mass spectrometry

Kebarle's measurements on ion/solvent clusters lead to new understanding of the importance of ion solvation for the energetics and reactivities of solvated ions. Further, in a long series of papers, Kebarle and his coworkers obtained fundamental data, such as proton affinities, hydride ion affinities, and electron affinities, on isolated molecules. These kinds of data, significantly expanded by other workers, now constitute a central data base that is of fundamental importance in many fields, including protein molecular modeling, physical organic chemistry, and analytical methods like biochemical mass spectrometry.

Source: Paul Kebarle, personal communication

Kenney-Wallace, Geraldine ♀

b. London, England
Physicist; President of McMaster University, Hamilton, Ontario
Founded the first ultrafast laser laboratory at a Canadian university

Kenney-Wallace became fascinated with science when Russia launched the Sputnik satellite in 1957. She went on to study and conduct research at Oxford University, England. Later, she travelled to Canada, where she earned her PhD at UBC in 1970. In 1974, Kenney-Wallace organized Canada's first ultrafast laser lab at the University of Toronto, Ontario. By 1987, she had achieved time scales of 6×10^{-14} seconds for research on molecular motion and optoelectronics. Kenney-Wallace has also taught at the École Polytechnique in Paris, France, at Yale and Stanford Universities in the USA, and has done research in Japan. Her achievements have led to many honours. She was the chair of the Science Council of Canada, is a Fellow of the Royal Society, and has received twelve honorary degrees.

Source: *Claiming the Future*, 1991

Kimura, Doreen ♀

Behavioural psychologist; world expert on sex differences in the brain

See full profile in the Profiles section.

Krebs, Charles J. ♂

Ecologist; famous for writing *Ecology*, a textbook used worldwide, and for his work on the Fence Effect

See full profile in the Profiles section.

Laidler, Keith James ♂ 🧪

b. 3 January 1916, Liverpool, England
Professor Emeritus of Chemistry, University of Ottawa, Ontario
A pioneer in the field of chemical kinetics and activated-complex theory

Laidler received his BA from Liverpool College, England (1934), his MA from Oxford University, England (1938), and his PhD from Princeton, New Jersey (1940). After working as a scientist in England for Canada during World War II, he eventually became a professor of chemistry at the

University of Ottawa in Canada (1955). His specialty, chemical kinetics, concerns the energy disposition of molecular reactions. He is also an expert on activated complex theory, which involves the mechanism whereby starting materials, and sometimes catalysts, combine to form intermediate complex states that go on to become the reaction products. He has applied his expertise to the chemistry of enzymes and other biochemical processes and written numerous books, including *Chemistry of Enzymes* (1954); *Principles of Chemistry* (1966); and *The World of Physical Chemistry* (1993). He has received many awards, including the Tory and Centenary Medals from the Royal Society of Canada.

Sources: Canadian *Who's Who*, 1993

Laird, Elizabeth Rebecca

b. 1874, Owen Sound, Ontario
Physicist; professor
Among the first to study X-rays

After studying at such prestigious schools as the University of Berlin, Germany, and Cambridge University, England, Laird received her PhD from the University of Toronto, Ontario, in 1927. For 36 years, Laird served as the head of the physics department at Mount Holyoke University, Massachusetts. During this time she studied the properties of "soft" X-rays, which occur in the electromagnetic spectrum between known x-rays and the extreme ultraviolet.

Source: *Who's Who in Frontier Science and Technology*, 1984

Langlands, Robert P. ♂ 〽

b. 6 October 1936, New Westminster, British Columbia
Professor of Mathematics, Institute for Advanced Study, Princeton, New Jersey
Developed mathematical theories of group representations and number theory

Langlands studied at UBC (BA, 1957; MA, 1958) and Yale University, New Haven, Connecticut (PhD, 1960) and has received several honorary degrees. He is known for his work in group representations and number theory, which involves mathematical symmetries and conjectures about pure number (such as: every number above the number 4 can be expressed as the sum of two primes). He has received many awards, including the Commonwealth Award, the Cole Prize, and the National Sciences Academy Award in Mathematics, and is a member of the Royal Society of Canada.

Source: *Canadian Who's Who*, 1993

Laurence, George Craig ♂ ⚛

b. 21 January 1905, Charlottetown, Prince Edward Island; d. 6 November 1987, Deep River, Ontario
Physicist
First person to attempt to build a fission reactor

Laurence was educated at Dalhousie University, Halifax, Nova Scotia, and Cambridge University, England, under Ernest Rutherford, the famous English nuclear physicist. In 1939 in Ottawa, he attempted, virtually alone, to build a graphite-uranium atomic reactor. He went to Montreal, Quebec in 1942 and joined the Anglo-French research team that built the ZEEP reactor, the first outside the USA. Then he went to Chalk River, Ontario in 1945 and served in the Canadian delegation to the UN Atomic Energy Commission (1946 to 1947). He became a senior scientist at the Chalk River Nuclear Labs. From 1961 to 1970 he was president of the Atomic Energy Control Board in charge of Canada's nuclear energy program.

Source: *The Canadian Encyclopedia*, 1988

Le Caine, Hugh ♂ ⚛

d. 1977
Physicist, NRC
Invented electronic musical instruments

Le Caine spent his life inventing and composing. At work, he was a physicist at the NRC. At home he pursued his consuming interest in electronic music and sound generation. During the 1940s, he designed a number of instruments, including the Sackbut synthesizer, which is now recognized as the first voltage-controlled musical instrument of its kind. Eventually Le Caine was allowed to bring his private interests to work at the NRC. His full-time involvement with music produced a legacy of new instruments and compositions, the most well known of which is *Dripsody*, a piece of music which consists only of the sound of falling water drops.

Source: *The Canadian Composer*, December 1989

Leblond, Charles Philippe ♂

b. 5 February 1910, Lille, France
Professor of Anatomy, McGill University, Montreal, Quebec
Improved the resolution of radioautography

Leblond received degrees from the University of Paris, France (MD, 1934), the Sorbonne, Paris (DSc, 1945) and McGill University (PhD, 1942). In 1946, with L. F. Bélanger, Leblond started experimenting to improve the resolution of radioautography – a method of using radioactive tracer elements to create images of biological tissues. Photographic emulsion was melted and poured on the tissue section so as to make a thin coat that hardened as it cooled, and acted as a photographic plate to the radioactive parts of the tissue section. The method became widely used as a tool in cell study and is now used in the electron microscope. The method can trace the activity of substances in the body. Leblond's experiments challenged much of established cell theory at that time. For example, he demonstrated that cells are continuously active, and do not alternate between repose and activity, as was thought. He was nominated for the Nobel Prize and received many honorary degrees and awards, including the Gairdner Foundation Award of Merit, and the Royal Society of Canada's Flavelle Medal in 1961.

Sources: *American Men in Science*, 1973-1978; *Canadian Who's Who*, 1993; *The McGill Reporter*, 25 January 1996

Lemieux, Raymond ♂ ⚗

b. 16 June 1920, Lac La Biche, Alberta
Chemist; University Professor Emeritus, University of Alberta, Edmonton
First to synthesize sucrose and many blood chemistry compounds

Lemieux received his BSc from the University of Alberta and his PhD from McGill University, Montreal, Quebec. Afterwards he went to Ohio State University to study the degradation of streptomycin. Lemieux first achieved fame for the synthesis of sucrose, or ordinary sugar. This is important because, though sugar is a simple carbohydrate, it has a three dimensional structure, and Lemieux perfected techniques that allowed him to synthesize molecules in their correct 3D configurations. His second major contribution was pioneering work on configurational determination by Nuclear Magnetic Resonance (NMR) spectroscopy. He invented the olefin cleaving reagent with von Rudloff in 1955, and invented many other reagents throughout his career. He also made many discoveries concerning antibiotics, and started a couple of research companies, including Chembiomed Ltd. with the University of Alberta. In 1973, he began his famous work on the synthesis of human blood group determinants, and in 1975 published the first synthesis of the B human system trisaccharide. He later synthesized the carbohydrate sequences for six different blood group determinants. These achievements are important to the chemistry of immunology. Lemieux's current work deals with molecular recognition in biological processes. He has received numerous awards, including the Albert Einstein World Award in Science in 1992, and the Gairdner Foundation International Award in 1985.

Source: Raymond Lemieux, personal communication

Levine, Martin David ♂ 〰

b. 30 March 1938, Montreal, Quebec
Computer scientist; engineer; professor; Director, McGill Research Center for Intelligent Machines, Montreal
Developed early theories of computer vision and artificial intelligence

Levine was educated at McGill University, Montreal (BEng, 1960; MEng, 1963) and at the Imperial College of Science and Technology, University of London, England (PhD, 1965). His research involves biomedical image processing, computer vision, intelligent robotics, and artificial intelligence. Levine's work is important for the understanding of vision in general and for machine applications of vision such as robotics and automated manufacturing systems. He is the author of *Vision in Man and Machine* (1985) and co-author of *Computer Assisted Analyses of Cell Locomotion and Chemotaxis* (1986). He was the founding president of the Canadian Image Processing and Pattern Recognition Society and he served on the technical staff of the Jet Propulsion Lab. He has received fellowships from numerous engineering and computer societies.

Source: *Canadian Who's Who*, 1993

Levy, Julia ♀ 〵

Immunologist; co-discovered photodynamic anti-cancer drugs

See full profile in the Profiles section.

Lewis, Walter and Memory Elvin-Lewis ♂+♀ 〵

Ethnobotanists and biochemists; husband-and-wife team famous for targeting medicinal plants in the tropical rainforest

See full profile in the Profiles section.

Li, Ming ♂ 〰

b. Hong Kong
Computer scientist; Professor, Department of Computer Science, University of Waterloo, Ontario
Applied the theory of Kolmogorov complexity

Li received his PhD at Cornell University in New York. He is playing a key role in developing and demonstrating the power of Kolmogorov complexity, a theory of randomness. His book (co-authored with Paul Vitányi), *An Introduction to Kolmogorov Complexity and Its Applications*, was the first comprehensive book in this field. It is used to teach graduate seminar courses all over the world. The power of Kolmogorov complexity is that it allows scientists to quantify the randomness of individual objects in an objective and absolute manner. This is impossible using classical probability theory. For example, in computer science it is often necessary to determine how fast a certain program runs. Using conventional methods, this is very difficult because the program must be run with a large number of inputs, each result analyzed, and an average time arrived at. Using Kolmogorov complexity, only one input is needed to complete the analysis. In one area of his current research (which also includes machine learning and computational biology), Li is extending the use of Kolmogorov complexity in the analysis of computer programs, DNA sequencing, physics, and computation. Others are following his lead. Li received a Steacie Memorial Fellowship in 1996.

Source: NSERC

Ling, Victor ♂ ⚕

b. not available
Medical biophysicist; Vice-President of British Columbia Cancer Research Center, and Assistant Dean of the
  Faculty of Medicine, UBC
Discovered the membrane transport protein P-glycoprotein

Ling's 1974 discovery of P-glycoprotein, which is encoded by the multidrug resistant gene (MDR) made him world famous. It is now known that P-glycoprotein is not only important clinically, as it confers multidrug resistance in many cancers, it also can protect the brain from poisonous substances. P-glycoprotein is the first protein discovered in humans that belongs to a group of membrane transport proteins called the ATP Binding Cassette (ABC). ABC is very important in maintaining normal cell functions. Mutations in this group of proteins cause many well known diseases. One example is the Cystic Fibrosis Transmembrane Regulator (CFTR), which is responsible for cystic fibrosis. Ling has won many international awards including the 1990 Gairdner award, the 1991 General Motors Cancer Research Foundation award, the Kettering Prize, the 1991 Joseph Steiner Cancer Research award, and the 1993 American Association of Cancer Research scientific award. Ling is the only person in the world to have won both the Kettering and Steiner awards, the highest honours in cancer research.

Source: Victor Ling, personal communication

Mak, Tak Wah ♂ ⚕

Immunologist; discovered the T-Cell Receptor

See full profile in the Profiles section.

Marcus, Rudolph Arthur ♂ ⚗ Ⓝ

b. 21 July 1923, Montreal, Quebec
Chemist; Arthur Amos Noyes Professor of Chemistry, California Institute of Technology, Los Angeles, California
Contributed to the theory of electron transfer reactions in chemical systems

Marcus received his PhD in Chemistry at McGill University, Montreal, in 1946. In 1949 he went to the USA, and became a naturalized citizen there in 1958. Beginning in 1956, and extending over a nine-year period, he wrote a series of papers developing what is now called the Marcus theory of electron transfer reactions, which was later experimentally verified. Marcus theory explains such phenomena as photosynthesis, electrically conducting polymers, chemiluminescence, and corrosion, as well as many other chemical reactions. Marcus won the Robinson Medal of the Royal Society of Chemistry, the Wolfe prize in 1985, the US National Medal of Science in 1989, and the 1992 Nobel Prize for Chemistry.

Sources: *Physics Today*, January 1993; *Who's Who in America*, 1994

Marie-Victorin, Frère (Conrad Kirouac) ♂ 🍃

b. 3 April 1885; d. 15 July 1944, Kingsey Falls, Quebec
Botanist; Professor, University of Montreal, Quebec
Founded the famous Montreal Botanical Gardens

Frère Marie-Victorin was the name in religion of Conrad Kirouac. He entered the Order of the Roman Catholic Brothers of the Christian Schools in 1901 at age 16. He was educated at the University of Montreal and became Professor of Botany there in 1920. He was a founder and director of the Montreal Botanical Institute in 1922, as well as founder of the Montreal Botanical Gardens in 1936. He is the author of many works, including his authoritative book on Quebec's botany, *La Flore Laurentienne* – 917 pages filled with 2,800 illustrations. As a major political and intellectual figure in Quebec, Marie-Victorin was honoured with the Prix David in 1923 and 1931.

Sources: *The Canadian Encyclopedia*, 1985; *Encyclopedia Canadiana*, 1977; NRC Hall of Fame

Masui, Yoshio ♂ 🍃

b. Japan
Zoologist; Professor, University of Toronto, Ontario
Discovered the cell growth switch

Masui and his students, working with basic equipment and modest funding, succeeded in isolating materials that control the process of cell division in all organisms. Masui credits some of his success to an advisor at Yale University, who recommended he concentrate on low-budget research techniques that would allow him to perform good work despite limited funds. At the University of Toronto's Department of Zoology, Masui invented many original techniques to assist his studies of cell division: a quantitative method for microinjection in 1971; microextraction in 1976; cell-free in-vitro mitosis in 1983. Masui's microinjection technique enabled him to directly transfer into cells controlled amounts of Maturity Promoting Factor (MPF) that initiates cell division and the cytostatic factor that stops it, confirming their role in cell growth. Masui won the 1990 Manning Award.

Sources: The Manning Awards; NSERC

Melzack, Ronald ♂

b. 19 July 1929, Montreal, Quebec
Neurophysiologist; Research Director, Pain Clinic, Montreal General Hospital; Professor of psychology, McGill University, Montreal
Developed the gate-control theory of pain

After studying for his PhD in 1954 with Donald O. Hebb at McGill University in Montreal, Melzack began to work with patients who suffered from "phantom limb" pain – pain felt in an arm or leg that has been removed. He found that pain often has little survival value, and some pains are entirely out of proportion to the degree of tissue damage, sometimes continuing long after injured tissues have healed. While still a postdoctoral student, Melzack began collecting "pain words" and putting them into classes that belonged together, like "hot," "burning," "scalding," and "searing." In 1975, this pursuit led to the development of the McGill Pain Questionnaire, now used in pain clinics and cancer hospices around the world. In 1965, at MIT, Melzack with his colleague Patrick Wall developed the gate-control theory of pain which states that pain is "gated" or modulated by past experience. Gate-control theory led to the valuable discovery of endorphins and enkephalins, the body's natural opiates. Melzack's recent research at McGill indicates that there are two types of pain, transmitted by two separate sets of pain-signaling pathways in the central nervous system. Sudden, short-term pain, such as the pain of cutting a finger, is transmitted by a group of pathways that Melzack calls the "lateral" system, because they pass through the brain stem on one side of its central core. Prolonged pain, on the other hand, such as chronic back pain, is transmitted by the "medial" system, whose neurons pass through the central core of the brain stem. Melzack is the author of several textbooks on pain, and is co-editor of *The Handbook of Pain Assessment* (1992). He has also published books of Eskimo stories and won the Canada Council Molson Prize in 1985.

Sources: NSERC; *Psychology Today*, August 1987; *Saturday Night*, December 1988

Menten, Maude ♀ ⚗

b. 1879, Harrison Hot Springs, British Columbia; d. 1960
Chemist
Developed the Michaelis-Menten equation for enzyme kinetics

Menten was one of the most versatile, innovative investigators in chemistry in the early part of the century. She received her BA (1904) and her MD (1911) from the University of Toronto, Ontario. She was a demonstrator of physiology in MacCallum's laboratory at the University of Toronto, but had to leave Canada to pursue a career as a research scientist. In those days women were not allowed to do research in Canadian universities. She became a research fellow at the Rockefeller Institute, and a research fellow at Western Reserve University. Then she went to study with Leonor Michaelis in Berlin, Germany, where they developed the Michaelis-Menten equation. This equation gives an expression for the rate of an enzyme reaction and became fundamental to the interpretation of how an enzyme reacts on its substrate. Ultimately, Menten earned a PhD in biochemistry at the University of Chicago, Illinois. She later became a professor on the faculty of the University of Pittsburgh School of Medicine in Pennsylvania. Her publication in 1944 of a new technique for the demonstration of the enzyme alkaline phosphatase ushered in the new azo-dye method.

Source: Computational Laboratory for Environmental Biotechnology, University of Virginia

Morawetz, Cathleen Synge ♀

b. 5 May 1923, Toronto, Ontario
Mathematician; Director, Courant Institute, New York
Developed mathematical applications of partial differential equations

Morawetz received her BA at the University of Toronto in 1945 and her PhD at New York University in 1951. She became the first female director of the Courant Institute, a famous school for mathematics. She has written numerous articles about applications of partial differential equations, especially transonic flow and scattering theory. She was a Guggenheim Fellow in 1967 and 1979.

Source: *Who's Who in America*, 1994

Morley, Lawrence Whitaker ♂ 〽

b. 19 February 1920, Toronto, Ontario
Engineer; President, Teledetection International
Pioneered Canadian remote sensing

Morley studied at the University of Toronto, Ontario (PhD, 1952) and became an engineer and scientist. In 1963 he proposed the theory of magnetic imprinting of ocean floors by the earth's reversing magnetic field, which led to the theory of plate tectonics – the idea that the earth's crust is made of a system of floating plates that grind together to create earthquakes. Morley instigated the Aeromagnetic Survey Plan and Resource Satellite Planning for Canada, and became the founding director general of the Canadian Centre for Remote Sensing. He was also the founding director of the Institute for Space and Terrestrial Science. He received the McCurdy medal in 1974 and is a fellow of the Royal Society of Canada.

Source: *Canadian Who's Who*, 1993

Newton, Margaret ♀ ◊

b. 1887, North Nation Mills, Quebec; d. 1971, Victoria, British Columbia
Plant Pathologist
Expert in wheat stem rust

Newton earned money to attend university by teaching and entered MacDonald College in Montreal, McGill University's agricultural school. She earned top marks, won the Governor General's medal, and decided to major in plant pathology, the study of plant diseases. She received her BA in 1918, followed by her MA the next year. None of these achievements were easy. As a woman, she had to fight for equal access to the labs with male students. Newton's graduate work was done in Minnesota and Saskatchewan with two wheat rust experts, E.C. Stakeman and W.P. Thompson. She received her PhD in 1922 – the first Canadian woman to receive a doctorate in agricultural science – and taught at the University of Saskatchewan in Saskatoon. In 1925, Newton was appointed head of the new Dominion Rust Research Laboratory at the University of Manitoba in Winnipeg. Newton became the best-known Canadian expert in stem rust, a fungus which destroys wheat, and her work helped find ways to fight the disease. Crop losses, which had once been at least 30 million bushels, fell to almost nothing. She was the first graduate from an agricultural college to be awarded the prestigious Flavelle Medal from the Royal Society of Canada. She was also given the Outstanding Achievement Award from the University of Minnesota in 1956. In 1969, the University of Saskatchewan made her an honorary Doctor of Laws.

Source: *Despite the Odds*, 1990

Ogilvie, Kelvin Kenneth ♂ ⚗

b. 6 November 1942, Summerville, Nova Scotia
Chemist; President and past Professor of Chemistry, Acadia University, Wolfville, Nova Scotia
Synthesized RNA (ribonucleic acid)

Ogilvie received his BSc (Honours) at Acadia University, in Wolfville, Nova Scotia in 1964, then his PhD at Northwestern University, Evanston, Illinois in 1968. He is famous for synthesizing RNA, important to many areas of medical research. This feat took him 20 years of research to achieve. Synthetic RNA could lead to cures for diseases caused by viruses. In medical research, synthetic RNA is making possible the development of new drugs that were previously beyond the reach of science. These drugs will consist of RNA sequences tailor-made to attach to certain types of viruses and interfere with their ability to replicate themselves. In 1980, Ogilvie also invented the automated gene synthesizer, or gene machine, which made it possible to build DNA sequences in a matter of hours rather than in months. He is the author of 12 patents including a drug called Glanciclovir, which fights the cytomegalovirus, a type of herpes. Ogilvie won the Buck-Whitney Medal in 1983, and the Manning Principal award in 1991.

Sources: *Canadian Who's Who*, 1993; *Maclean's*, 24 October 1988; NSERC

Osler, Sir William ♂ ⚕

b. 12 July 1849, Bond Head, Ontario; d. 29 December 1919, Oxford, England
Physician; Professor of Medicine, Johns Hopkins University, Baltimore, Maryland
Best-known physician in the English-speaking world circa 1900

Osler trained in medicine at the University of Toronto, Ontario, and McGill University, Montreal, Quebec (MD, 1872), and began his teaching career at McGill. In 1889 he became the founding professor of medicine at Johns Hopkins University. He was particularly expert in diagnosis of diseases of the heart, lungs, and blood. His book, *The Principles and Practice of Medicine* (published in 1892 and frequently revised), was the preeminent medical textbook for more than 30 years. He helped create the system of postgraduate training for physicians that is followed today. His description of the inadequacy of treatment methods for most disorders was a major factor leading to the creation of the Rockefeller Institute for Medical Research in New York City. He moved to Oxford, England, in 1905, and was created a baronet in 1911. His ashes rest in the Osler Library, Montreal.

Source: *The Canadian Encyclopedia*, 1988

Peebles, Phillip James E. ♂ ⚛

b. 25 May 1935, Winnipeg, Manitoba
Physicist; cosmologist; Albert Einstein Professor of Science, Princeton University, New Jersey
Important cosmologist and astrophysicist

Peebles received his BSc at the University of Manitoba, Winnipeg (1958) and his PhD from Princeton University (1962). He is considered by some to be the single most important cosmologist of the last 30 years. With Robert Dicke and others he predicted the existence of cosmic background radiation and planned to seek it just before it was found by A. Penzias and R. Wilson. He has investigated characteristics of the radiation, and clustering and superclustering of galaxies. He has calculated the universal abundances of helium and other light elements, demonstrating agreement between big-bang theory and observation. He has provided evidence of the existence of large quantities of dark matter in the haloes of galaxies. His two books on physical cosmology have had a significant impact in convincing physicists that the time has come to study cosmology as a respectable branch of physics. He is a recipient of numerous honorary degrees and awards, including the A.C. Morrison award, the Eddington Medal, the Heineman Prize and the 1995 C.W. Bruce medal of the Astronomical Society of the Pacific.

Sources: *Who's Who in America*, 1994; Phillip Peebles, personal communication

Penfield, Wilder Graves ♂ ⚘

b. 26 January 1891, Spokane, Washington; d. 1976
Neurosurgeon; founder, Montreal Neurological Institute, McGill University, Montreal, Quebec
Mapped out the functional areas of the cerebral cortex of the brain

Penfield studied at Princeton University in New Jersey (LittB, 1913), Oxford University in England (BA, 1913, MA and BSc, 1920) and Johns Hopkins University in Baltimore, Maryland (MD, 1918). His early research focused on improving the treatment of focal epilepsy by gentle electrical stimulation. He mapped out new functional areas of the human cerebral cortex, and discovered that stimulating parts of the cortex could evoke vivid and specific memories, including sounds and smells. Penfield was a founder of the Montreal Neurological Institute. He wrote many books on brain physiology and received the Lannelongue Medal of France in 1958, the Lister Medal of the Royal College of Surgeons in 1961, and the British Order of Merit.

Source: *Modern Men of Science*, 1966

Person, Clayton Oscar ♂ 🍃

b. 16 May 1922, Regina, Saskatchewan
Geneticist
International authority on genetics of host-parasite relations

Person was educated in Saskatchewan and Alberta. He became an expert on the genetics of host-parasite relations, and his theoretical methods have been widely applied in the management of parasitic diseases in agriculture and forestry. He received the BC Science Council's Gold Medal in 1981, the Royal Society of Canada's Flavelle Medal, and the Genetics Society of Canada's Award of Excellence in 1982. He became a member of the Order of Canada in 1986.

Source: *The Canadian Encyclopedia*, 1988

Pielou, Evelyn C. ♀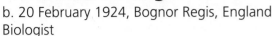

b. 20 February 1924, Bognor Regis, England
Biologist
Invented mathematical ecology

Pielou studied at the University of London, England (BSc, 1951; PhD, 1962; DSc, 1975). Eventually she became a professor at Dalhousie University, Halifax, Nova Scotia, and was the Oil Sands Environmental Research Professor at the University of Lethbridge, Alberta. She contributed significantly to the development of mathematical ecology and wrote several books, ranging from *Introduction to Mathematical Ecology* (1969) to *After the Ice Age* (1991). She received the Lawson Medal of the Canadian Botanical Association in 1984, the Eminent Ecologist Award from the Ecological Society of America in 1986, and the Distinguished Statistical Ecologist Award from the International Congress of Ecology in 1990.

Source: *Canadian Who's Who*, 1993

Plaa, Gabriel Leon ♂

b. 15 May 1930, San Francisco, California
Toxicologist; retired professor and Director, Interuniversity Centre for Research in Toxicology, University of Montreal, Quebec
Pioneered toxicology in Canada

Plaa was educated at the University of California (BSc, Berkeley, 1952; PhD, San Francisco, 1958). He came to Canada in 1968, joining the faculty of the University of Montreal, where he has served as chairman of the Department of Pharmacology and vice-dean of the Faculty of Medicine. He was one of the first researchers to study the toxic effect of chemicals on the liver, particularly the way chlorinated hydrocarbons like chloroform and carbon tetrachloride kill liver cells. He is the recipient of the Thienes Award (1977), the Henderson Award (1969), the Society of Toxicology's Achievement Award (1967), and the Lehman Award (1977).

Source: *Who's Who in America*, 1994

Polanyi, John C. ♂

Chemist; won the 1986 Nobel Prize for Chemistry for Chemiluminescence

See full profile in the Profiles section.

Poussart, Denis Jean-Marie ♂ 〽

b. 3 October 1940, St. Denis D'Oleron, France
Electrical Engineer; Professor of Electrical Engineering Laval University, Quebec City, Quebec
Researches computer vision

Poussart came to Canada in 1952. He was educated at Laval University, Quebec City (BSc, 1963) and MIT in the USA (MSc, 1965; PhD, 1968). He became a professor of electrical engineering and an expert in computers and robotic systems. He is known for his work in computer vision and intelligent sensors for use in intelligent manufacturing systems and remote control robots. He heads many boards and research groups involved in computers and robotics, and has published widely on the subject.

Sources: *Who's Who in America*, 1994; Denis Poussart's webpage

Rapoport, Anatol ♂ 〽

b. 22 May 1911, Lozovaya, Russia
Mathematician; Professor of Peace Studies, University of Toronto, Ontario
One of the main originators of conflict theory, game theory, and peace research

Rapoport studied piano, composition, and conducting in Vienna, Austria, but came to the USA in the mid-1930s and became a mathematician of biology and behavioural science. He received degrees from the University of Chicago, including a PhD in Mathematics in 1941. His research has focused on game and conflict theory – the mathematics of decision making. Rapoport went to Toronto in 1970. He is the author of *Two-Person Game Theory* and *N-Person Game Theory*, among many other well-known books on fights, games, violence, and peace. He is the recipient of the Lenz International Peace Research Prize (1976), and has been a member of many boards and committees involved in mathematics and peace research.

Source: *Canadian Who's Who*, 1993

Rapson, (William) Howard ♂ 〽

b. 15 September 1912, Toronto, Ontario
Professor Emeritus of Chemical Engineering, University of Toronto
Global authority on pulp and paper chemistry

Rapson was educated at the University of Toronto (BASc, 1934; MASc, 1935; PhD, 1941). He became an expert in pulp and paper chemistry, which involves the manufacture and purification of wood pulp and cellulose for making paper. His particular specialty was the use of the chlorite ion (ClO_2-) in pulping and bleaching, a process which he developed during World War II when the usual pulping agent, sulfuric acid, was in short supply. He holds 33 patents in 45 countries and has received numerous awards from the pulp and paper industries of several countries, as well as the Eadie Medal from the Royal Society of Canada in 1981, and the Izaak Walton Killam Memorial Prize from the Canada Council in 1986.

Sources: *Canadian Who's Who* 1993; Howard Rapson personal communication

Reeves, Hubert ♂ ⚛

b. 13 July 1932, Montreal, Quebec
Physicist; cosmologist; administrator
World famous cosmologist and science communicator

Reeves was educated at the University of Montreal (BA, 1950, BSc, 1953) and McGill University, Montreal (MSc 1955), and Cornell University, New York (PhD 1960). He worked for several years as a professor at the University of Montreal, and in 1965 he became Director of Research for the French National Centre of Scientific Research (CNRS) in Paris, France. He still maintains an associate professorship at the University of Montreal and teaches courses there each year. Reeves studies the thermonuclear reactions in the cores of stars, the fate of stars, the elements created within them, and, ultimately, the origin and fate of free energy in the universe. Reeves has published many scientific books and papers; he is best known, particularly in the French speaking world, for his many popular books (*Compagnons de Voyage* 1992, *Malicorne* 1990) and films (*Un soir, une étoile*, and *La vie dans la universe*) on cosmology and astronomy. Reeves has won many awards including the Grand Prix de la francophonie décerné from the Acadamie Francaise in 1989, and the Chevalier de la Legion d'Honneur (France) in 1986.

Sources: *Canadian Who's Who* 1993; *Unesco Courier*, January 1993

Ricker, William ♂ ◖

Fisheries biologist; invented Ricker Curve for describing fish population dynamics

See full profile in the Profiles section.

Robert, André ♂ ⊬

b. 28 April 1929, New York, New York; d. 18 November 1993
Climatologist
First Canadian Scientist to successfully perform a simulation of the atmosphere's general circulation using a computer model

Robert emigrated to Canada – Grand Mère, Quebec – in May 1937. His university education took place at Laval University, Quebec City, (BSc, 1952), the University of Toronto, Ontario (MSc, 1953), and McGill University, Montreal, Quebec (PhD, 1965). He started his career as a weather forecaster with the Meteorological Service of Canada, but in 1959 transferred to research, where he was engaged in the development of atmospheric models for short- and medium-range forecasts. His chief accomplishments were to develop and implement efficient numerical techniques to solve the interacting time-dependent partial differential equations that govern the evolution of the atmosphere. Robert was the only scientist in the world between 1963 and 1970 to attempt to produce meteorological forecasts with a spectral model combining existing Lagrangian methods with his own scheme. In contrast to many scientists in this field, who aim primarily at improving accuracy, he always devised efficient numerical methods to attain a given degree of precision with the least amount of computation. The methods that he developed are now used in models at the world's largest weather prediction and climate research centres.

Source: Personal communication from John Digby Reid, Canadian Meteorological and Oceanographic Society

Ruse, Michael ♂ ⌇

b. 21 June 1940, Birmingham, England
Biologist; philosopher; Professor, Departments of Philosophy and Zoology, University of Guelph, Ontario
Contributed major ideas about the philosophy of biology and Darwinism

Ruse received his BA from the University of Bristol, England (1962), his MA from McMaster University, Hamilton, Ontario (1964), and his PhD at the University of Bristol in (1970). He is known for his numerous books on the philosophy of biology, particularly on Darwin's theory of evolution, including *Molecules to Men* (1990), *The Darwinian Paradigm* (1989), and *Taking Darwin Seriously* (1986), also issued in Spanish, Italian, Portuguese, and Polish; and *Is Science Sexist?* (1981). He has tried to define the difference between science and pseudo-science. Ruse was called to testify as an expert witness in the celebrated creationism trial in Arkansas in the 1980s, in which a federal judge ultimately ruled that a law requiring the teaching of biblical creation in high school was unconstitutional. Ruse's testimony was probably an important factor in the judge's decision on a definition of science.

Source: *Canadian Who's Who*, 1993

Saunders, Sir Charles Edward ♂ ⌀

b. 2 February 1867, London, Ontario; d. 25 July 1937, Toronto, Ontario
Chemist; plant breeder; cereals experimentalist
Developed Marquis wheat for the Canadian West

Charles Saunders was educated at the University of Toronto, Ontario, and Johns Hopkins University, Baltimore, Maryland. Briefly a professor of chemistry, he studied music and teaching of voice for nine years until 1903, when his father, William Saunders, who had created Canada's Dominion Experimental farms in 1886, appointed him an experimentalist there. Over a period of 19 years, Saunders developed Marquis wheat, the strain that made Canada famous for its hard red spring wheat, which matures early, produces high volume, and is excellent for bread. Saunders also applied his single-line breeding methods to barley, oats, peas, beans, and flax, and introduced several new excellent varieties of each kind of crop. In 1922, Saunders' health broke down and he moved to Paris where he studied French literature for three years. He was knighted in 1934.

Source: *The Canadian Encyclopedia*, 1988

Scriver, Charles ♂ ◊

b. not available
Geneticist; Medical Doctor at Montreal Children's Hospital
Discovered the importance of vitamin D in rickets, a children's skeletal disease

Vitamin D is put into Canadian milk thanks to Scriver's study of rickets in Quebec children. He also worked on identifying genetic predisposition to disease and raising nutritional standards. His recommendations have had great impact on Quebec's health care system, which became the first in the world to provide a system for identifying genetic diseases and nutritional information to help overcome these conditions. He was also involved in the inception of the Human Genome Project, though his research focus has been more towards genetic variation than gene identification and cloning. Another result of Scriver's work, the Interuniversity Institute for Research on Populations (IREP), maintains a database on the Quebec population and is able to track genes such as phenylalanine hydroxylase, which is involved in a form of mental retardation that can be avoided with early treatment. Scriver has won the Wilder Penfield award and Prix du Québec Science.

Source: *The McGill Reporter*, December 7, 1995

Seguin, Fernand ♂ ⊞

b. 9 June 1922, Montréal, Quebec
Biochemist; Professor, University de Montreal
Popularized science

Seguin conducted biochemical research in Chicago, Paris and Montreal, and in 1950 founded the Biochemical Research Department at Saint-Jean-de-Dieu Hospital, where he specialized in schizophrenia research. He won the Prix Casgrain-Charbonneau for his MA thesis about a method to determine aminopyrine in the blood. In 1954 he abandoned his research career and began a long series of radio and TV programs that sparked scientific curiosity in Quebec and inspired scientific careers. In 1977 he became the first Canadian to receive UNESCO's highest award for scientific popularization, the Kalinga Prize.

Source: *The Canadian Encyclopedia,* 1988

Selye, Hans ♂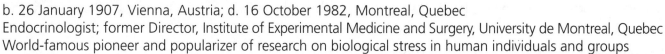

b. 26 January 1907, Vienna, Austria; d. 16 October 1982, Montreal, Quebec
Endocrinologist; former Director, Institute of Experimental Medicine and Surgery, University de Montreal, Quebec
World-famous pioneer and popularizer of research on biological stress in human individuals and groups

Hans Selye was educated in Prague, Paris, and Rome. He was the first director of the Institute of Experimental Medicine and Surgery, University of Montreal (from 1945 to 1976). After retiring from the university, he founded the International Institute of Stress in 1977, in his own home in Montreal. His controversial theory, General Adaptation Syndrome, was based on much experimentation with rats. He concluded that stress plays some role in the development of every disease and that failure to cope with "stressors," which can be any stimuli, can result in "diseases of adaptation" such as ulcers and high blood pressure. He wrote several books describing his theories, including *The Stress of Life* (1956). Selye came up with the idea of "eustress," an ideal amount of stress that is necessary to keep the body's immune system in tune, but not enough to overwhelm it. Selye was appointed a Companion of the Order of Canada.

Source: *The Canadian Encyclopedia,* 1988

Smith, Michael ♂

Chemist; won the Nobel Prize in Chemistry for site-directed mutagenesis

See full profile in the Profiles section.

Steacie, Edgar William Richard ♂ ⚗

b. 25 December 1900, Montreal, Quebec; d. 28 August 1962, Ottawa, Ontario
Chemist; educator; former President of the NRC (National Research Council)
Pioneered research into chemical reactions and helped found university research programs in Canada

Steacie was educated at McGill University, Montreal (BSc, 1923; PhD,1926), where he began his teaching career and conducted ground-breaking research in free radical chemistry. He extended his research into photochemistry and chemical kinetics after joining the NRC as Director of the Division of Chemistry in 1939. He played a leading role in British-Canadian collaboration in atomic energy, which led to the construction of the Chalk River reactor, the first to be built outside the USA. In 1950 Steacie became vice-president of the NRC, then president two years later. He is perhaps best known as an administrator and statesman of science for Canada, since he was very instrumental in building up university research in Canada and was the architect of enduring programs to support industrial innovation. Various awards have been established in his honour, including the Steacie Memorial Prize, which recognizes the achievements of young Canadian scientists.

Source: NRC

Stewart, Robert William ♂

b. 21 August 1923, Smoky Lake, Alberta
Oceanographer; professor; administrator
Studied turbulence spectra in oceanography

Stewart received degrees from Queen's University, Kingston, Ontario (BSc, 1945; MSc, 1947) and Cambridge University, England (PhD, 1952). He became an oceanographer, and is particularly known for his studies in turbulence. He recognized the importance of exchange processes between the oceans and the atmosphere, and was one of the first to study the two as a combined system. Stewart has served as an administrator of numerous scientific bodies and governmental departments and has received numerous awards and medals, including the Order of Canada, the Sverdrup Gold Medal, the Patterson Medal, and the Tully Medal.

Source: *Canadian Who's Who*, 1993

Stoicheff, Boris Peter ♂ ⚛

b. 1 June 1924, Bitol, Yugoslavia
Physicist; Professor Emeritus, University of Toronto, Ontario
Discovered inverse Raman effect spectroscopy

Stoicheff came to Canada in 1931 and received his university education at the University of Toronto (BASc, 1947; MA, 1948; PhD, 1950). He discovered generation of sound by light, and the inverse Raman effect. His research interests include lasers, atomic and molecular spectroscopy and structure, light scattering processes, two photon absorption, and nonlinear optics. He has received the Gold Medal of the Canadian Association of Physicists, the Tory Medal of the Royal Society of Canada, and the Ives and Meggers Medals of the Optical Society of America.

Source: *Canadian Who's Who*, 1993

Suzuki, David T. ♂

b. 24 March 1936, Vancouver, British Columbia
Zoologist; geneticist; professor; science communicator
Famous popularizer of science and ecological issues

Suzuki received his university education at Amherst College, Massachusetts (BA, 1958), and the University of Chicago, Illinois (PhD, 1961). Although he worked in genetics, his research has been superseded by his fame as a popularizer of science, and particularly ecological, issues. He has written several books and many articles, and has been host of numerous TV and radio shows on science since 1979, notably CBC TV's "The Nature of Things." He has received numerous awards, including the Royal Canadian Institute's Sanford Fleming Medal (1982); UN Environmental Program Medal (1985); the Governor General Award for Conservation (1985); UNESCO's Kalinga Prize (1986); and the Biological Society of Canada's Gold Medal Award (1986).

Source: *Canadian Who's Who*, 1993

Taube, Henry ♂

b. 30 November 1915, Neudorf, Saskatchewan
Physical chemist; Professor of chemistry, Stanford University, Stanford California
Won the 1983 Nobel prize in chemistry for studying electron transfer reactions

Taube studied at the University of Saskatchewan, Saskatoon (BSc, 1935; MSc, 1937), and the University of California, Berkeley (PhD, 1940). He has spent his life conducting experiments to understand the behaviour of ions in solution. His most famous work has been in electron transfer reactions, for which he won the Nobel Prize for chemistry in 1983. His current work continues in this area, and includes studying the reactivity of inorganic substances, mixed-valence molecules, and the systematic study of back-bonding. In addition to the Nobel Prize, he has received numerous awards and honours, including as the Linus Pauling Award in 1981.

Sources: *Who's Who in Frontier Science and Technology*, 1984-85; *Modern Men of Science*, 1966

Taylor, Richard ♂ ⚛

b. 2 November 1929, Medicine Hat, Alberta
Physicist; Professor, Stanford University, Stanford, California
Won the 1990 Nobel Prize for Physics for verifying the quark theory

When Taylor entered the University of Alberta in Edmonton, he registered in a special program emphasizing mathematics and physics. He became interested in experimental physics while working on his MSc there. He went to Stanford University in California to study towards a PhD, but after two years, stopped working on it to join the High Energy Physics Laboratory and build a new linear accelerator. Eventually, he went back to Stanford to get his PhD. By the early 1960s he was designing the experimental areas of the Stanford Linear Accelerator Center, helping to build the equipment and taking part in electron scattering experiments. Between 1967 and 1973, Taylor conducted a series of experiments together with Jerome Friedman and Henry Kendall of MIT, in which they used the powerful new accelerator to smash protons and neutrons to pieces. They discovered that these elementary particles, once believed to be indivisible, are made up of quarks, thus proving the existence of these theoretical and as yet undiscovered building blocks of nature. The Nobel committee described it as finding a "new rung in the ladder of creation," and awarded Taylor, Friedman, and Kendal the 1990 Nobel Prize for Physics.

Sources: *Science*, October 1990; *Science News*, October 27, 1990; *The Canadian Encyclopedia,* 1988

Terzopoulos, Demetri ♂ 〰

b. 29 February 1956, Pirgos, Greece
Computer scientist, University of Toronto, Ontario
Pioneers research in fields of computer vision, artificial life, and computer graphics

Terzopoulos received his university education at McGill University, Montreal, Quebec (B.Eng., 1978, M.Eng., 1980) and MIT (PhD, 1984). He does pioneering work in artificial life, an emerging field that combines computer science and biological science. He devises computer models of animal locomotion, perception, behaviour, learning, and intelligence. Professor Terzopoulos and his students have created artificial fish, virtual inhabitants of an underwater world simulated in a powerful computer. These autonomous, lifelike creatures swim, forage, eat, and mate on their own. Terzopoulos has also done important work on human facial modelling. He has produced what is widely recognized as the most realistic biomechanical model of the human face to date. Expressive synthetic faces are useful in entertainment and human-computer interaction, but they can also play a role in planning reconstructive facial surgery, as well as in automated face recognition and teleconferencing systems. Terzopoulos is widely known as the inventor of deformable models, a family of shape modeling algorithms that have bridged the fields of computer vision and computer graphics and have opened up new avenues of research in medical imaging and computer-aided design. Among his numerous awards, Terzopoulos won an NSERC Steacie Memorial Fellowship in 1996.

Source: NSERC

Tsui, Lap-Chee ♂ 〵

Molecular geneticist; discovered the cystic fibrosis gene

See full profile in the Profiles section.

Tulving, Endel ♂ ◊

Cognitive psychologist; expert on human memory

See full profile in the Profiles section.

Tutte, William ♂ ⌇

b. 14 May 1917, Newmarket, England
Mathematician; Professor Emeritus, University of Waterloo, Ontario
Discoverer of Tutte's Theorem

During his early schooling, Tutte became fascinated with prime numbers, as well as articles on astronomy and other sciences in a children's encyclopedia. He studied the natural sciences at Cambridge University in England (BA, 1938; MSc, 1941; PhD, 1948), but became more and more interested in mathematics. His experience cracking secret codes during World War II gained him a fellowship at Trinity College, where he became particularly well known for his papers on Graph Theory – the mathematics of the combinations of connections between points on a plane or in other dimensions. He was a professor of mathematics at the University of Toronto, Ontario, from 1948 to 1962, then fellow mathematician H.M.S. Coxeter helped him get a post at the University of Waterloo, where he worked until retirement in 1985. He is the author of several books, including *Graph Theory* (1984). Tutte received the Tory Medal of the Royal Society of Canada in 1975, and the Izaak Walton Killam Memorial Prize in 1982.

Sources: *In Celebration of Canadian Scientists*, 1990; *Canadian Who's Who,* 1993

Uchida, Irene ♀ ◊

Cytogeneticist; expert on Down syndrome

See full profile in the Profiles section.

Unruh, William George ♂ ⚛

b. 28 August 1945, Winnipeg, Manitoba
Physicist; cosmologist; professor, UBC; Director, Cosmology, Canadian Institute for Advanced Research
Contributes to theories on gravity and black holes, early cosmology, and quantum phenomena

Unruh received his university education at the University of Manitoba, Winnipeg (BSc, 1967), and Princeton University, New Jersey (MA, 1969; PhD, 1971). In his research, Unruh applies quantum mechanics to study gravity and the forces that existed at the moment of creation according to big-bang theory. He is also examining the process of black hole evaporation discovered by the great English physicist, Stephen Hawking, which is still a mystery. Unruh won the Rutherford medal of the Royal Society of Canada (1982); the Herzberg Medal of the Canadian Association of Physics (1983); the Steacie Prize (1984); a Steacie Fellowship (1984-86); and the BC Science Council Gold Medal (1990).

Source: *Canadian Who's Who*, 1993

White, Mary Anne ♀ ⚗

b. 28 December 1953, London, Ontario
Physical chemist; Professor, Dalhousie University, Halifax, Nova Scotia
Developed a new class of heat-absorbing chemicals

White received degrees from the UWO (BSc, 1975) and McMaster University, Hamilton, Ontario (PhD, 1980). Over five years she developed a new class of chemicals which absorb waste heat from industrial processes, and which can also be used to insulate homes.

Sources: *Focus* vol. 2, no. 2; *Canadian Who's Who*, 1993; *Canadian Women: Risktakers and Changemakers*, 1994

Whitehead, Lorne A. ♂ ⚛

b. not available
Physicist; Professor, UBC
Invented and developed the Prism Light Guide System

Whitehead received his degrees at UBC (BSc, 1977; MSc, 1979; PhD, 1989). In 1978, while he was still a student, he began working on the light pipe after making a key discovery. He showed theoretically that the "total internal reflection" effect used in optical fibres could be harnessed in large hollow pipes if they could be coated with precise gem-like prisms. His research on structured surface physics – the study of interfaces containing precision structures on a scale of 0.1 to 100 micrometres – led to the prism light guide. His system is important because it can make use of either sunlight or electric light as a source and carry it with very little loss to a distant room or object. His physics research continues to generate innovations in lighting, image display technology, optics, electromagnetic filters, and thin, flexible sound sources. Whitehead received the 1984 Manning Award, and the 1995 BC Science and Engineering Gold Medal in Industrial Innovation.

Sources: The Manning Awards; Lorne Whitehead's homepage; Science Council of British Columbia

Wiesner, Karel ♂ ⚗

b. 1919, Prague, Czechoslovakia; d. 28 November 1986, Fredericton, New Brunswick
Organic chemist; Professor, University of New Brunswick, Fredericton
Greatest Canadian natural products chemist

Wiesner received his PhD in Prague, Czechoslovakia, where he studied polarography at Bulovka Hospital. He came to the University of New Brunswick in 1948 and developed Canada's leading school of natural products chemistry – the extraction and characterization of naturally occurring chemicals from plants and animals. His former students are found at most of the major chemistry schools in Canada. He determined the chemical structure and synthesis of very complicated alkaloids, and made major contributions to the fields of terpenoids and steroids. He received the highest honour of the Chemical Institute of Canada in 1963, and became a Fellow of the Royal Society of Canada in 1957.

Source: *The Canadian Encyclopedia,* 1988

Wilson, John Tuzo ♂ 〽

b. 24 October 1908, Ottawa, Ontario; d. 1992
Geophysicist
Pioneer in the study of plate tectonics

Wilson received the first BA in geophysics ever granted at the University of Toronto, Ontario, then went on to acquire graduate degrees at Cambridge University, England (1932, 1940) and Princeton University, New Jersey (1936). After working with the Geological Survey of Canada from 1936 to 1939, he became Professor of Geophysics at the University of Toronto (1946 to 1974). While searching for unknown Arctic islands in 1946, he became the second Canadian to fly over the North Pole. He was internationally respected for his work on glaciers, mountain building, the geology of ocean basins, and the structure of continents, but his greatest contribution lies in his explanation of plate tectonics – the notion that the earth's crust is made up of a series of floating plates. He also pioneered the use of air photos in geological mapping and was responsible for the first glacial map of Canada. Wilson served on the National Research Council from 1958 to 1964, and was also an author for popular audiences. His books include two on China that helped reopen relations between China and Western countries. Wilson was the recipient of numerous awards, and was a Companion of the Order of Canada.

Source: *The Canadian Encyclopedia,* 1988

SOURCES FOR SHORT BIOGRAPHIES

Ainley, M.G. *Despite the Odds: Essays on Canadian Women and Science*. Vehicule Press, Montreal, 1990.

American Men of Science. Bowker, New York, 1973-1978.

Asimov I., *Asimov's Chronology of Science and Techonology*. HarperCollins, New York, NY, 1994.

Asimov, I. *Asimov's Biographical Encyclopedia of Science and Technology*, (2nd rev. ed). Doubleday, Garden City, N.Y., 1982.

Bohnert, B., *Canadian Women: Risktakers and Changemakers*. The Women Inventors Project, Etobicoke, Ontario, 1993.

The Canadian Who's Who, 1993, 1994.

Encyclopedia Canadiana, 1977.

Hacker, C. *The Indomitable Lady Doctors*. Clarke, Irwin, Toronto, 1974.

Kenney-Wallace, G. et al., eds. *In Celebration of Canadian Scientists: A Decade of Killam Laureates*. Charles Babbage Research Centre, Ottawa, 1990.

May, E. *Claiming the Future: The Inspiring Lives of Twelve Canadian Women Scientists and Scholars*. Pembroke Publishers, Markham, Ontario, 1991.

McLeod, C. *Legendary Canadian Women*. Lancelot Press, Hantsport, N.S., 1983.

Millar, D. *Chambers Concise Dictionary of Scientists*. Press Syndicate of the University of Cambridge, New York, 1989.

Modern Men of Science. McGraw-Hill, New York, 1966-68.

Ogilvie, M. B. *Women in Science: Antiquity Through the Nineteenth Century*. MIT Press, Boston, 1986.

The Canadian Encyclopedia. Hurtig, 1985, 1988.

Who's Who in America, 1994.

Who's Who in Frontier Science and Technology, (1st ed). Marquis, Chicago, Ill., 1984.

Who's Who in Science and Engineering. Marquis, Chicago, Ill., 1992.

Glossary

EACH SCIENCE HAS ITS OWN LANGUAGE of special words. This glossary is an alphabetical list of many of the special words used in the long profiles in the first half of this book.

2D Two-dimensional or flat. Having only width and length. A flat surface is 2D.

3D Three-dimensional. Having width, length, and height. Space is 3D.

A

Acetic acid solution (CH_3COOH)   The simplest carboxylic acid dissolved in water. Also known as vinegar.

Activity budget An accounting of the time spent on various activities by a focal animal under observation in an anthropology experiment.

AIDS (Acquired Immune Deficiency Syndrome)   A severe immunological disorder caused by the retrovirus HIV. People with AIDS have weakened immune systems and cannot protect themselves against disease. AIDS victims usually end up dying of rare infectious diseases. AIDS is transmitted primarily sexually, or by exposure to blood or blood products from an infected individual.

Airborne Something that is carried in the air, like dust or pollen.

Allergenic A substance such as pollen that causes an allergy, an abnormally sensitive reaction characterized by sneezing, itching, or rashes on the skin.

Amazon The world's second longest river, which begins in Peru and empties into the Atlantic ocean in Brazil. It carries more water than any other river in the world, and traverses the world's largest rainforest, which bears the same name.

Amino acid A type of organic molecule found in living things. It has an amino (NH_3) group on one end, and a carboxylic acid (COOH) group on the other. Amino acids are linked together by enzymes to form proteins, which are essential building blocks of all living things.

Angstrom A unit of length equal to 10^{-10} meters or 0.1 nanometers (a nanometre is a billionth of a metre).

Anthropology The study of humankind through evolution, culture, and social structures.

Antibody (antibodies) An immune system protein which gloms onto bacteria thereby inactivating them or their toxins, making them easier to kill by other immune system molecules.

Antigens A substance that is foreign to the human body and stimulates an immune response. Some antigens are toxins, bacteria, foreign cells, dust, dirt, chemicals, and pollen.

Aphasia   A speech disorder that occurs when people's brains are damaged by some kind of accident or disease. For instance, a person with aphasia might be able to tell you everything about oranges and even write the word orange, but for some strange reason would not be able to say "orange." There are many different kinds of aphasia.

Arthritis   A disease involving inflammation of the joints and connective tissues.

Atmosphere   The gas layer surrounding a planet. On earth it's the air and everything that goes with it, like clouds, rain, and storms.

Atmospheric turbulence   Eddies and winds caused by pockets of air of different pressures and temperatures.

Atmospheric Data Analysis Title of a 1991 book by Roger Daley. It is considered to be one of the primary sources for computerized weather models.

Atom (atoms)   The smallest part of an element that can exist. Atoms consist of a nucleus of protons and neutrons surrounded by a cloud of electrons.

Auto-immune diseases Any of a number of diseases caused by a malfunctioning of the immune system. Allergies are a common example.

Average A number that is typical of a large set of numbers often calculated by adding all values and dividing by the number of values.

B

Bacterium, bacteria Single-cell organisms that can cause disease in plants and animals.

Balmer lines Characteristic vertical dark lines on a spectrogram. Named after the Swiss high school teacher who first described them mathematically in 1885.

Base pair A pair of nitrogenous bases linked by hydrogen bonds connecting the complementary strands of the DNA molecule. The base Adenine always pairs with Thymine, and the base Guanine always pairs with Cytosine.

Base pair deletion A mutation that arises as a result of the deletion of one base pair in a DNA chain.

B-cells A type of white blood cell; part of the human immune system. When stimulated, they produce antibodies which kill specific antigens.

Behavioural psychologist A scientist who studies how brains work in order to understand how people differ from each other.

Bering Sea A northward extension of the Pacific Ocean between Siberia and Alaska.

Bertrand Russell The great English philosopher and educator who lived from 1872 to 1970. His most famous book, *Principia Mathematica*, demonstrated that mathematics could be explained by the rules of formal logic. He won the Nobel Prize for Literature in 1950. He was a pacifist and was jailed twice for his activities on behalf of peace and nuclear disarmament.

Big-bang theory Currently accepted by most cosmologists, this theory about the origin of the universe says that about ten billion years ago, all matter in the universe was created in an instant in one tremendously hot explosion originating from nothing.

Biochemistry The study of chemical compounds and reactions occurring in living organisms.

Biology The study of living things.

Biotechnology The use of microorganisms such as bacteria or yeast to produce commercial products such as drugs, foods, and so on. Also for the treatment of wastes and oil spills.

Black hole theory The concept of a region of space that has so much mass concentrated in it that nothing can escape its gravitational pull, including light. Hence the name "black hole."

Blood type (blood group) The classification of human blood based on its immunological qualities. Persons must receive blood transfusions of the same blood group or they will have an adverse immune response. Blood type is passed on genetically from parents to their children.

Borneo A tropical island in the western Pacific Ocean; the third largest island in the world. The country of Brunei is on the northwest coast while the rest of the island is divided between Indonesia and Malaysia. Biruté Galdikas lives and works in the Indonesian part of Borneo.

Botanist A person who specializes in botany, the study of plants.

BPD (BenzoPorphyrin Derivative) A second generation photodynamic drug that is undergoing trials for approval in the treatment of cancer, eye disorders, and auto-immune diseases.

C

Caffeine A bitter white alkaloid most often found in tea or coffee and used as a minor stimulant.

Cancer A disease that happens when certain cells in the body begin growing in an uncontrolled manner creating a tumour that upsets the function of one or more parts of the body.

Cassava root The root of a tropical shrub. It has large tubers that are eaten as a staple food after leaching and drying to remove cyanide.

Carbon dioxide (CO_2) A gas which is the main product of burning, including the combustion of fossil fuels like oil, gas and coal.

Catalysis A process that speeds up chemical reactions by the introduction of a molecule or atom which promotes the chemical reaction but is not consumed by it.

Catalytic RNA A special kind of RNA that acts like an enzyme. First discovered by Sid Altman.

Cell (cells) The smallest structural unit of an organism that is capable of independent functioning. A simple cell consists of a nucleus and cytoplasm, and is enclosed by a cell wall.

Centrifuge An apparatus consisting of a device that can spin test tubes around at very high speed. Used to separate contained materials or to precipitate out by gravity the solids suspended in a liquid.

Chemical A substance with a distinct molecular composition that is produced or used in a chemical process or reaction.

Chemical reaction   A change or transformation in which a chemical decomposes, combines with other chemicals or shares atoms or groups of atoms with other chemicals.

Chemiluminescence   The feeble emission of light from colliding molecules during a chemical reaction.

Chemist   A person who studies chemistry.

Chemistry   The science of the composition, structure, properties, and reactions of matter, especially atomic and molecular systems.

Chicha drink   A sour-tasting beverage made by native women in the Peruvian jungle. They chew a kind of tapioca root and spit it into a huge bowl, then let it stand for a while to ferment.

Chinook   A type of salmon native to the Pacific Northwest. Also known as spring salmon.

Chloride ion   The negatively charged ion of the element chlorine. Usually found in aqueous solution.

Chromosome spread   Also known as a karyotype, a set of chromosomes from a cell that has been fixed and spread out on a glass slide for analysis.

Chromosome band   The characteristic banding of chromosomes helps cytogeneticists identify them. Banding is caused by different types of DNA and associated proteins.

Chromosomes   Threadlike strands found in the nuclei of animal and plant cells. Chromosomes are made of DNA molecules and associated proteins and they carry hereditary information about the organism.

Classical geometer   A mathematician who studies classic geometrical structures such as points, lines, angles, surfaces and solids.

Cognition   The mental processes of knowing.

Cognitive psychology   A branch of psychology dealing with how the brain processes information, especially concerning perception, memory, knowing, awareness, reasoning, judgment and learning.

Cognitive functions   How brains process information, especially with regard to perception, memory, knowing, awareness, reasoning, judgment and learning.

Coho   A type of salmon native to the Pacific Northwest. Also known as silver salmon.

Collimate   To line up, as in a parallel beam of radiation.

Complex number   A number that has a real part and an imaginary part. The imaginary part is something like the square

root of a negative number which by ordinary logic is impossible.

Congenital   Some thing or condition that you have at birth.

Coordinates   A way of specifying a point's location in space with numbers. For instance, on a two-dimensional plane, you need two numbers, one to show how far to the right or left and one to show how far forward or backwards the point is from some other location on the plane.

Cosmology   A branch of physics concerned with the origins of the universe, its history, structure and dynamics.

Crystal structures   The regular pattern of atoms or molecules in a solid crystalline substance.

Culture   The socially transmitted behaviour patterns, arts, beliefs, and knowledge as an expression of a particular community, period, class, or population.

Cystic fibrosis (CF)   A fatal disease that kills about one out of every 2000 Canadians, mostly children. Cystic fibrosis is the most common genetic disease among white people.

Cytogenetics   The study of chromosomes in cells. It concentrates on the behaviour and identification of chromosomes.

D

Data   Factual information organized for analysis or used to reason and make decisions or conclusions.

Data collection   Recording observations from experiments for later analysis.

Deoxyribose   A type of sugar ($C_5H_{10}O_4$) that is a constituent of DNA.

Diagnose   To distinguish or identify something, often a disease, by observing symptoms.

Diagnosis   The act or process of identifying the nature and cause of a disease or injury through evaluation of patient history, examination, and review of laboratory test data.

Dimension   A mathematical concept concerning how many numbers you need to specify uniquely a point in space. On a flat surface you need two numbers. It's called a two-dimensional space. We live in 3D or three-dimensional space where you need three numbers to tell exactly where you are.

Dimensional analogy   The process of stretching geometrical shapes into higher dimensions.

DNA (DeoxyriboNucleic Acid)   The molecule that encodes the genetic information which tells cells how to function and grow.

Down syndrome A congenital disease caused by the accidental tripling of chromosome number 21 during conception. Affected people have mild to moderate mental retardation, short stature, and flat facial features.

Dye A substance used to colour materials.

E

Ecology The study of natural systems of plants and animals through the experimental analysis of their distribution and abundance.

Electron A subatomic particle with a unit of negative electric charge. A constituent of all atoms which are composed of one or more electrons orbiting the atom's nucleus in a sort of electron cloud.

Electrophoresis A standard laboratory method for separating chemical compounds. A few drops of a material in solution are dropped onto a glass plate on which there is a thin layer of gel and the plate is then exposed to a strong electric field. This causes the various compounds to move different distances through the gel over a period of time, thereby separating them.

Element A substance composed of atoms all having the same number of protons in their nuclei. Elements cannot be reduced to simpler substances by chemical means. There are about 110 known elements, of which 94 occur in nature.

Emeritus Retired but retaining an honorary title the same as the one held before retirement. Usually applied to university professors.

Encoding a memory The recording or laying down of a memory in the brain.

Energy The capacity of a physical system to do work.

Enzyme A protein that promotes chemical reactions in living organisms through catalysis.

Epithelial A type of cell that forms the membranous covering of most internal and external surfaces of the body and its internal organs. For instance, skin cells are epithelial cells. Other epithelial cells in the nose and mouth and other parts of the body secrete mucous.

Ethnobotanist A person who practices ethnobotany, the study of plants by obtaining information from people around the world.

Event horizon The point of no return for matter or light falling into a black hole. At this distance from the singularity at the centre of the black hole, gravity is so strong that nothing can escape. To an outside observer, the event horizon appears as the surface of the black hole.

F

Fence or Krebs Effect The population explosion and crash that results from fencing in an area in the wild where rodents live.

Ferment The energy producing process used by some microorganisms to break down sugar molecules, often (but not only) resulting in the products of ethyl alcohol and carbon dioxide.

Fetus (Fetuses) The unborn young still developing in the womb.

Fibre-optics The science or technology of light transmission through very fine flexible glass or plastic fibres.

Fibre-optic scope A device for peering into the body or other hard-to-reach place. It uses fibre-optics to transmit the image from the remote site to the end user.

Fisheries biologist A biologist who studies fish habitat and population.

Fish population dynamics The rise and fall of fish populations as a result of natural effects and fishing.

Focal animal An animal subject that is the focus of the research in an anthropology experiment.

Folk medicine Traditional medicine as practiced by non-professional healers, generally using natural and especially herbal remedies made from local plant materials.

Fourth dimension We experience the world in three dimensions, but it is possible to imagine a world with four or more dimensions. The fourth dimension could be time or maybe it's where ghosts come from.

Fraser River A major river in British Columbia. It begins in the Rocky Mountains and drains into the Straight of Georgia near Vancouver.

Free radical A transition molecule created briefly in a chemical reaction when molecules come together and transform themselves into something new. Free radicals last only for the length of time it takes for their constituent atoms to rearrange themselves with other molecules into new molecules – a few millionths of a second.

Fungus Plant-like organisms that lack chlorophyll. They include yeasts, molds, smuts and mushrooms.

Fur trading company In the early days of North America fortunes were made by trading with First Nations peoples and European trappers for animal furs. The furs were made into coats and hats for sale mostly in Europe. The Hudson's Bay Company is probably the oldest and best known fur trading company.

G

Gene A hereditary unit that occupies a specific place on a chromosome and determines a particular characteristic of an organism.

Genetic code The sequence of nucleotides in a DNA molecule that specifies the amino acid sequence in the synthesis of proteins. Each amino acid is coded by three nucleotides. For instance, glutamic acid is coded by the sequence Guanine, Adenine, Adenine.

Genetic engineering Using molecular biological techniques to alter the genes in organisms so that they produce or express certain substances or qualities that are desirable or commercially valuable.

Genetics A branch of biology concerned with genes and heredity and how inherited characteristics are transmitted among similar or related organisms.

Genome The complete set of genes for an individual organism.

Genomics The sequencing of the DNA of an organism to understand how it works.

Geometer A person who does geometry.

Geometrical coordinates A way of specifying a point's location in space with numbers. For instance, on a two-dimensional plane, you need two numbers, one to show how far to the right or left and one to show how far forward or backwards the point is from some other location on the plane.

Geometry A branch of mathematics that deals with points, lines, angles, surfaces and solids.

Geophysical Having to do with the physics of the earth, including oceans, land and atmosphere. Represented by the sciences of seismology, oceanography, and meteorology, respectively.

Glass slide A small flat piece of glass used for mounting samples to be viewed under a microscope.

Global warming The idea that coal, oil and gas burning might cause a large enough increase in carbon dioxide in the atmosphere over the next 100 years to cause a "greenhouse effect," whereby carbon dioxide in the atmosphere traps infrared radiation and warms the planet by a few degrees centigrade.

Graph A diagram such as a pie chart that illustrates numerical relationships.

Green Book A book written by William Ricker in the 1950s

and updated in the 1970s. It presents a mathematical system for the computation of fish population statistics. The Green Book is still used to determine allowable catches for fisheries in many countries, including Canada.

Greenhouse effect The process whereby increasing carbon dioxide in the atmosphere traps infrared radiation and warms the planet by a few degrees centigrade, allowing the polar ice caps to melt and cause great flooding all over the planet.

Grid A framework of horizontal and vertical lines forming squares on a map, chart, photograph or the ground.

H

H.G. Wells Herbert George Wells (1866-1946), the great English author and science fiction writer who wrote books like *The Time Machine* and *War Of the Worlds*.

Haemoglobin The iron-containing pigment in red blood cells that carries oxygen to cells.

Hell's Gate Falls A deep gorge with rapids and waterfalls in the Fraser River Canyon between Hope and Lytton, British Columbia.

Helper T-cell A special T-Cell that activates other cells in the immune system to mount a defensive response against invading antigens in the body.

Hexagonal Having six sides.

Hydrogen (H_2) A colourless, very flammable gas. The lightest of all gases and the most abundant element in the universe.

Hypercube The four-dimensional version of a cube. A four-dimensional hypercube is analagous to a three-dimensional cube. Also known as a tesseract.

Hyperdimensional geometry Geometry that goes beyond the three dimensions of ordinary space.

I

Immune system The system of organs and cells in our bodies that is concerned with protecting us from invading organisms or molecules such as germs, dirt, viruses and bacteria.

Immunologist A person who studies immunology, a branch of medicine or biology concerned with the structure and function of the immune system.

Incubator An apparatus or a chamber for maintaining living organisms in an environment that encourages growth.

Infrared spectrometer A device used to measure emission or absorption of infrared light.

Inner Horizon In a black hole, the point beyond which you cannot see out.

Ion An atom or molecule with a positive or negative electric charge caused by gaining or losing one or more electrons.

K

Kaleidoscope An instrument that uses mirrors and bits of glass to create an endlessly changing pattern of repeating reflections.

Kantian doom The idea that we are doomed because even though we know that something is bad for us, we do it anyway because everyone else is doing it. Immanuel Kant was a German philosopher who in the last half of the 1700s wrote a lot about the meaning of existence and morality. Kant's supreme principle of morality is called the *categorical imperative* and is a way of testing the morality or quality of our behaviour. In simple terms, Kant tells us to ask ourselves before we do something: what would happen if everyone acted like this?

Karyotype A spread of chromosomes on a glass slide, often photographed, sorted and analyzed.

Killer T-Cells A special large T-Cell that attacks and kills invading target cells bearing specific antigens.

Knockout mice Mice with missing genetic instructions for making just one protein.

L

Lemming A small thickset rodent that lives in the North and is known for periodic devastating population crashes in which almost all the lemmings die.

Light-year The distance that light travels in one year, or 9.46 trillion kilometres.

Line of natural replacement In the Ricker Curve, a line that represents spawners (adult fish who lay eggs or fertilize them) being replaced by an equal number of progeny (fish who grow up to be adults).

Lipoproteins Complex protein molecules that carry fatty material in blood. For instance, lipoproteins are responsible for carrying cholesterol to various parts of the body.

Live-animal trap A little cage that traps animals without harming them so that animal ecologists can measure and tag the animals for experimental study.

Lynx A type of wildcat that lives in northern North America and Eurasia. They are identified by their tufted ears, and black-tipped tails.

M

Macrophage A specialized cell that's part of the immune system. Like a garbage truck in the body, macrophages go around collecting bits of living and dead cells and other material to present them to T-Cells for identification.

Marlborough man The rugged male character employed by the RJ Reynolds tobacco company to create an image of the type of person who smokes Marlborough brand cigarettes. He is typically shown wearing a cowboy hat, and situated alone (or with a horse) in wide open country.

Maser (Microwave Amplification by Stimulated Emission of Radiation) Like a laser but radiating microwaves instead of light. Giant distant masers can be seen from the earth in far away galaxies.

Mast cells Cells in the body that release substances in response to a disease or injury and can help the body repair itself.

Maximum sustainable catch The point on a Ricker Curve that shows the maximaum number of fish you can catch to sustain the stock of fish for future years.

Medicinal plant A wild plant that can be the source of a drug or medicine. For instance, willow bark was the original source of the drug aspirin.

Memory The mental faculty of retaining and recalling past experiences.

Metaphysical Of or relating to metaphysics, a division of philosophy that is concerned with the fundamental nature of reality and existence.

Meteorologist A person who studies the atmosphere and in particular, weather.

Meteorology The study of the earth's atmosphere and weather.

Methane (CH_4) An odourless colorless flammable gas, the main constituent of natural gas.

Methylene (CH_2) A hydrocarbon molecule consisting of a carbon atom with two hydrogen atoms, one on either side. Methylene has two free electrons, making it a very reactive free radical.

Microbiology A branch of biology that deals with living things on a microscopic scale.

Microscope An optical device that uses a combination of lenses to magnify small objects that cannot be seen by the naked eye.

Models Mathematical representations of systems – like the atmosphere or the nucleus of an atom – that account for their properties and may be used to study or predict their characteristics.

Molecule (molecules) The smallest particle of a substance that retains the properties of the substance and is composed of one or more atoms.

Molecular Having to do with molecules.

Molecular biology Biology on the molecular level; the physics and chemistry of molecules in biological systems.

Molecular ions A group of atoms with a net electric charge caused by gaining or losing one or more electrons.

Molecular geneticist A person who studies genetics at the molecular level – in particular, the molecules of DNA and associated compounds.

Mongoloid The old term for persons with Down syndrome. They were called mongoloid because the disease causes features of a flattened nose, wide eyes and short stature, which in the past were thought to be of mongoloid racial origin.

Multiple sclerosis A chronic degenerative disease of the central nervous system in which patches of the protective myelin sheath around nerves are lost. The cause is unknown and symptoms include disturbances of vision, speech, balance, and coordination. There is no cure, but some drugs can reduce its severity.

Mutagenesis The formation or development of a mutation.

Mutate The process of mutation whereby an organism changes in character or quality as a result of a change in its DNA.

Mutation A change of the DNA within a gene of an organism that results in the creation of a new character or quality not found in the parents of the organism.

N

Nanometre A billionth of a metre, or 10^{-9} metres.

N-dimensional Having up to *n* dimensions, as in 1-dimension, 2-dimension, 3-dimension, and so on. Up to any number (n) dimensions.

Nebulae Interstellar dust or gas visible as luminous patches or areas of darkness in outer space.

Neon A rare inert gas. The tenth element. It is inert but glows reddish orange in an electric discharge. Used in neon display signs.

Nervous system The brain, spinal cord, nerves and related tissues in a person or animal.

Neuropsychological tests Tests that uncover relationships between the brain and mental functions such as language memory and perception.

Neutron An uncharged elementary particle that has a mass similar to a proton. Protons and neutrons are present in the nucleus of all atoms (except hydrogen which only has one proton and no neutrons).

Nuclear physics The physics of atomic nuclei and their interactions, with particular reference to the generation of nuclear energy.

Nucleotides The basic chain link of a DNA or RNA chain composed of a backbone phosphate sugar part and a purine or pyrimidine base linking part. The four nucleotides Adenine, Thymine, Cytosine and Guanine are the building blocks of the genetic code.

Nursery A place where plants are grown for sale, transplantation or experimentation.

O

Oligonucleotide A short chain of nucleotides.

Orangutans Great apes who live in the tropical rainforests of Borneo (Indonesia).

Osmosis The tendency of fluids to diffuse through a permeable membrane until the concentration of the fluid is the same on both sides of the membrane.

Ova A female reproductive germ cell, or egg.

Ozone (O_3) A form of oxygen gas that has a slight blue colour. Formed by the exposure of air or oxygen to ultraviolet radiation or an electrical discharge. It is unstable, poisonous, powerfully bleaching and smells like the air around a lightning storm.

Ozone holes Gaps in the upper atmosphere that appear seasonally over the north and south polar ice caps. They are probably caused by the presence of chlorofluorocarbons released into the atmosphere. Chlorofluorocarbons are synthetic gasses used in refrigeration and as propellants in spray cans. Under the influence of ultraviolet radiation, they react with air to desroy ozone in the upper atmosphere, something which seems to be happening more often above the earth's poles.

P

Peruvian Of or having to do with Peru, a country in north-western South America.

PET scanner A machine that shows what parts of your brain are especially active while you are doing or thinking something. PET stands for Positron Emission Tomography.

Philosopher A person who studies philosophy, the search for a general understanding of meaning, values, beliefs and reality.

Photodynamic therapy Treating disease with new drugs that are activated by light.

Photofrin A first-generation photodynamic drug developed by QLT PhotoTherapeutics Inc. in Vancouver, British Columbia.

Photosensitive Something that is sensitive to light. Upon being exposed to light, it changes or reacts in some way.

Physical anthropologist A person who studies the physical evolution of the human species.

Physical chemist A person who studies the physics of chemical reactions and compounds.

Physics The study of the laws that determine the structure of the universe and all the matter and energy within it.

Pi or π A mathematical constant that is roughly 3.14159 and represents the ratio between the radius and circumference of a circle. Pi is a transcendental number which means it keeps on going and the digits never end or repeat in a pattern.

Pie chart A type of pie-shaped graph that shows the relationship between numerical quantities as parts of a whole. The parts look like wedges of a pie.

Pink Salmon A Pacific salmon fish also known as humpback salmon.

Pollen Fine powderlike material that is produced by the anthers of seed plants.

Polygon A plane figure with a number of sides, such as a square (4) or a hexagon (6).

Polyhedron A solid bounded by polygonal faces, such as a tetrahedron (4 triangular faces) or a cube (4 square faces).

Polytope Higher dimensional versions of a hypercube.

Population explosion The rapid geometric expansion of a biological population of animals (including people).

Population crash The sudden fall of a biological population due to natural causes.

Precursor RNA An intermediate form of RNA that is one of at least six kinds of RNA involved in the process of transcribing the genetic code from DNA to make protein molecules.

Prism A transparent body usually made of glass in a triangular shape and used for separating white light or other electromagnetic radiation into a spectrum.

Protein (chain, or molecule) A large complex organic molecule composed of one or more chains of amino acids. Proteins are fundamental components of all living cells and include many substances such as enzymes, hormones, antibodies and cell wall structures.

Proton An elementary particle that is stable, has a positive charge and can be found in the nuclei of all atoms.

Psoriasis A noncontagious skin disease characterized by recurring reddish patches covered with silvery scales.

Psychological subject A person who participates in a psychological experiment usually involving some test of perception, memory, behaviour or other cognitive function.

Psychology The science that studies behaviour and thinking.

Q

Quantum mechanics A mathematical system of describing the behaviour of very small particles such as atoms and molecules. In quantum mechanics you cannot describe precisely where a thing will be. You can only express the probability of it being someplace at a particular time.

Quantum theory A relatively modern theory of physics which is based on the idea that certain properties such as energy occur in discrete amounts or quanta.

R

Radiation Energy traveling in the form of electromagnetic waves or particles – for example, light or neutrons or X-rays.

Radioactive nuclear pile The core of a nuclear reactor in which a controlled fission reaction takes place. A source of neutrons.

Rainforest The tropical jungle that girdles the earth at equatorial latitudes, and typically has rainfall greater than 2.5 metres per year. Temperate rainforests also exist in the North

American Pacific Northwest, Chile, and New Zealand.

Reaction dynamics A field of chemistry concerned with the motions and energies of molecules during the course of a chemical reaction.

Relativity A mathematical system of mechanics developed by Einstein in the early 1900s. It is based on the idea of describing the motion of a body in a manner which is independent of the motion of any observer who may be studying the body. In other words, no absolute frame of reference exists.

Retrieving a memory The process by which the brain recalls memories which it has previously encoded.

Rhombus A rhombus is a squashed square. It has sides of equal length.

Ricker Curve A mathematical model of fish population dynamics developed by William Ricker and used to determine allowable fish catches worldwide.

RNA (ribonucleic acid) A molecule that is part of the biological system in a cell that decodes instructions in DNA.

Rotation Turning around a central point. One rotation would be one time around the circle.

Rotational energy The energy in a particle, atom or molecule arising from its spin.

S

Salmon A type of food and game fish (of the genera Salmo or Oncorhynchus) found in northern waters. They have delicate pinkish flesh and return from the sea to spawn in freshwater rivers and creeks.

Sample group A randomly selected group of subjects for an experiment. It could be people, rabbits, bacteria, genes, rocks or anything. The important thing is that they are chosen to represent the typical variability you might find in the total population from which the sample group is chosen.

SAT Scholastic Aptitude Tests National university-entry level exams taken by high school students wishing to study in universities in the USA.

Simulation An imitation or a representation of one system by another, as in a computer model of the weather.

Singularity An infinitely massive point in space.

Site-directed mutagenesis A technique developed by Michael Smith that allows geneticists to make a genetic mutation precisely at any spot in a DNA molecule.

Snowshoe hare A medium-sized rabbit with large furry feet that lives throughout the northern latitudes. The snowshoe hare's fur is brown in summer and white in winter.

Social behaviour The relationships and behaviours among individuals in a community of animals.

Sockeye A type of salmon native to the Pacific Northwest, characterized by very bright red oily flesh.

Solar mass An astrophysical unit which is the mass of our sun (Sol). A solar mass is about 330,000 times the mass of the earth.

Solid state physics The study of the physical properties of solids such as crystals, rocks, gems, and so on.

Spawners Mature adult mating fish.

Spawning grounds The shallow creek beds where female salmon lay eggs which male salmon then fertilize.

Spectrogram The photograph of a spectrum that is obtained with a spectrograph.

Spectrograph A device that is a spectrometer with a camera mounted on the eyepiece so that you can take photographs of spectra (see definition of spectrum below).

Spectrometer A device that measures the angle, wavelength or energy of light or other type of radiation.

Spectroscopy The study of radiant energy emitted or absorbed by a burning chemical.

Spectrum The distribution of radiant energy emitted or absorbed by a substance, as in a rainbow. The plural of spectrum is spectra.

Spherical harmonic expansion A computational technique developed by Roger Daley for atmospheric simulation models of weather patterns.

Structural brachiators Animals that swing from branches with their arms, like monkeys and orangutans.

Superstring theory The idea of describing the building blocks of matter with tiny line-like strings instead of point-like particles and waves.

Synthetic Something produced in a test tube. Not naturally occurring.

T

T-cell A principal type of white blood cell that is responsible for identifying foreign antigens in the body and activating other immune cells to attack the antigens.

T-cell receptor A protein structure on the surface of a T-Cell that is a specific match for one of trillions of possible eight-amino-acid protein chain particles derived from invading viruses and other foreign material in a body.

Telescope A device usually made of lenses and mirrors and used to look at distant objects such as planets and stars.

Test tube Small glass tubes with one sealed end. Used by chemists and biologists to conduct small experiments.

Thymus A small glandular organ behind the breastbone; part of the immune system responsible for T-Cell development.

Time travel The notion of physically moving forward or backward to different times.

Toxin A poison, usually a protein, produced by living cells capable of causing disease or killing other cells.

Tracer atoms Radioactive isotopes of atoms that have been substituted for normal atoms in biological molecules so that the molecules will become mildly radioactive and detectable by various experimental methods.

Translational energy The energy in a chemical reaction arising from the motion of atoms or molecules from point A to point B.

Tribal elders Wise men or women who generally lead or act as a repository of knowledge for a tribe, a group of families typically of aboriginal origin.

Triple-axis neutron spectroscope The spectroscope developed by Bert Brockhouse for which he won the Nobel Prize in 1994.

Trisomy The tripling of a chromosome during conception. Trisomy results in genetic diseases such as Down syndrome.

t-RNA (transfer-RNA) One of a group of RNA molecules involved in the transcription of the genetic code from DNA into protein molecules.

V

Velocity The speed of motion.

Vertex A point in a geometrical shape that is at the end of a line or is the intersection of two or more lines – for instance, the corner of a cube or a square.

Vibrational energy The energy in a molecule arising from the in and out stretching of chemical bonds.

Virus A simple submicroscopic parasite that causes disease in animals and plants. Viruses consist of just RNA or DNA within a protein coat. They can only replicate inside a host cell, so they are not considered to be living things.

Vole Rodents like mice but with shorter legs and heavier bodies.

W

Wavelength The distance between one peak of a wave of light, heat, or other energy and the next peak. A measure of the colour or energy of radiation or light. Long wavelengths are red and of low energy. Short wavelengths are blue and beyond. The shorter the wavelength, the higher the energy content of the wave.

Weather satellite A satellite orbiting the earth and collecting information about the atmosphere with various cameras and sensors that can be used to predict the weather.

Weather forecaster A person who predicts the weather based on historical and present conditions.

Wildlife biologist A scientist who studies animals in the wild.

Wormhole A rift in the space-time continuum which leads to a parallel universe.

X Y Z

X and Y chromosomes The chromosome associated with male and female characteristics. Females have two X chromosomes, while males have one X and one Y chromosome.

X-ray A powerful form of radiation similar to visible light, but with a shorter wavelength. X-rays can pass through solids and act on photographic film as light does.

Zoologist A person who studies zoology.

Zoology The study of animals.

Index

(Note: **Bold** page numbers point to the main source of information for a topic while page numbers in *italic* indicate that an illustration accompanies the text.)

2D (two dimensional)   33
3D (three dimensional)   33

A

Abbott, Maude   125
Acetic acid solution   117
Achuar Jivura   77, *79, 80*
Activated-Complex   157
Affleck, Ian Keith   125
Aguayo, Albert Juan   126
AIDS   79, 84
Airborne pollen   79
Alcock, Alfred John   126
Alkaloid   180
Allergenic pollen   76, 79,
Alouette Earth satellite   135
Alloys   155
Altman, Sidney   7, 13, **14**
Amazon rain forest   77,
American Psychological Society   61, 111
Amino acids   85, 87, 102, *103-104*, 106,
Amphetamine   143
Analytical chemistry   150
Anatomy   130, 159
Ancaster, Ontario   22
Angstrom   24
Angular momentum   53
Anthropology, anthropologist   43, **45**, 130
Antibiotic   160
Antibody (antibodies)   83
Anticancer drugs   73
Antigens   87, 147
Aperiodic tiling   35
Apes   45
Aphasia   63
APL programming language   154
Archaeometry   144
Archeology, archeologist   156
Arthritis   73, 85, 138
Artificial cell   134
Artificial Intelligence   161, 177
Artificial life   177
Asimov, Isaac   12
Astronaut   131
Astronomy   152, 171
Asymmetry, physical   63
Atmosphere   38, 39, 171, 175
Atom   23, 89, 141
Atomic Energy   23, 149, 159, 174
Atrium of heart   139

Atwood, Harold Leslie   127
Auto-immune diseases (see AIDS)   73, 85,
Axons   148

B

Bacteria   86, 102, 138
Ballistics   134
Balmer lines   53
Bancroft, George Michael   127
Banting, Sir Frederick Grant   7, 127
Barr, Murray Llewellyn   128
Base-pair   101,
B-cells   83, **86**,
Beatty, Sam   32
Bell, Alexander Graham   13, 128
Belyea, Dr. Helen   129
Benzoporphyrin Derivative   73, 74
Berkely, Dr. Edith   129
Best, Charles Herbert   130
Bienenstock, John   130
Big-bang theory   56, 167
Biochemistry, biochemist   97, 100, 137, 165
Bio-Economics   136
Biofilm   138
Biophysics   148, 162
Biotechnology   97,
Black, Davidson   130
Black hole   55, 56, 57, **58**, 178
BLAST search for DNA sequence   103
Bleach for pulp and paper   170
Blue bottle technology   144
Blood Serum   130
Blood type (blood group)   109, 160
Bolton, James Robert   131
Bondar, Roberta Lynn   131
Bone disease   137
Borneo   43, 44
Botany, Botanist   76, 139, 163
Boyd, Dr. Gladys   131
Boyle, Willard   132
BPD (BenzoPorphyrin Derivative)   74, 75
Brachiators   46
Brain   9, 21, 63, 113, 143, 168
Brenner, Sydney   18
Brimacombe, J. Keith   132
British Columbia Science Council   72, 97
Brockhouse, Bertram Neville   7, 22
Brooks, Harriet   133
Bruckner   31
Bruton, Len   133
Buchwald, Manuel   106
Buckley Prize   22
Bull, Gerald   134
Buyers, William James Leslie   134

C

Caffeine   80
Calcitonin   137
Calcium in the body   138

Camcorder   132
Canadian Association for Women in Science   61
Canadian Association of Physics   55
Canadian Geological Survey   129
Canadian Meteorological Centre   38
Canadian Psychology Assoc.   61
Canadian Salmon Commission   93
Canadian Society of Zoologists   66
Canadian Space Agency   131
Canadian Weather Service   38
Cancer   72, 73, 75, 147, 155
Carbon-14 dating   156
Carbon dioxide   40
Cardiac disease   125
Cardiomyoplasty   136
Cashion, Ken   89, *90*
Cassava root   77
Catalytic RNA   17, 18, **20**
CD-ROM   14
Cell assembly theory   150
Cell growth switch   163
Cells   83, 117, 160
Cenozoic research   130
Centrifuge   117
Cerebral cortex, mapping   168
Cervix, cancer of   73
CFC reclamation   143
CFTR protein   108, 162
Chang, Han   106
Chang, Thomas Ming Swi   134
Chapman, John Herbert   135
Charge Coupled Device   132
Chemical kinetics   157, 174
Chemical reaction   50, 89, 158, 174
Chemiluminescence   88, 89, **91**, 163
Chemistry   17, 49, 97, 140, 146, 158, 160, 166, 176, 180
Chemotherapy   87, 149
Chicha drink   77
China   82, 130, 141
Chinook Salmon   94
Chitty, Dennis Hubert   66, 68, 135
Chiu, Ray Chu-Jeng   136
Chlorinated flourocarbons (CFC)   143
Chlorine gas   90
Chloride ions   108
Chown, Bruce   116
Chromatin   128
Chromosome   *108, 117*, **119**
Clark, Colin Whitcomb   136
Clemens, W. A.   92
Clinical depression   143
Cobalt-60   142, 155
Cocaine, pharmacology   143
Codon   102
Cognitive psychology   63, 111, **113**
Coho Salmon   94
Cold Virus   21

Here are entertaining and educational products that complement Great Canadian Scientists:

Website
Great Canadian Scientists is on the World Wide Web at www.science.ca. In 1996, this site was voted one of the "Top 5 Per cent of the Web" by New York's Point Survey, and it has been listed as a top-ten Canadian site by Southam News. Updates to the profiles in this book, plus new profiles and information, may be found at the website. Access is free.

CD-ROM
A companion CD-ROM for Macintosh or PC complements the *Great Canadian Scientists* book with video clips of scientists speaking, interactive computer games and a quiz with 100 questions. Users play the CD like a video game. The CD is searchable and content can be copied to other applications. $20 Cdn.

Teachers' Resource Guide
A 150-page illustrated guide to the book helps teachers plan lessons on Canadian scientists and science. Dozens of fun creative classroom activities come on single 8.5x11 pages for easy photocopying as class handouts. Other resources include science vocabulary, quiz questions, a list of local science centres across the country, and much more. $20 Cdn.

Call 1-800-779-6357 to order by Visa or Mastercard, or send this order form with a cheque to the address below. Please include $4.50 shipping and handling per item, plus 7% GST.

Name: ---

Address: --

-- Phone: ---

Item	Price	Quantity	Total per Item
CD-ROM	$20 + $4.50	x -------------------------	$ ----------------------
Teacher's Guide	$20 + $4.50	x -------------------------	$ ----------------------

Total Order $ --------------------- x 7% GST = $ ---------------------

Mail orders to:
Softshell Small Systems Inc.
4692 Quebec St.
Vancouver, BC V5V 3M1

For enquiries, or to order in the USA, call: 604-876-5790, or e-mail: info@science.ca

Barry Shell is Research Communications Manager for the Centre for Systems Science at Simon Fraser University. He has written for a variety of magazines and papers, including *Equinox*, *Adbusters*, *The New York Times*, and the *Globe and Mail*. In 1987 he founded Softshell Small Systems Inc., which began as a software training and development company but now specializes in science communications. Barry lives with his family in Vancouver, BC.

Bright Lights from Polestar

Polestar Book Publishers takes pride in creating books that enrich our understanding of the world and introduce readers young and old to exciting writers and ideas. We support independent voices that illuminate our history and stretch the imagination.

Non-Fiction

Long Shot: Steve Nash's Journey to the NBA
by Jeff Rud
1-896095-16-X
$18.95 (Canada)
$16.95 (USA)
"There's no glorification of the ... super-hyped world of the NBA. Special focus is placed on Nash's work ethic, his tremendous devotion and the support of his family."
– Quill & Quire

Celebrating Excellence: Canadian Women Athletes
by Wendy Long
1-896095-04-6
$29.95 (Canada)
$24.95 (USA)
A collection of biographical essays, interviews and photographs showcasing over 200 women athletes who have achieved excellence in their chosen sports.

Seeing the Forest Among the Trees: The Case for Wholistic Forest Use
by Herb Hammond
0-919591-58-2
$46.95 (Canada)
$39.95 (USA)
Here is the definitive forest ecology handbook, presented with the lay reader in mind. Winner of the Roderick Haig-Brown Non-Fiction Award.

Fiction

DogStar
by Beverley Wood and Chris Wood
1-896095-37-2
(ages 11 and up)
$8.95 (Canada)
$6.95 (USA)
Jeff, a 1990s teen, finds himself transported to 1930s Juneau, Alaska, accompanied by a Bull Terrier named Patsy Ann. Jeff soon discovers that all is not right on the Alaska frontier. But what can he do to help? And how can he return home? Check out the Patsy Ann website: http://home.istar.ca/~bever/patsyann.htm

Witch's Fang
by Heather Kellerhals-Stewart
0-919591-88-4
$9.95 (Canada)
$7.95 (USA)
Three teens risk their lives in this mountain-climbing adventure.

Dreamcatcher
by Meredy Maynard
1-896095-01-1
$9.95 (Canada)
$7.50 (USA)
A 13-year-old boy comes to terms with the death of his father.

Polestar titles are available from your local bookseller. For a copy of our catalogue with a complete list of our books, contact:

Polestar Book Publishers, publicity office:
103-1014 Homer Street
Vancouver, British Columbia
Canada V6B 2W9
polestar@direct.ca
http://mypage.direct.ca/p/polestar